It was by far the most intimate experience she'd ever had.

This man, this…stranger, with a few words, had opened himself up to her more than any other human being Galen had ever known.

"Sorry," she heard Del whisper, his voice gruff.

She lifted her eyes again, meeting his, her heart pounding. "For what?"

She saw him suck in a fast, deep breath, shake his head. "Nothing." Another breath, a ghost of a smile. "Nothing. Forget it."

And when she let herself, for the dozenth time, drift in those incredibly honest eyes, she thanked God she wasn't going to be around for more than a few days. Because she knew, on some level so deep and so pure that the knowledge fairly hummed inside her, she could lose herself in those eyes.

Dear Reader,

The year is ending, and as a special holiday gift to you, we're starting off with a 3-in-1 volume that will have you on the edge of your seat. *Special Report,* by Merline Lovelace, Debra Cowan and Maggie Price, features three connected stories about a plane hijacking and the three couples who find love in such decidedly unusual circumstances. Read it—you won't be sorry.

A YEAR OF LOVING DANGEROUSLY continues with Carla Cassidy's *Strangers When We Married,* a reunion romance with an irresistible baby and a couple who, I know you'll agree, truly do belong together. Then spend 36 HOURS with Doreen Roberts and *A Very...Pregnant New Year's.* This is one family feud that's about to end...at the altar!

Virginia Kantra's back with *Mad Dog and Annie,* a book that's every bit as fascinating as its title—which just happens to be one of my all-time favorite titles. I guarantee you'll enjoy reading about this perfect (though they don't know it yet) pair. Linda Randall Wisdom is back with *Mirror, Mirror,* a good twin/bad twin story with some truly unexpected twists—and a fabulous hero. Finally, read about a woman who has *Everything But a Husband* in Karen Templeton's newest—and keep the tissue box nearby, because your emotions will really be engaged.

And, of course, be sure to come back next month for six more of the most exciting romances around—right here in Silhouette Intimate Moments.

Enjoy!

Leslie J. Wainger
Executive Senior Editor

Please address questions and book requests to:
Silhouette Reader Service
U.S.: 3010 Walden Ave., P.O. Box 1325, Buffalo, NY 14269
Canadian: P.O. Box 609, Fort Erie, Ont. L2A 5X3

Everything But a Husband

KAREN TEMPLETON

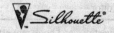

INTIMATE MOMENTS™

Published by Silhouette Books

America's Publisher of Contemporary Romance

This book is dedicated to all those parents who daily face,
and meet, with grace, courage and a never-ending sense of
humor the challenge of raising "special" children;

and to Jack, who has, for more than twenty years,
tirelessly supported my quest to be everything I want to be.

 SILHOUETTE BOOKS

ISBN 0-373-27120-4

EVERYTHING BUT A HUSBAND

Copyright © 2000 by Karen Templeton Berger

All rights reserved. Except for use in any review, the reproduction
or utilization of this work in whole or in part in any form by any
electronic, mechanical or other means, now known or hereafter
invented, including xerography, photocopying and recording, or in
any information storage or retrieval system, is forbidden without
the written permission of the editorial office, Silhouette Books,
300 East 42nd Street, New York, NY 10017 U.S.A.

All characters in this book have no existence outside the imagination of
the author and have no relation whatsoever to anyone bearing the same
name or names. They are not even distantly inspired by any individual
known or unknown to the author, and all incidents are pure invention.

This edition published by arrangement with Harlequin Books S.A.

® and TM are trademarks of Harlequin Books S.A., used under license.
Trademarks indicated with ® are registered in the United States Patent
and Trademark Office, the Canadian Trade Marks Office and in other
countries.

Visit Silhouette at www.eHarlequin.com

Printed in U.S.A.

Books by Karen Templeton

Silhouette Intimate Moments

Anything for His Children #978
Anything for Her Marriage #1006
Everything But a Husband #1050

Silhouette Yours Truly

*Wedding Daze
*Wedding Belle
*Wedding? Impossible!

*Weddings, Inc.

KAREN TEMPLETON

is the mother of five sons and living proof that romance and dirty diapers are not mutually exclusive. Her first book for Silhouette appeared in 1998; just two years later, she was thrilled to see her work make the Waldenbooks series bestseller list. A transplanted Easterner in serious denial, she spends far too much time coaxing her Albuquerque, New Mexico, garden to yield roses and something resembling a lawn, all the while fantasizing about a weekend alone with her husband. Or at least an uninterrupted conversation.

She loves to hear from her readers, who may reach her by writing c/o Silhouette Books, 300 E. 42nd St., New York, NY 10017.

IT'S OUR 20th ANNIVERSARY!
**December 2000 marks the end of our anniversary year.
We hope you've enjoyed the many special titles already
offered, and we invite you to sample those wonderful titles
on sale this month! 2001 promises to be every bit as
exciting, so keep coming back to Silhouette Books,
where love comes alive....**

Desire

#1333 Irresistible You
Barbara Boswell

#1334 Slow Fever
Cait London

#1335 A Season for Love
BJ James

#1336 Groom of Fortune
Peggy Moreland

#1337 Monahan's Gamble
Elizabeth Bevarly

**#1338 Expecting the
Boss's Baby**
Leanne Banks

Romance

**#1486 Sky's Pride and
Joy**
Sandra Steffen

#1487 Hunter's Vow
Susan Meier

**#1488 Montana's Feisty
Cowgirl**
Carolyn Zane

#1489 Rachel and the M.D.
Donna Clayton

**#1490 Mixing Business...with
Baby**
Diana Whitney

#1491 His Special Delivery
Belinda Barnes

Special Edition

#1363 The Delacourt Scandal
Sherryl Woods

#1364 The McCaffertys: Thorne
Lisa Jackson

**#1365 The Cowboy's
Gift-Wrapped Bride**
Victoria Pade

#1366 Lara's Lover
Penny Richards

#1367 Mother in a Moment
Allison Leigh

#1368 Expectant Bride-To-Be
Nikki Benjamin

Intimate Moments

#1045 Special Report
Merline Lovelace/Maggie Price/
Debra Cowan

**#1046 Strangers When We
Married**
Carla Cassidy

**#1047 A Very...Pregnant
New Year's**
Doreen Roberts

#1048 Mad Dog and Annie
Virginia Kantra

#1049 Mirror, Mirror
Linda Randall Wisdom

#1050 Everything But a Husband
Karen Templeton

Chapter 1

"*B*ecause you had a choice."

Brow knotted, Galen dropped onto the rush-seated ladder-back chair in front of Gran's desk. That's all it said, the note wrapped around the large brown envelope, one of those old-fashioned kinds that tied in the back. That, and her name, marching across the front in her grandmother's distinctive angular scrawl.

She'd had to pry it out of the top right-hand drawer of the desk, wedged as it was behind a cache of loose change and old receipts, a wad of tangled gumbands and at least two dozen long since dead pens. The old woman had refused to let her touch any of her personal stuff. Just because she couldn't walk so good anymore—or see, or hear, Galen had silently added—didn't mean her mind was gone, she'd said. Long as she was still breathing, she could handle her own damn finances. Except "damn" came out "dumb" in her thick Slovak accent.

Well, Gran had stopped breathing a week ago, twelve days short of her ninety-first birthday, leaving Galen to sort everything out. And find things, too. Like long brown envelopes with her name printed on them.

The phone—an antique of sorts, left over from the late forties—jangled on the back of the desk. Galen answered it, tucking a stray hank of hair back behind her ear as she distractedly informed the hyper telemarketer that she seriously doubted her grandmother needed another charge card.

She rattled the receiver into its cradle, stared again at the envelope.

"Because you had a choice."

Now what on earth d'you suppose she meant by that? Well. There was only one way to find out, wasn't there? Yet...a perverseness not unlike Gran's stilled her fingers, kept her from untwisting the thin string, opening the envelope.

Or maybe it was more than perverseness?

Galen sighed, squinting out the naked paned window at the flanneled November sky, absently worrying a loose thread dangling from the hem of her sweatshirt. Never could convince her grandmother to splurge on curtains in her bedroom, the old woman insisting the vinyl roller shade was perfectly adequate. Odd how they'd always done that to each other, her grandmother and her. Goaded each other. Driven each other batty. Peculiar way of showing they cared, when she thought about it. Still, all they'd had was each other, for the last three years, a pair of widows keeping each other company in the tiny South Side Pittsburgh house her grandmother had lived in her entire married life.

Now Galen didn't even have that.

A small, tight knot of anxiety twisted in her stomach.

She dropped the envelope, pushed herself up from the desk. Her hands lifted to the back of her neck, where she released her thick, straight hair from its tortoiseshell barrette, only to immediately finger-comb it back, reclip it. Her gaze lit on the sagging double bed in the center of the room, still shrouded in its yellowing chenille bedspread. Tears pricked behind her eyelids.

Maybe she'd returned to the house where she'd spent so much of her childhood because it seemed she had no choice. Because, after Vinnie died, his medical bills had eaten up whatever there might have been, leaving her flat broke. And without the opportunity she'd naively assumed would be hers. But she'd stayed because she'd wanted to. Somehow, Gran had mellowed in Galen's absence, allowing a gentleness and sense of humor to rise to the surface of an otherwise dour personality Galen had sure never seen during those interminable years of living with her grandparents after her parents' deaths. Had Gran's iron-handedness simply been a reflection of her grandfather's? She supposed so. After all, most women of her grandmother's generation and cultural bent felt it their duty to defer to their husband's decisions. And together, they'd certainly done all they could to clip a young girl's wings. No makeup, no dating, no going off by herself… To this day, she wasn't sure how she managed to talk them into letting her take that job at Granata's, one of Pittsburgh's most popular Italian restaurants. Four evenings a week, waiting tables. Which was where she met Vinnie, the youngest of the four Granata brothers, already thirty to her sixteen.

Another twist to the gut, this one sharper. Colder. To be sure, he'd courted her slowly. Sweetly. Secretively. Never touched her, except for the occasional stroke of her cheek, a squeeze of her hand, when no one else was around, and not even that the first year. Blinded by the dazzling glare of first love, Galen had been living a dream, hardly daring to believe that this handsome, older man really wanted her. That he might rescue her from the prison of her grandparents' overprotectiveness. But he did. Enough to keep their secret for two years. The morning of Galen's eighteenth birthday, they eloped.

He'd cheated her out of a wedding. Too.

A sharp breeze rattled the windows; with a sharp sigh, Galen turned back to the desk, saw the envelope.

"Because you had a choice."

Yes, it was true. After all, she could have gotten a job—*any* job—and tried to make a life of her own. After all, it wasn't as if there were any children—Galen shut her eyes, waiting out the tug of self-pity.

So. She could have refused her grandmother's offer to come live with her. Just until she got on her feet, Gran had said.

Except that within five minutes of moving back, Galen realized the indomitable woman she'd feared so much as a child had somehow turned into a frail and needy old lady. Still domineering, still set in her ways, to be sure, but now someone Galen could love.

But. Now Gran was gone, and Galen found herself back at square one. All she had, besides this house and a couple of not-exactly-impressive bank accounts, was a neurotic terrier-mix who piddled whenever she got too excited, and whatever was inside this envelope. She couldn't imagine what it might be: Gran had insisted on putting Galen's name on everything some time ago, insisting she didn't want any "rigamarole", as she put it, with the government, when the time came. Said there'd be little enough as it was, no sense making things complicated on top of it.

The old chair squawked as she sank back onto in it, began untwisting the strings on the suddenly blurred envelope. She knuckled away a tear, supposing when your very last relation dies on you, when, at thirty-five, you find yourself childless and husbandless and careerless and *life*less, it's hard not to feel a little down in the dumps.

Steam hissed from the radiator squatting underneath the window, startling awake the walking mop. Speaking of personal effects. Eyes bulging, the tiny dog hopped out of her basket and clicked over the bare wooden floor to Galen, whimpering to be picked up. Gran's dog, Baby, a cross between a Chihuahua and a Yorkie. Maybe. Not an attractive animal. For several seconds, dog and woman stared at each other.

With a weighty sigh, Galen scooped the raggedy thing into her lap, then finally undid the envelope, pulled out the contents. Oh. A life insurance policy, looked like. She scanned the first page. Blinked. Heard her heart begin to pound in her ears.

"Jiminy Christmas," she said on a long, slow whisper, only to yelp like she'd been goosed, the mutt flying off her lap, when the phone rang again.

Galen managed a strangled "Hello?" as the dog made her

stiff-legged way back to her basket, into which she flopped with a little doggy groan.

"Galen, baby? It's Cora. You know, you've been on my mind so much the past couple of weeks, and it's been way too long since I've heard from you, so I finally figured I'd better just go on ahead and call before I drove myself crazy. What's going on, honey?"

The rich, soothing voice of her mother's old friend swept over her. Just like that, Galen saw the frown pleating the coffee-brown forehead, remembered long-ago Saturday mornings in Cora Mitchell's base housing living room in Norfolk, playing dress-up with Cora's daughters to the comforting hum of their mothers' conversation a few feet away.

Tears swam in Galen's eyes, as her throat went dry and tight. She'd been out so seldom during the three years she'd spent with her grandmother, she'd lost touch with what few friends she had. Other than the parish priest and a few neighbors who'd hesitantly inquired about her grandmother, she'd talked to no one this past week. Not that she'd ever exactly been a party girl, but still—

"Oh, Cora!" spilled out on something between a sob and a sigh.

"Galen! What is it? What's happened, baby?"

So she told the only real friend she had left in the world about her grandmother's passing, about how things had changed between them, about how much she missed the old bat—this said on one of those crying laughs that happens when your emotions get all tangled up in your head like that wad of gumbands in Gran's desk—which brought the expected moans of commiseration and sympathy. Galen honked into a stiff, scratchy generic tissue—Gran never would pay extra for the good stuff—then pointed out that Gran *had* been nearly ninety-one, after all.

"Still," Cora said, and Galen could feel the hug. "Things had really changed that much? Between you?"

"Amazing, huh?"

"A blessing, is what I'm thinking."

Barely eight years old, Galen had been staying overnight

with Cora while her father, home on leave after six months at sea, whisked Galen's mother off to New York for a quick second honeymoon. It was Cora, tears tracing silver tracks down dark cheeks, who'd gently told her that her parents had died because some drunk had run head-on into them, just on the other side of Dover, Delaware, on their way back. And, ultimately, it had been Cora and her husband who'd delivered Galen to her never-before-seen grandparents in Pittsburgh. Her father's parents, they of the stoic, strict Slovak extraction, her mother's Irish parents having both passed away some time before.

Now, if anyone had bothered to ask Galen her druthers about who she wanted to live with, she would have chosen Cora—who was more than willing—over her grandparents any day. The court, however, ruled in favor of blood over druthers, and that was that. Cora had stayed in touch anyway, even after her husband retired from the military and they moved back to her native Detroit, figuring she was still Galen's honorary aunt.

Hearing Cora's voice…well, it was a Godsend, is what it was. Not just because Galen was still getting over her grandmother's death, but because—it all came back to her, now—there was the little matter of just having discovered she was the sole beneficiary of a life insurance policy worth a *quarter of a million dollars*.

She burst into tears.

"Oh, hell, honey…Oh, shoot, I wish I was there! Talk to me, baby. Get it out, that's it, get it all out."

So, between assorted choked sobs and blubbers, she did.

Cora went understandably, if uncharacteristically, silent for several seconds. Then she said, "And you had no idea?"

"N-none. And I have no idea how she did this, *why* she did this, where she got the money to make the payments on the policy…" Galen shook her head, pushing that stray wisp behind her ear. "I suppose I'll never know, now. Thing is, though, I keep thinking I'm reading it wrong."

"Okay. Tell me what it says. Word for word."

She did.

"You're not reading it wrong," came the dry pronouncement across the wire. "So can I hit you up for a loan? This house I bought's about to bleed me dry."

Good old Cora.

"So...what're you going to do with all that money?"

Galen blew out a sigh, stared again at the policy. Heavens. She was rich. Well, maybe not *rich.* But certainly not *poor.* She realized she was shaking. And that her head felt like a fly was caught inside it. "I have no idea," she said over the buzzing. "Buy some new underwear, I suppose."

"Don't knock yourself out, now."

Galen felt a smile twitch at her mouth.

"Hey! How about blowing some of it on a plane ticket?"

"To?"

"Here. For Thanksgiving."

Thanksgiving? Oh, yeah...that was next week, wasn't it? Galen's stomach knotted. "Oh, goodness, Cora. I don't know. I haven't even thought about it."

"Now, don't you tell me you were planning on spending the day alone?"

"I hadn't *planned* on anything. Besides, people do, you know," she said, only to be cut off by an indignant *hmmph.*

"Give me one good reason why you can't come up here."

A harsh, startled laugh tumbled out of her mouth. But no excuses.

"Uh-huh, that's what I thought. Look, my girls can't get out here—Willa's too busy and Lynette's too pregnant—and I can't go to either of their places without putting the other one's nose out of joint, so I'm staying here, and I *hate* spending Thanksgiving alone. Gets too damn depressing, buying one of those pathetic little turkey breasts just for yourself. So, you wanna come out Tuesday or Wednesday?"

Galen felt the corners of her mouth lift. Right. Knowing Cora, she probably had a million friends she could spend the holiday with. But leave it to her to twist things around to make it sound like Galen would be doing *her* a kindness, not the other way around.

The house did suddenly seem extraordinarily empty. And quiet.

But...

She shifted in the chair, making it squawk again. "Oh, I don't know... I've still got so much to do. About Gran's stuff 'n' that."

"It'll still be there when you get back, baby."

True enough. "But what about getting plane reservations this late?"

"Hey, if it's supposed to happen, the way will be made clear, you hear what I'm saying?"

Then the dog propped her chin on the edge of her basket, gave her *doleful*. Right. "I can't leave the dog."

"What dog?"

Galen let out a weighty sigh the same time the dog did. "This mutt of Gran's."

Doleful turned to *indignant*.

She tucked the phone to her chest. "Well, you are," she said, only to realize she was justifying herself to a dog. An ugly one, at that.

"Last time I checked," Cora said, "they allowed dogs in Michigan."

Michigan. Crikey. Galen couldn't remember the last time she'd been out of Pittsburgh, let alone to another state. Something suddenly leeched all the air from her lungs. "Oh...I don't know. This just seems so last minute—"

"For heaven's sake, girl—you ever hear of the concept of *spur of the moment?* Besides, you live alone now. You can do things just because, and nobody's drawers are going to get in a knot about it. So. Tuesday or Wednesday?"

Galen stood up, stretched, looked around the bleak little room. Realized she could go. Or she could stay. It was completely her decision.

That, for the first time in her life, she didn't have to answer to a living soul.

"I'll...call you back after I make the reservations," she said, then laughed, nervously, at Cora's squeal in reply.

Mirroring his increasingly dreary mood, a cold light drizzle began to mottle Del Farentino's truck windshield as he pulled out of the Standish's driveway. Two days before Thanksgiving, with four clients wanting/needing/demanding Del complete their remodeling projects by this afternoon.

He shoved his perpetually too-long hair off his forehead, glancing at the dashboard clock. Ten-o-three. Not bad, actually, considering he'd had a devil of a time getting his four-year-old daughter Wendy dressed and out of the house this morning. Something about the purple sweater—which had been her favorite up until five minutes before he tried to get it on her body—being itchy, and she only wanted to wear the pink one, which was buried underneath several strata of dirty clothes in the laundry basket. It had not been a pretty scene, but the last thing he needed this morning was to be late for his eight o'clock appointment with the Goldens, potential new clients with a large house out past Shady Lakes.

Now there was a bright note. Hot *damn*, would he love to get his mitts on that one. A complete redo, not just a kitchen remodel or add-a-room project. The architect had been there— a youngish woman who understood how to blend practicality with innovation—and the plans made his mouth water. A job like this would be a real feather in his cap. Prove to the world he was more than a handyman. Not that he was complaining about all the smaller jobs that seemed to drift his way. Between Wendy's special classes and what-all, not to mention full-time daycare, the kid ate up his income faster than a dog ate steak. Money was money, and he'd take whatever he could get. But it sure would be nice to move up to the big leagues. Which, if these people accepted his bid, just might happen.

Damp gravel crunched underneath his tires as he pulled up in front of Cora Mitchell's mongrel house, close to the center of town. It had a porch and some eaves and a gable or two and a couple of stories, more or less, but you couldn't exactly call it anything. Except old. Cora, a long-widowed, vociferous, black earth mama in her late fifties, had worked her way up from temp to managing his step-mother's Realty office. She'd recently bought the fixer-upper for some outrageously low price, only to discover the repair costs would be equally out-

rageous. Del pictured this project being on the periphery of
his, or somebody's, to-do list for years.

Cora was in a dither when he arrived, as only Cora could
get herself into. According to Maureen, the woman was the
epitome of order and decorum in the office, but for some reason—maybe because she'd be fixing up this house well into
old age—this project seemed to keep her off-balance. This
morning, she was a mess. Muttering something about a guest
arriving that afternoon and she hadn't yet gone to the store
and did Del think the rain might change to snow, she barely
allowed a glance in his direction as she tromped from room
to room, eventually stopping long enough to shroud herself
within a long woolen cape the color of a grape Popsicle.

From the basement, he heard reassuring clunks and clanks
as his guys changed out her old furnace. They'd already tackled the leaky roof and the sagging living room ceiling where
some overly enthusiastic soul had attempted to make a great
room out of two smaller rooms by removing a load-bearing
wall.

"Who's the guest?" he asked.

"What?" Silvery eyes, startling against her dark skin, stared
at him blankly for a moment. "Oh, you mean Galen," she
said, her breath frosting in front of her face in the cold house.
They hadn't intended on replacing the furnace until the spring,
but the furnace had other ideas. Cora hooked the cape together
at her throat. "Her mama and I were friends when our husbands were stationed in Norfolk, oh, Lord, more than twenty-
five years ago, now. Galen and my girls used to play together,
you know?"

She picked up her purse from the hall table, clicked it open,
grunted, then clicked it shut again. "Anyway, Galen's mama
and daddy died in a car accident when she was maybe eight
or so. Bill and I would've taken her ourselves, but whoever
makes these sorts of decisions decided she should go with her
grandparents instead. We kept in touch, though. The girls and
I even went to Pittsburgh to see her, couple of times." She
hesitated, gazing at the doorknob, her brows drawn. "Strange,
the way these things happen," she said, more or less to herself,

then looked again at Del. "In any case, I'm not gonna bore you with all the details, 'cause I know you got things to do and, God knows, so do I, but her grandmother died a couple weeks ago, and that was the only living relative she had left, so I strong-armed her into coming up here for Thanksgiving. Since I can't get out to California this year to see the girls, you know, what with this house sucking every penny out of me like it is. And I didn't figure there was any reason for her to just sit in that big old empty place of her grandmother's down in Pittsburgh all by herself. I mean, can you *imagine?*"

Without waiting for Del's response—clearly, one wasn't expected—she tugged open the glass-paned front door and clomped out onto the slate gray porch, the surface marred with smudged workboot footprints. Del followed. The drizzle had turned to sleet, clicking on the porch overhang, bouncing like tiny white bugs off the winter-dry grass out in the yard; Del frowned, silently questioning the wisdom of Cora's driving on what could easily become icy roads. He also knew better than to call her on it.

"So," she said, her face smothered in breath clouds as she looked out over her whitening lawn. She yanked on a pair of driving gloves, taking her time smoothing them over her broad knuckles. "You gonna bring the baby to Elizabeth's for Thanksgiving?"

Del stuffed his fingers in his jeans pockets, grateful he hadn't yet removed his down vest if the woman was going to conduct a conversation outside. Elizabeth Louden Sanford was his stepsister, his father Hugh having married Elizabeth's mother Maureen about a year and a half ago. To make things more complicated, Elizabeth's husband Guy not only brought three children of his own to the marriage, but was the youngest of five sons. In what had to be either the world's most courageous or dumbest moment, Elizabeth had volunteered to host Thanksgiving for *everybody*. At last count, Del's father had said, the guest list was about to pass fifty, and still climbing.

"I haven't decided," he finally said. "That's a lot of people to subject a certain someone to. I'm just not sure…"

Uh-oh. Cora was giving him her Look. "I swear to Heaven,

child—when they pass out the award for Overprotective Father of the Year, you'll win, no contest. You really gotta do something about those trust issues weighing you down, you know? Wendy loves being with people. She'll be fine, if Paranoid Papa will give her half a chance. Okay, baby," she continued without waiting for Del's response, since clearly, nothing he could possibly say was worth listening to. "I'm going on to the store, then out to the airport. I should be back by one at the latest. You need me for anything?"

Del swallowed a smile. Cora drove his guys to distraction. Knowing she'd be gone for three hours would probably make their day.

"Nah. I think we can manage. I'll be in and out myself, though. What with the holiday coming up and everything, we're busting butt all over town today."

"Huh," Cora said, not paying any attention. She glanced at her watch, invoked the Almighty's name and vanished. Del yelled, "Drive carefully," as soon as he was sure she couldn't hear him.

He stood on the porch for a moment, thinking about the conversation. About Wendy. About his—yeah, he'd admit it—obsessive need to protect her. He supposed it was only natural, considering. Still, Cora was right. Putting Wendy into a new situation was always harder on Del than it was on his daughter. But even though his kid was a fighter—yeah, a champ!—and even though it would take far more than throwing her into a crowd of strange kids to knock her for a loop...

He let out a long, ambivalent sigh.

Two clients later, in the midst of assuring Mrs. Allen that her stove would indeed be ready to go by that afternoon, his cell phone chirped at him. He'd no sooner said, "Yo," than he was assaulted by a torrent of words from one really mad woman. The connection wasn't wonderful, but he made out several choice cuss words, an injunction against nature in general and ice storms in particular, and two very distinct phrases: "won't be ready until late today" and "her plane's due in forty-five minutes!"

"Cora?"

"Well, who the hell else would be calling you to go pick up someone at the airport?" That came through clearly enough.

Uh-oh.

"Cora—why on earth are you calling *me*? I'm backed up clear to Canada—"

"Baby, you think I don't know that? And I'm really sorry, I am, but I've called everybody else I can think of and you're the first person to answer their damn phone."

Great.

"Cora, I—"

"Oh, thank you, baby! And I'll make it up to you, I swear. It's just that the child's all broken up about her grandmother and everything, you know—?"

Del didn't have the heart to point out the "child" had to be significantly over thirty.

"—anyway, you got something to write down the flight number?"

With a sigh, Del pulled out a small notebook and pen he always carried with him from his back pocket, duly recorded the information. Clearly, strong-willed females were part of his karma.

"So, what's she look like? Galen?"

"Oh, Lord. I haven't seen her in years. She sent me a wedding picture, though. Poor baby. She's a widow, did I tell you? Oh! And another picture, maybe four, five years ago. Don't imagine she's changed much since then. Longish red hair. Dark, like she uses henna on it except this is natural. Real fair skin, some freckles, maybe, I don't exactly remember. Kinda tall, I guess. Slender. Eyes like those pictures of the Caribbean. Green blue. Pretty girl. You can't miss her. Okay, this man is giving me a look like I don't want to know how much this is going to cost me. I'll see you back at the house."

Well, that was that. Del hooked the phone back onto his belt, one eyebrow crooked. Red hair and green-blue eyes, huh?

"Mr. Farentino?"

Mrs. Allen was standing far too close, mouth pursed, hands

clasped, one of those women to whom lipstick and a housecoat meant "presentable."

"Does this mean you're leaving? Before my stove is installed?"

"Now, Mrs. Allen," Del said in his divert-the-potential-hysteria voice, flashing her his famous, and woefully unused, female-snagging smile. He fetched his vest from where he'd draped it over the back of a kitchen chair, slipped it on. "You gonna trust me here or what? I promise, Dan and Lenny'll get you all fixed up, okay? By three o'clock this afternoon, you'll be baking pumpkin pies in that baby, no problem."

He was out the back door before she had a chance to point out the stove hadn't even arrived yet.

Chapter 2

Where was Cora?

Swallowing down yet another surge of the nausea that had plagued her since the plane left Pittsburgh, Galen scanned the waiting room, already filling with passengers for the next flight out. She felt like a pack mule. Her purse strangled her diagonally from left shoulder to right hip, her carry-on bag and winter coat crushed the fingers of her right hand, while a beleaguered whimper floated up from the small plastic pet carrier clutched in the other. Amazing, how heavy it was, considering the animal in it weighed about as much as a hoagie. A *small* hoagie. A hank of hair had slipped out of its clip to torment her cheekbone, but if she put everything down, she'd never figure out how to pick it all up again. Underneath her five-year-old black sweater, she shivered. And not from cold.

All around her, winterized bodies swarmed and jostled each other, the cacophony of voices drowning out intermittent PA announcements and tinny music. Heavens—she hadn't actually seen Cora in something like twenty years. Tears bit at Galen's eyes as something close to panic tangled with the queasies. Baby whined again; Galen automatically offered some vague reassurance, as if the thing could hear, let alone understand, her.

She shut her eyes, hauled in a lungful of air. She'd been cloistered even more than she'd thought if a simple trip could throw her this much. True, she'd only flown once before—with Vinnie to St. Thomas for their honeymoon—but she was a grown woman, for heaven's sake. Not a little kid. Her stomach heaved again; sweat broke out on her forehead, trickling down the side of her face.

"This is crazy," she muttered to herself, beginning to rethink dumping at least some of her load before her fingers fell off. One corner of her lower lip snagged between her teeth, she craned her neck, her eyes darting around the terminal. *Okay, Volcek. Get a grip. You're just stressed and woozy. She'll be here—*

"Galen? Galen Granata?"

She jumped a foot at the sound of the deep masculine voice a foot away, whirled around to find herself face-to-chest with a '63 Buick of a man, nicely packaged in plaid flannel and navy blue nylon. Her gaze drifted upward over a thick neck, a squared chin, a smile both tentative and cocky, and a pair of heavy-lidded, thickly-lashed, puppy-dog brown eyes that all but screamed Latin or Mediterranean or something equally threatening.

And then—oh, my—there was that headful of nearly-black hair at least three weeks past needing a haircut.

This was not Cora.

"I'm sorry," rumbled the voice again. The kind of voice that, when you hear it over the phone, immediately conjures up, well, someone who looks like this. Except, in real life, you discover, eventually and with profound disappointment, the person attached to the voice really looks like Barney Fife. "I must have the wrong person..."

There he went again. Talking. Galen shook her head at the not-Cora, not-Barney-Fife person, which turned out to be a huge mistake. Served her right, she supposed, for holding everything down for two hours. But losing her cookies into a barf bag at thirty-thousand feet was just so...public. She wobbled for a second, both grateful and irked when a firm, large hand grasped her elbow. She caught a whiff of aftershave, and everything heaved inside her.

"Whoa—you okay?"

Reflex jerked her elbow from the man's grasp, which was another mistake. Her coat and bag slithered and thunked to the floor as she clamped her hand over her mouth, her eyes going wide. The next few seconds were a blur as whoever-this-was scooped up her belongings, clamped one arm around her waist, and propelled her down the hall to the ladies' room. She shoved the carrier at him, grabbed the carry-on, then lurched inside, narrowly missing a mother with toddler twins just coming out.

"I'll wait here," she thought she heard as the door whooshed shut behind her a split second before she catapulted into the nearest stall.

Well, *that* wasn't a moment too soon. Del let out a sigh of relief, leaned against the wall outside the restroom door. He'd never seen anyone actually turn green before.

A redhead, Cora had said. Check. Caribbean-green eyes. Pretty girl. Can't miss her. Check, and check, and *hoo*-boy.

Then a sardonic smile twisted his mouth. Yeah, right… Cora's car skidded on the ice, she was stuck at the service station, she just couldn't get anyone else to answer the phone…

Woman was about as subtle as Ru Paul's makeup.

Of course, all the women he knew—and half the men—had been trying to fix him up ever since he moved to Spruce Lake, three years ago. Thus far, he'd been able to deflect everyone's good intentions with either a grin or a glower, depending on his mood. But like the slow, torturous shift and grind and upheaval of the earth's plates, so Del's thoughts had begun to shift over the years, leading him to think that, mmm, well— he scrubbed a palm over his chin, hardly believing he was admitting this to himself—he might actually be open to the idea of marrying again.

Well. He'd finished the thought and his heart was still beating. But it was true. He was tired, dammit. Tired of trying to figure out his precocious, inquisitive, hyper daughter by himself, tired of having nothing but the TV to keep him company after she went to bed, tired of waking up alone. Not that he didn't love his daughter with everything he had in him, mind, but...

But.

He let out a sigh loud enough to make some woman coming out of the ladies' room give him a funny look.

Yeah. *But.*

What did he think, he could order up a wife from Spiegel's or something? Criminy. Look how long it had taken him to find *one* woman willing to hitch herself to a guy smart enough to get a college education but not smart enough to use it, who clearly preferred living in near poverty—but, hey, calling the shots—than sucking up to some boss just for some minor thing like, oh, security. Like there was actually another woman on this planet that crazy?

One willing to take on, besides the promise of continued financial instability, the exhausting, often thankless task of raising someone else's child?

Especially one as strong-willed and independent as Wendy.

Find another wife? Sure, why not? Piece of cake.

Let's see...if Wendy was four and a half now, and she left home at eighteen, that meant...only thirteen and a half more years of celibacy.

That brought the old mouth down into a nice, tight scowl.

He jumped each time the restroom door opened. Three women gave him the eye, one looked as though she was willing to give him far more than that. Galen finally emerged, slightly less green but still frighteningly pale, hugging her carry-on to her stomach like a drowning woman a log. He thought she might have run a comb through her hair, splashed water on her face, if the damp tendrils hugging her temples and clumped eyelashes were any indication. Those incredible turquoise eyes met his; a flush swept up from underneath the baggy, high-necked sweater—black, severe, a startling contrast with her fair skin, the dark red hair.

''Thank you,'' she whispered, a smile flickering over almost colorless lips.

''Rough flight?''

Her gaze darted to his, vulnerable and embarrassed. A breath-stealing urge to put his arm around her swamped him again; he handily fought it back.

She nodded, shifting from foot to foot. Even without makeup, her complexion was flawless, the skin as clear and fine as a teenager's. Only the hairline creases bookending her mouth hinted that she was older. And yes, Cora, there were freckles. Just a few, nicely arranged.

''We hit—'' she swallowed ''—turbulence over the lake.'' Another smile played peekaboo with her lips. Nice mouth, even if a bit on the anemic side. Geez…how long had it been since he'd noticed a woman's mouth? Hell, since he'd noticed a woman's anything? Or, in this case, *everything*.

At first glance you'd say, okay, sure, she's pretty—definitely pretty—but in an ordinary way for all that, y'know? Just…average. Average height, average weight, averagely clothed in sweater and jeans. Very average hair, except for the color. Straight, parted in the middle, clipped back. Strictly utilitarian, right? On second glance, however, you'd say, ''Hmm.''

On second glance, you'd notice the delicacy of her bone structure, the way one tawny eyebrow sat slightly higher than the other, that the loose sweater, the no-frills jeans, really didn't hide what he suspected was a spectacular figure as much as she probably thought it did. That her ears were absolutely perfect. If red rimmed.

She held out her hand for the carrier. Short nails. No polish. No rings. ''Here, I'll take that back—''

''No, it's okay, I've got it.'' He lifted it up, peeked inside for the first time. Managed not to wince. Huge, batlike ears, buggy eyes, hairy—the thing looked like a Furby. Before they perfected the prototype.

''She was my grandmother's,'' Galen said on a sigh, as if that explained it. Which, in a weird sort of way, it did. ''Now she's mine, I guess.''

Del lowered the carrier. "Lucky you."

That got a tiny smile. And another blush. "Well. Talk about your inauspicious beginnings," she said, traces of blue-collar Pittsburghese tingeing her speech patterns. She jerked her head back toward the restroom door, cleared her throat. "So. You know I'm Galen. And you are?"

Del snapped to, now tried to take her bag as well. Wariness flared in her eyes as she inched away, choking it more closely to her. He swallowed a grin. The dog, he immediately surmised, he could have. Whatever was in that bag, though, she'd fight to the death for. "Del Farentino. I'm the contractor doing some work on Cora's new house."

"Oh. The one that's costing her way too much money?" She flushed even brighter. "Th-the house, I mean. Not the contractor…"

"I think she'd probably agree with you on both counts," Del said with a grin, wondering what it was about this woman that was making him feel…good. Like something remotely human, even. "Well, we might as well get a move on." Del started down the concourse, assuming Galen would follow.

She didn't. Del turned around, got bumped from behind by a foreign tourist. He frowned at the not unwarranted suspicion in Galen's eyes. "What?"

"Why couldn't Cora pick me up?"

Del took a step back to her, resisting the urge to glance at his watch. "Well, the story is, she went to do some shopping, her car skidded off the road, messing up the muffler or something, so she couldn't pick you up. And I was the only person to answer the phone. Can we go—?"

She stayed put, squinting at him with an expression caught neatly between guarded and nervous. "How do I know you're telling me the truth?"

Ah, hell.

"Oh, *I'm* telling the truth, honey, trust me. It's whether *Cora's* telling the truth we have to consider." He gave her the reassuring smile he'd given Mrs. Standish earlier. She didn't smile back. Del took a step closer. The dog yipped. Del's hand streaked through his hair as minutes ticked by like race cars. "You afraid to get in the truck with me, what?"

"Uh, yeah." Caution stiffened her features, shadowed her eyes. But not, he thought, from experience as much as...lack of it. That's what it was, he realized. She was like a child on the first day of school, excited and fearful all at once. She shifted the bag, which was clearly heavy. "Kinda got that drummed into me by the time I was three. It stuck."

It wasn't that he didn't understand—he hoped his daughter would grow up to be half this streetsmart, which he doubted, which he decided he did not need to think about just now— but he still had a lot of work to do and it was Thanksgiving week and he had to pick Wendy up from the sitter's at four and, frankly, he wasn't in the mood. Hadn't he just explained who he was? Did she really think he made all that up, somehow? Still, he plastered on another smile. "Honey, I just got you to the john before you threw up all over the terminal floor. You can trust me to get you to Cora's with both your reputation and body parts intact, okay? I mean, come on, already— do I look like someone you should be afraid of?"

She drew her bottom lip between her teeth, color pinking her cheeks. Shook her head. But that was it.

Del huffed out a sigh. "Okay, here's the deal. Trust me, and I'll get you to Spruce Lake in just under an hour, no hassles, and for free. Otherwise, take your chances with a taxi. And remember. It's two days before Thanksgiving. And the weather sucks."

He pivoted on his heel, started to walk away, figuring if this tactic worked at least fifty percent of the time with a four-year-old, he might have a shot of it working with a grown woman.

Five seconds later, he turned back, undecided whether to throttle or comfort the basket case in front of him. Then he lifted both hands, the carrier dangling like a suspended Ferris wheel basket. "For crying out loud, I know who you are, I know who Cora is, I didn't run off with your dog when I had the chance—" he jerked the carrier to prove his point, which he noticed did provoke a small, startled reaction on her part, not to mention the dog's ''—so why are you so afraid of me?''

''It's not that...''

He sighed. Mightily. But he walked back, dumped the carrier and her coat, then fished his wallet from the vest's inside pocket. As what seemed like the entire population of the Great Lakes region milled around them, he flipped it open to his driver's license, which happened to sit opposite a picture of his daughter. ''Okay, here. I don't know what this will prove, but what the hell.''

She never even noticed the license, he could tell. She tucked a stray piece of hair behind her ear, a soft ''Oh'' falling from her lips. ''Is that your little girl?''

Suddenly, he wasn't quite so ticked with her. Suddenly, he was aware of her shiny, fragrant hair, the way the part wasn't quite straight, that she was just the right height to fit neatly under his chin, if he were to hug her.

That this feeling-like-a-human business could easily get out of hand.

After a stunned moment or two, Del angled his head to look at the shot, one of those a-thousand-photos-for-fifteen-bucks JC Penney specials. Wendy's fourth birthday portrait, all deep brown eyes and dimples. A twinge of something like fear hobbled through his gut, as images of strapping, hormone-sodden teen males—guys just like he had been, once upon a time—popped into his head.

God, she looked so freaking much like Cyndi, although the dark eyes were definitely Farentino stock. And everytime he saw Wendy, or even a photo of her, it socked into him how long it had taken him, was still taking him, to come to grips with her mother's death. Yeah, Cyndi had been the most bull-headed woman he'd ever known, but he'd loved her from the bottom of his heart, and her death had damn near devastated him. He and God were still on the outs about that one. In fact, he pretty much figured if he did get married again, it would be more for companionship—and, okay, sex—than for love. It wasn't that he was saying he'd *never* love again, exactly, as much as he just wasn't sure he *could*. Not the way he'd loved Cyndi, that was for sure.

But then, the next Mrs. Farentino—should there ever be such a creature—would be nothing like Cyndi. She'd be...

Demure. That's it.

Did women even come in *demure* anymore? Or had that concept gone the way of avocado kitchen appliances?

He glanced at Galen.

Huh.

"Uh, yeah," he finally said before she wondered if he'd fallen in a hole or something. "Wendy. She's four and a half. All we've got is each other."

Now why the hell did you say that?

He could feel Galen's gaze dust his cheek, sweep back to the photo. "What a sweetheart."

"She has her moments."

Seconds passed. Del wondered if you could get drunk from just smelling someone. If letting too many hormones flood the bloodstream too fast could give you the bends.

"She has your eyes," Galen said at last, softly, which, for some odd reason, seemed to settle things in her mind, as they decidedly unsettled things in his. Without warning, she took off, leaving Del grabbing for the carrier, then double-stepping to catch up.

He switched everything to one arm, then took her bag from her; she actually didn't protest. "You got any other luggage?"

She shook her head, her russet hair gleaming in the overhead lights as she walked. "I'm only here for the weekend. Oh!"

She swayed again, as if being tossed on a wave. Del reached again for her elbow; she moved away. "I'm fine."

"What you are, is full of it."

"Not any more." She bobbled again, but the hell with her. She didn't want him to touch her, he wouldn't touch her. Well, unless she listed more than twenty degrees, in which case, he was there.

"You didn't eat before you boarded, did you?"

A herd of teenagers, all talking and laughing at the top of

their lungs, swarmed past, forcing Galen to step closer to him or risk being trampled. Close enough to catch another whiff of her hair. Of her. Floral-scented pheromones. A few more hormones surged forth, like an army determined to breach the enemy's stronghold.

The throng of kids passed, Galen reclaimed her space, and the hormones ebbed.

"No, really. I'm okay." Except she went all wobbly again, coming damn close to passing the twenty degree mark.

His hand shot out, grabbed her elbow. "Come on," he said, steering her toward a coffee shop. What the hell—the day was blown, anyway. As long as he was back in time to pick up Wendy, it wasn't as if the guys couldn't cope without him. "You need a cup of tea, something to settle your stomach—"

"Don't tell me what I need!" She squirmed away from his touch, yet again, digging in her heels. Perplexed, Del was startled to see something almost like fear glittering in those turquoise eyes. "I told you, I'm fine." Criminy—they were talking a lousy cup of *tea.* What was with this woman? "If you don't mind, Mr.… Farentino, was it? I'd really just like to get to Cora's."

First he couldn't get her to leave, now he couldn't get her to stay. Del stared her down, ignoring—or so he told himself—the odd prickling sensation in various parts of his body when their gazes locked. "Okay, answer me one thing." The higher of the two slender brows lifted in question. "If you'd just about upchucked all over Cora and *she'd* suggested getting a cup of tea, would you be giving *her* a fight about it?"

She looked away, and Del felt like she'd just broken an electrical connection. "I'm sorry," she said after a moment, her words coming out on a long breath. "I know you mean well. It's just…" She flushed, color staining her pale cheeks. "Please?"

Something slammed into him, although he couldn't have put a name to it. Something about the way she said "Please," as if she'd had to beg one too many times for things she shouldn't have had to. Ten seconds ago, he'd been damn close to lusting after this woman—at least, he thought that's what it was, since it had been so long he wasn't all that sure he recognized the signs anymore—and now he felt like girding those errant loins of his and going to battle for her, slaying dragons or jerks or whatever had put that apprehension in her eyes.

With a nod, he shifted everything to one arm, then reached out to take her elbow; she flinched again. He lifted his free hand. "Sorry."

There went the fear again, flickering across her features. But a smile, too. Shaky, insecure, but a smile. "You're just one of those touchy types, aren't you?"

"What can I tell you? I'm Italian."

The poor little grin petered out. "Oh, that much I know," she said softly, then hitched her purse up onto her shoulder, took a deep breath and headed down the concourse, leaving him once again to follow.

She should have taken her chances with the million other passengers and gotten a taxi. Getting in a confined space with this man was pure lunacy. Not because she was afraid he'd murder her or anything quite that dramatic, but because…

Because…

Spit it out, Volcek.

Because only once before had she been this sexually attracted to a man, and look how that had turned out.

But it made no sense. Not just the part about her blood zinging to parts of her body she'd pretty much decided would need shock treatment to be brought back to life—over a man she'd just met, no less—but because…

Trotting along behind Del through the parking garage, she told herself the flight, the stress of the past few days, had left her addle-brained.

There was no reason Del Farentino should remind her of Vinnie. None. Vinnie was suits and ties. Vinnie was never a hair out of place, manicures and pinky rings, expensive men's cologne and an accent carefully culled of any hint of its working-class roots. Vinnie was culture and class and money, the quintessential product—like his three older brothers—of the American dream. His grandparents might have come to the

States on the great immigration tide at the turn of the century, but they worked their fingers to the bone so their children would have it better than they did, their grandchildren better than that. The four boys, like their parents before them, may have been restaurateurs, but they could hold their own in a conversation anywhere and with anyone.

Del Farentino, on the other hand, was solid blue-collar stock, as average as any other guy she'd ever known in her grandparents' working-class neighborhood. The guys her grandparents wouldn't let her date, the guys they declared weren't good enough for her. Yet, despite what she knew were surface differences, there was…something—a quality? an attitude?—that made her husband and this ordinary, slightly disheveled enormous man striding beside her more alike than different. She just couldn't put her finger on it. And then there was this crazy, unwarranted attraction. To a complete stranger. Sure, he was good looking. And nice, if a little full of himself. And, granted, she'd lived like a nun for three years. Longer, since she and Vinnie hadn't been intimate for some years before his death. But still, it wasn't as if she'd been languishing from sexual frustration all this time. She'd never really thought all that much about it, frankly. Sex 'n' that.

Until about twenty minutes ago.

Caution hummed through her, warning her she needed to…what?

Protect herself.

She started at the thought, not comprehending. For heaven's sake, she was only going to be here for a few days. She probably wouldn't even see him again. Yet, as she watched him lope to the truck, his strides sure and strong, yet oddly reckless, she was again struck by the differences between Vinnie and this man. She couldn't even imagine him in a suit. Not that there wasn't a certain grace to his broad movements, like the movements of a wild beast. But the word "elegant" was not the first word that came to mind when you looked at Del Farentino.

Actually, the first word that came to mind was "hot".

Oh.

Oh, my.

While she stood there, mulling over why her brain had run away with her libido, like the dish with the spoon, Del opened the door to the extended cab, settled all her things, and the dog, in the back, then hooked a hand on her elbow to usher her up to her seat.

His heat sizzled right through her sweater, dancing along her skin clear up to her ears, which must be downright glowing. She told herself she was still feeling the aftereffects of her upset tummy.

He strode around to his side, yanked open his door, climbed in. Yup. Just as she expected. This cab was much too small.

"Put your seatbelt on," he growled, and she shot him a look.

He looked back, heavy black brows dipped. They'd only been outside for a minute, but the sharp, biting wind had done a real number on his shaggy hair. He shoved it back off his forehead. It fell right back. "What?"

She yanked on the belt, drawing it across her chest to ram it into place. There it was. What had reminded her of her husband. The one thing that should easily negate whatever this physical business was. "I'm not a child, Mr. Farentino," she said quietly, directing her gaze out the window. Away from those intense eyes. "I don't need to be told what to do."

His sigh seemed equal parts frustration and contrition. She risked a quick peek at the side of his face as he put the truck into reverse, started to back out of the parking space. His mouth had thinned, but the corner was tilted into kind of a smile. "Sorry." She flinched when his long arm suddenly slammed across the back of the seat, his hand landing right behind her head, as he shifted to see behind him. "Force of habit. Hey…" The truck lurched to a stop, half-in, half-out of the space. "You okay?"

She gasped. The parking garage, redolent with exhaust and gasoline, combined with the tension of unwelcome feelings and even less welcome memories had threatened the fragile peace with her stomach. But she would have been fine had Del not jerked to a stop like that. "I was."

"Ah, hell—you're white as a sheet. You gonna lose it again?"

She couldn't tell if he sounded more annoyed or worried. She sucked in a slow, steadying breath. "No," she said tightly. "I'll be okay as soon as we get out of here and into some real air."

"You sure?"

"I don't need to be coddled," she bit out, hot, dumb tears needling her eyes. "I just need some air, okay?"

His skepticism practically vibrated between them, but he slowly completed the maneuver, carefully driving the truck out of the garage and, within a minute or so, onto the highway. At the moment, despite the heavy, solid clouds still crouched overhead like a huge cat waiting to pounce, the bad weather had called a truce of sorts. She cracked the window, breathing in the damp air. Willing herself to feel normal again.

To feel safe.

"You can open it more, if you want. I don't mind."

She did, afraid to speak, to admit the air wasn't helping at all. To admit she felt, again, like a helpless child, alone and ill in a stranger's truck.

She heard Del chuckle, which she might have enjoyed, actually, were it not for the fact that she really felt like yesterday's garbage and that she had the definite feeling the chuckle was aimed at her. But the words that followed couldn't have been more gentle.

Like Vinnie's used to be.

"Okay, since my pointing out that you're being stubborn would probably only make you feel worse, I'm just gonna say that anytime you want to stop, you only have to say the word, okay?"

Her stomach heaved. How, she didn't know, because there wasn't a blessed thing inside it. She rolled down the window some more.

"How long did you say until we get to Spruce Lake?" she managed, inexplicably angry. At her body, for betraying her in a hundred ways. At herself, for feeling petulant. At Del, for reminding her of Vinnie.

The Vinnie she'd thought she was marrying, anyway.

"Little less than an hour."

An hour? Her eyes burned. How on earth would she make it that long? Oh, why had she let Cora talk her into this? A chill raced up her spine, exploding into a cold sweat at the back of her neck, her forehead.

"*Stop!*"

Del pulled smoothly up onto the shoulder, was out of the truck and to her side before she even got the door open. Then she was on her knees in the wet winter weeds by the side of the road, Del holding her shoulders as she heaved to the sound of traffic whizzing by them.

Could the gauge on her mortification scale possibly sink any lower?

"Better?" she heard in her ear.

Well, apparently, since she started to bawl, there was indeed another point or two left on the bottom of that scale. About what, she had no idea. Nothing. Everything. Barfing in public and losing her grandmother and having no family and embarrassing herself in front of a complete stranger and realizing how really, really bad she was at being alone. And how she had no one but herself to blame for getting herself into such a sorry state.

"Hey, hey…c'mere, honey." Squatting beside her, Del tucked her under his chin, one arm still clamped around her shoulders. "These things happen, y'know? Nothin' to be embarrassed about."

"Oh, right," she said on a shaky breath, not liking how much she liked the way his chin nestled on top of her head. How good it felt to have a man's arm around her again. How this whole man-woman thing was such a crock. "I suppose this kind of thing happens to you all the time."

"Actually, you might be surprised. I do have a four-year-old, you know."

At that, she drew away enough to look up into his eyes. And immediately regretted it. Not because she didn't like what she saw, but because she did. Not just the way the skin crinkled around his eyes when he smiled, or even the profound goodness she sensed behind the smile. No, it went far, far deeper than that, because she suddenly figured out another reason why this man reminded her of Vinnie. Actually, of every man she'd ever known.

Del Farentino, she realized with the force of a thunderclap, was a Protector. Too. The kind of man whose mission, as he saw it, was to take care of all the females in his life, to ensure their health, safety and well-being. On the surface, a desirable enough trait, until the down side of having a man look out for your every need smacks you between the eyes. Until you wake up one day and realize you've never made a single important decision on your own.

Heck, that you've barely made any *little* decisions on your own.

And that, because of what you'd allowed to happen, you weren't considered capable of handling what should have been yours by right.

Vinnie had been a Protector. As had her grandfather. Granted, they had different ways of carrying out their mission, but the message was the same: a woman needed a man to take care of her, to give her what she needed, to guide her through life, to protect her from…herself. Maybe Vinnie had been a kinder, gentler example of the species, using sweet talk and presents to get his way, but get his way, he did. In everything. And how the heck was a completely sheltered eighteen-year-old who'd never even dated another man to know how detrimental such an attitude could be? That her husband's outdated ideas about men's and women's roles, his determination to shield her from the worries and cares of the everyday world— in other words, *life*—had also created the woman who now couldn't take a simple little trip without becoming violently ill?

She scrambled to her feet then, throwing off both Del's concern and his arm. True, she wobbled for a second, but ultimately forced everything to settle down.

Her body hadn't gone haywire because of the plane, or the exhaust smells or anything else physical. Not really. She was sick because she was petrified. Of being alone. Of being on her own. Of being unable to handle decisions other people—other women—handled without a second thought. With the money her grandmother had left her, she really could do pretty much whatever she wanted…and the prospect of being the only person responsible for her life absolutely terrified her.

The prospect, however, of being sucked into another relationship, of falling under another man's protection, terrified her far more.

Still, even though the men in her life could be, in large part, credited for the state in which she now found herself, she wasn't dumb enough or naive enough to consign the entire blame to them. For thirty-five years, Galen Volcek Granata had *let* men boss her around, one way or another. Strip her of her autonomy, her ability to function as a complete human being. For ill or good, she had made her own choices, all along.

Now she had the opportunity to fix things.

She stomped over to the truck, yanked open her own door before Del could, climbed in on her own steam.

"I guess that means you're ready to go?" he said at her window.

"More than I've ever been in my life," she said, chin raised, and the nausea simply vanished.

Chapter 3

Del ordered pizza—extra cheese, black olives, pepperoni—then turned to the stack of dirty dishes patiently waiting for him on the counter beside the sink. God bless Pizza Hut. What with having to pick Galen up at the airport and all, he'd had no choice but to drag Wendy along on his last-minute check-ins. But all was finished, all was fixed, all was well, and now he had five whole days with nothing to do but rest, watch TV, and play with his daughter.

Notice, he did not include *thinking about Galen Granata* on that list.

He rinsed off the last Corelle bowl from breakfast, slowly set it in the drainer. Of course, trying not to think about the redhead was like trying to ignore a mosquito bite. The woman was, without a doubt, the strangest creature he'd ever encountered. Whatever was going on in that gal's head, it was definitely scary. One second, she's looking at him like a lost puppy; the next minute, like he'd just threatened to sue her. Or she, him.

Del dried his hands, rummaged in one of the cupboards for a couple of paper plates. Once back in the truck, Galen had sat with her hands tightly folded in her lap, staring straight ahead, that luscious mouth of hers pulled in a straight line. He made a few lame attempts at conversation, but lighting wet wood would've been easier. After three or four tries, he'd given up.

What bugged him, though, was why her uncommunicativeness should bother him so much. So what? He'd only been doing Cora a favor, after all. Wasn't as if her houseguest was going to be around, someone he had to entertain or even put up with. And if Miss Caribbean Eyes had been actually rude, he probably wouldn't even be thinking about her now. She'd just been...unwilling to talk. As if getting to know him, or letting him get to know her, somehow put her in danger. As if she was trying to prove something to herself.

He wondered about her husband.

He wondered why he was wondering about things that were none of his business.

The phone rang, interrupting pointless musings.

"Yo."

His father, a successful developer, chuckled. "Real professional, Del. Good way to impress all those potential clients, you know?"

Del shrugged, sliding down onto a kitchen chair. "Hey— one, this is my personal number, and two, who the hell would be calling me about a job tonight?"

"Guess you have a point there."

"*Thank* you."

Hugh Farentino laughed again, making Del smile. Dad and he might have had their moments—still did—but he genuinely admired the man. Liked him, too. And he was glad his father, a widower for so many years, had found someone to make him happy. On the surface, Maureen Louden seemed no different than a hundred other well-heeled, Midwest born and bred, middle-aged lady Realtors—blonde and small and pretty and impeccably dressed, no matter what the occasion. But in the year-plus since his father's remarriage, Maureen had proven that, yeah, she was strong willed, to be sure, but also determined to wring every drop of passion out of her life—

and equally determined that everyone in her circle did the same.

It was also almost embarrassingly clear how much she loved Del's father.

Del's heart did this funny stuttering thing, making him frown. Was that a twinge of envy? For Dad and Maureen? Absurd.

"So. Cora told Maureen you hadn't decided whether or not to come to Elizabeth's," his father said.

If he wanted privacy, he'd have to move elsewhere. Like to a hitherto unnamed planet. "I don't know, Dad. Sounds like an awful lot of people…"

"Exactly. All those kids for Wendy to play with."

Apprehension pulled tight in his chest, as it did a hundred times a day. Wendy hadn't met most of these children, they wouldn't know—

"Del," Hugh said softly, interrupting his paranoia. "I know what you're thinking. But you've got to let Wendy start stretching her wings."

"She's not even five yet, Dad—"

That got a laugh. Which Del returned, somewhat. "Okay, yeah, I know she's a little advanced for her years—"

Hugh snorted.

"—but still. And she's also very sensitive…"

"Which doesn't have a damn thing to do with anything, and you know it. That's just the way she is. You were, God knows. And it's something she's going to have to learn to deal with, sooner or later. It'll be fine, Del. And Wendy will have a blast."

Wendy wandered into the kitchen, squeaking a chair across the floor as she yanked it back, sank into it, her face caught in her palms. Bored, would be Del's guess. Just the other day, in fact, she was begging to see Elizabeth's and Guy's kids, including their toddler daughter Chloe.

He was being silly. Wasn't he?

"Okay," Del said on a resigned sigh. "I guess we'll be there."

"Good. Give our girl a hug for us."

Del no sooner hung up than the doorbell rang. Wendy jumped up, holding out her hands for the money, which he retrieved from his wallet and handed to her. He opened the door and took the pizza, letting Wendy pay—keeping an eye on the delivery kid to make sure they got the right change back—his chest swelling with pride when she said a very clear "Thank you" to the kid as he left.

Galen looked up from unpacking her few things from her bag, blinking in astonishment at Cora, enthroned in an armchair in front of the heavily draped guest-room window. Somehow, in all the thousands and thousands of words they'd already exchanged since her arrival, Cora had overlooked these. Just as Galen had not mentioned Del Farentino, other than to thank Cora for sending him. She was having enough trouble figuring out her bizarre reaction to the man without throwing her surrogate mother a bone to gnaw on.

"What do you mean, we're going to somebody's house for dinner on Thanksgiving?" The dog jumped up on Cora's guest-room bed; Galen pushed her off before the beast's sharp nails snagged the comforter's ivory satin cover. Nonplussed, Baby pranced over to Cora, who scooped her up onto her broad lap. "What was all this about not wanting to spend the holiday alone?"

"And you believed me?"

Galen let out a weary sigh, then carried her sweaters over to the bureau drawer.

"See, Elizabeth and Maureen are doing the turkeys—"

Galen turned so fast she nearly put out her shoulder. "*Turkeys?* Plural?"

"Well, yeah, since one bird ain't gonna feed fifty people—oh, close your mouth. It'll be fun. And then everybody else is bringing the side dishes." One maroon-nailed hand drifted up to toy with a processed wave artfully draped across a forehead smooth as the polished walnut headboard on the bed. "'Course, with Elizabeth, you can't call it *potluck,* since she wouldn't likely see the humor in a table full of twenty-five pumpkin pies and nothing else. So she assigned people food groups."

With a smile, Galen turned back to the bed, fishing her underwear from the bag. She'd already heard a lot about this woman and her tendencies toward obsessive-compulsiveness. And how her marriage to Guy Sanford, a free spirit with three young children and no discernible fashion sense, had loosened her up quite a bit in the past couple of years. "And what did you get?"

"Green vegetables." Clutching the dog to her impressive bosom, she tugged the hem of her loose red sweater back over her thighs. "'Cept when I suggested bringin' a mess of greens, she kinda blanched. Oh, she's too polite to say anything, but she sure did brighten up when I mentioned as how a green bean casserole might hold up better, you know? Oh, honey…"

Galen looked up. "What?"

"I see you didn't get to buy yourself that new underwear after all."

Galen glanced down at the white cotton undies in her hands. "Sure I did. See?" She waved a bra. "Still has the tag and everything."

Cora heaved herself from the chair, canine in tow, and snatched the bra from Galen's hand. Glowered at it. "You mean, you just inherited two hundred fifty *thousand* dollars, and you bought underwear from K mart?"

"What's wrong with that?"

"Well, child, if you have to ask, there's your answer right there." Cora tossed the bra back like it was a snake, then *hmmphed* through her nose. "What are you now? Thirty-four, thirty-five? And still dressing like they just let you outta the convent. Girl, I would kill for that figure you got, and there you go, keeping it all covered up like it was some kinda sin to let the world see how gorgeous you are. And then have the nerve to wear that sorry stuff underneath."

Galen felt her cheeks flame. "It's cotton. I like it."

It's what good girls wear. Good women. The kind of woman I married, Galen.

Over another hmmph behind her, Galen added, "Besides,

it's not like I've got anyone to exactly, well..." To her cha-
grin, she blushed even more. "Wear it for," she finally finished. And no, that was not Del Farentino's hooded, appreciative gaze that just popped into her head.

And call it instinct, but somehow she had the feeling Del
wouldn't tell her only cheap women wore fancy, lacy underwear.

She also had the feeling she was losing it, hooking up Del
and sexy underwear in the same sentence when she no earthly
reason to be thinking about either of them at all.

"Who said anything about anybody else?" Cora was saying. "A woman wears pretty things next to her skin because
they make *her* feel good. Like a *woman,* you hear what I'm
saying? At least, that's the first reason to wear 'em. Any other
reason that might happen to come along's just frosting on the
cake."

Her cheeks still burning, Galen quickly tucked the garments
in the drawer, slamming it shut maybe a little harder than she
meant to. Somehow, she knew what was coming.

"Anyway, you didn't wear anything pretty for your husband?"

*What the hell is this? If I'd wanted someone cheap, I
would've married one of the Ruscetti girls. So you just take
that stuff back to the store. If they give you a hard time, tell
'em your husband said he didn't like it....*

"They...all wore out."

Cora plopped back down into the chair, laughing low in her
throat. Her "uh-huh" laugh. Galen knew Cora didn't mean
her reaction to sting, but the truth was...

The truth was, Galen really didn't feel like thinking about
the past tonight. Or ever. Far as she was concerned, there was
only the future, starting right this very minute. A future completely non-dependent on what kind of underwear she wore.
The eighteen-year-old girl who'd only bought the pretty lingerie because she thought it might please her husband, the
husband she loved more than she'd ever loved anyone in her
life, didn't exist anymore.

And the thirty-five-year-old woman who'd taken her place was perfectly happy with cotton.

Vinnie hadn't been mean about it, really. Or even angry. In fact, something like amusement had flashed in his dark eyes when she'd come to him, shyly untying the deep green satin robe she'd bought to go with the matching satin bikini panties, the push-up bra. No, he'd just looked at her—briefly—as he might have a child who'd put her shoes on the wrong feet. Then he'd pulled the robe closed, kissed her on top of her head, and calmly told her to go change.

And take back the underwear. Which of course she couldn't do because she'd worn it. If only for five minutes.

When she'd finally thrown it out, she didn't fully understand, not then, why she felt like something'd been stolen from her.

"Okay." Galen turned around, arms folded across her waist, mentally whapping at the heebie-jeebies. Wondering who she might have been, if she hadn't made some of the choices she had. If she hadn't let desperation cloud reason, all those years ago. How long, she wondered, could a seed remain dormant before it would no longer spring to life? Guess she was about to find out, huh? "You're doing green beans. What can I do?"

"Do?" Cora leaned back, her features twisted. "Baby, unless I'm very mistaken, this is the closest thing you've had to a vacation in years. Nobody expects you to so much as lift a finger while you're here."

Galen squinted at her. "You're forgetting. This is the woman who loves to cook, who hasn't had a chance to strut her stuff for nearly five years. Invalids and old ladies aren't very appreciative when it comes to anything fancier than custard and boiled chicken." She grinned, several possibilities swirling around in her brain. "You wouldn't have a pasta maker by any chance?"

Cora's eyes went wide. "You *make* pasta?"

"It's the only way."

"Uh, no. The only way is to buy stuff in boxes, throw it in boiling water, ten minutes later you eat."

"You'd make a lousy Italian, Cora."

"Not something that keeps me awake at nights, believe me." Cora stood again and tramped to the door, still hanging on to the moony-faced dog. "Besides, Miss Irish-Slovak Mutt, you weren't exactly born singing 'O Sole Mio' yourself."

"Minor point."

Cora chuckled, then said on her way out the door, "But, as it happens, I do have a pasta maker."

Galen followed, confused. "But you said—"

"Didn't say I used it." Cora started down the narrow stairs, one wide hand braced on what seemed to Galen to be a very flimsy banister. "Rod and Nancy—you'll meet them tomorrow, friends of Elizabeth's and Guy's, she's crazier than a loon but they're both just the sweetest people you'd ever want to meet—anyway, they gave me one when I moved in here. He's some sort of gourmet cook himself, you should *see* his kitchen, honey. Mm-*mm*. But back to what I was saying before..." Now at the bottom of the stairs, she turned back to Galen, brows drawn together. "You're supposed to be taking it easy."

Galen stopped, two steps from the bottom, hands tucked in her pockets. "For heaven's sake, Cora. I'm on vacation, not convalescent. So where's this pasta maker?"

"You don't have to do this—"

"Hey—you want me to go to this thing? You let me bring something."

"Oh, Lord." Shaking her head, Cora pivoted on the bare wooden floor, her leather-soled flats tapping against the boards as she made her way to the kitchen. "Now I'm beginning to remember what you were like as a child. Like to give your mama fits, what with you always getting a bee in your bonnet about one thing or another." She finally jettisoned the dog, then opened and closed several heavily enameled white kitchen cupboard doors before she found what she was looking for. She lugged the machine off the shelf, thunking it down onto a badly worn Formica counter in a hideous shade of aqua.

Galen *oohed* at the pasta maker for several seconds before

Cora's words sank in. She looked up, brow puckered. "What are you talking about?"

"Baby, you were a real piece of work when you were little. Stubborn? Hardheaded? Willful?" Cora laughed. "Take your pick." She nodded toward the appliance. "That okay?"

"What? Oh, yeah." Her brain spinning, Galen caressed the glistening surface of the appliance. "This is like the Rolls-Royce of pasta makers."

"Yeah?" Cora looked at it the way those people did on the "Antiques Road-show" when the appraiser told them the piece of junk that had been sitting in their great-aunt's attic for a thousand years was worth more than their house, then shrugged. "Still." Then she took off for the living room, leaving Galen, once again, to follow. Which she only did because she wanted Cora to tell her what the heck she was talking about.

Cora grabbed the clicker from the coffee table, settled herself on one end of the nubby, striped sofa. "Now, I'm not saying you were a bad child. Nothing like that. You never sassed your mama, least not that I ever heard. And you were always so good with my girls, even though they were so much younger than you. But you sure were a determined little thing. When you wanted something, you'd either drive your mama nuts until she gave in, or figured out some way to get whatever it was you wanted on your own." She angled her head, frowning. "You don't remember that?"

With a sigh, Galen sank into the overstuffed cushions beside Cora, her arms knotted at her waist. "Vaguely. But somewhere along the line..." She stopped, trying to figure out how to put what she felt into words. The dog hopped up onto her lap, bestowing two tiny kisses on her knuckles. Galen smiled in spite of herself. "I guess my parents' deaths shook me more than I even realized."

"Knocked all the fight out of you, in other words."

"Maybe. Yeah, I guess."

"Well, honey—" Cora aimed the clicker at the TV, surfing through several channels until she lit on some sitcom Galen had watched once and vowed to never watch again "—ain't nobody around to tell you what to do anymore, is there? You wanna make something for dinner, you go right ahead.'' Without waiting for a reply, she waved at the TV. ''You like this show?''

Galen reached around to finger a stray hair tickling the back of her neck. ''Actually…'' Cora pinned her with a look she'd seen a thousand times on her grandmother's face. ''Sure. It's…one of my favorites.''

''Good. I was hoping you'd say that.''

Galen just sighed.

Even though the brilliant flush of high autumn was long past, Thanksgiving decided to be clear and bright and crisp, a day to do Norman Rockwell proud. Around two, Cora's little Ford Probe slid in behind a conga line of minivans snaking around from the front of Elizabeth's and Guy's corner-lotted Victorian. They got out, carefully withdrawing the terry-blanketed casseroles from the floor behind the front seat: Cora's green-bean casserole and a dish Galen had learned to make on the sly by watching Vinnie's grandmother. Galen had dragged Cora all over creation for two hours yesterday before she found a store with the right kind of prosciutto ham, the Parmesan cheese—fresh, not the Kraft stuff—the ricotta. Then, this morning, she'd spent a couple more blissful hours in the kitchen, humming contentedly as she chopped and stirred and layered, while Cora made assorted ''better you than me, baby'' comments.

To tell the truth, Galen had often thought she preferred cooking to sex. A revelation she kept to herself, for obvious reasons. Sex had always left her feeling…what? Agitated, somehow. Like there should be more, but she couldn't quite put her finger on what the ''more'' should be. It wasn't that Vinnie was bad in bed as much as he just didn't seem all that interested.

So much for the passionate Italian lover theory.

Instead, she found incredible satisfaction in making even the most intricate, complicated dishes from scratch. When she was in the kitchen, rolling out pasta, chopping herbs, layering cheeses and meats in obscenely expensive pans, she was at peace. Since she'd been married to an Italian, she'd learned to cook Italian. Learned to cook it *well*.

Even if she rarely had the opportunity to show off her talents.

A gaggle of shrieking, laughing children swooped past them, tossing huge armfuls of curled, crinkly leaves in a hundred shades of brown at each other, as Galen and Cora waded through the arboreous debris up to the house, a dusty-blue-trimmed white Victorian with a wide wraparound porch on three sides. The house was set far back on a large lot overflowing with lush evergreens and the graceful skeletons of a dozen or more deciduous trees, slashes of charcoal against the sharp blue sky; a few blocks to Galen's left, she could see the glint of water sparkling at the end of what looked like a park. She inhaled deeply, delighting in the pungent-sweet scent of moldering leaves and fireplace smoke, even as a strange, inexplicable mixture of contentment, apprehension and regret swirled around her heart.

"Cora!"

A laughing woman's voice cut through Galen's thoughts. They'd just about reached the porch steps; she looked up to see a petite blonde standing in front of the open door. Slung on the woman's trim hip was a toddler in pink overalls and flyaway blond hair, guzzling something in a Sippee cup. This was one classy lady, Galen decided at once, feeling downright dowdy in her brown sweater and slacks, her hair pulled back in its standard clip. A finely knit, obviously expensive, heathery blue turtleneck sweater hugged the woman's slender figure, dipped into matching wool slacks. She wore her pale hair pulled into a neat twist at the back of her head, a few wisps floating around her delicately featured face. Simple pearl earrings glinted in her ears; her makeup was understated, perfectly applied. Her lightly glossed lips, however, were pulled up into a broad, welcoming smile. She held out her free hand...which is when Galen spotted the Popsicle stick turkey, enthusiastically and messily painted, pinned to one shoulder.

"You must be Galen," she said, her handshake firm and

warm. "Welcome to the funny farm. I'm Elizabeth, and this is Chloe, my daughter, and I'm not even gonna *try* to introduce you to everyone else! It's each person for him- or herself today."

Just then, a dark-haired man with the brightest blue eyes Galen had ever seen poked his head out the front door, a single gold stud gleaming in one ear. "There you are," he said to the blonde. "Wondered where you went."

"I escaped," Elizabeth announced. "Between your mother, my mother and Rod, that kitchen is way too crowded. Galen…Granata, isn't it?" Galen nodded, impressed she remembered. "My husband, Guy Sanford. Well, come on in," she said, sidling through the door, the baby beating on her shoulder with the empty cup. "We're still waiting on a few stragglers. In the meantime, we're setting everything up on the dining table."

The scent of roast turkey and spices and just-cleaned house washed over Galen as they walked through the high-ceilinged entry hall, the ivory walls splashed with splinters of sunlight from the cut-glass panes in the transom over the front door. Elizabeth glanced at Cora's foil-covered dish. "Green beans?"

"Well, I guess you'll just have to wait and see, won't you, Miss Nosybody?" And with that, she tromped off, leaving Galen standing alone with Elizabeth, feeling abandoned and awkward. Guy had also disappeared; Elizabeth lowered the fussy toddler to the floor, who headed toward the living room, a warm, cluttered collection of leather furniture and antiques in shades of golds and dark reds. The baby was making fast tracks toward the largest, scruffiest dog Galen had ever seen.

"Chloe?" The baby pivoted around, her mouth tucked into a "who, me?" expression. "Be nice to Einstein, okay?"

Chloe babbled something completely unintelligible, then resumed the pursuit of her quarry, who seemed not the least bit concerned he was about to be attacked by twenty pounds of unbridled affection.

Elizabeth watched for a moment as the dog slowly rolled to his back so the little girl could pat his stomach, sighed, then turned her attention back to Galen. "I know he's ten times bigger than she is, but those cute little hands of hers can be lethal. Come on back," she said, her low-heeled pumps soundless on the Oriental-patterned runner leading back to the dining room, then glanced back at the dish in Galen's hands. "More green beans?"

"Uh, no. Spinach and prosciutto pasta."

Brows lifted, Elizabeth stopped in her tracks, lifted a corner of the foil covering the dish. "Ooooh…that smells absolutely *wonderful*." She took the dish from Galen's hands, carrying it over to the lace-covered dining room table herself. "Hey, you two!" she said to a pair of little boys, one blond, one dark-haired, black olives tipping *all* their fingers. "Go on, scoot! It's not time yet—"

"Mama," the darker-haired boy said, stuffing three olives in his mouth, then tugging on her sleeve. "Look what Micah did to the pumpkin pie—"

"I did not!" the blond kid shot back. "It was already like that!"

"Oh, yeah? Then how come your breath smells like pumpkin pie?"

"Boys?" They both looked up at their mother. "Go *away*."

Exchanging half-hearted jabs, they did. Bracing Galen's casserole against her hip, Elizabeth scanned the table, already smothered in assorted baskets and casseroles and plastic bowls. "Here—move those rolls over there—yeah, that's right—and that bowl of…whatever it is, to the right of the Jell-O mold—" Galen smiled at the ill-concealed grimace "—there!" Elizabeth set the casserole down, clearly pleased with herself.

"Okay, where you want the ice?"

Galen whipped around to run smack into Del Farentino's startled smile.

"Oh, great!" Elizabeth said. "There's an ice chest…" She peeked around the corner of the table. "Ah. Right here. Just plop it on in there." She looked up, then from one to the other. "Oh, uh…you two already met?"

Galen folded her arms against her ribs, quickly taking in Del's unbuttoned, untucked plaid shirt casually framing a torso-hugging T-shirt disappearing into the waistband of a pair of worn jeans. "Del picked me up from the airport the other day," she said, silently pleading for him not to say anything else.

"Oh, that's right. Cora told me." Elizabeth snatched an olive herself, then headed toward the swinging door which Galen assumed led to the kitchen. "Where's Wendy?"

Del grinned. A little unsteadily, Galen thought. "God only knows. She saw the kids playing in the leaves, took off like a shot." Galen saw his glance swerve toward the table, after which he let out a long, low whistle. "Man oh man, that's a lot of food."

"Nobody'll leave here starving, that's for sure," Elizabeth agreed, then vanished through the door, leaving it swinging in her wake.

Leaving Galen alone with Del. She was gonna kill Cora when she saw her again. She laced her hands together, only to immediately unlace them. Then she turned to the table, fiddling with the pile of plastic flatware dumped on the corner. Ridiculous, the way her heart was pounding. Like she was interested or something. Jiminy Christmas.

"Wonder where everyone else is?" she said through a scratchy throat.

"Oh, that's easy. Kids are all outside, men are all in the family room watching a game and the women are either in the kitchen or upstairs criticizing the decor."

She smiled. But not at him.

He stepped closer, smelling of cold air and aftershave and some indefinable unique scent that made her want to smell more. That made her want to run away. She shut her eyes, reminding herself it was a trap, making men smell good. Nature's way of derailing a woman, making her believe in things that weren't real. Of making her miss the point. Not to mention the boat.

"Which one's yours?" he asked, looming over the table, his hands braced on his hips. "And please don't tell me it's the Jell-O mold."

Her own laugh surprised her. She'd really have to watch

that. Letting him make her laugh. Because then, see, she might discover she really liked him. And even that was too great a risk. "No. It's the one over there, by the cranberry sauce. Oh! What are you doing?"

Del had made an exaggerated show of peering over his shoulder before snitching one of the individually sliced rolls, holding it over the palm of his other hand as he munched. "Sampling," he said around the bite, then groaned.

Galen shrugged, trying not to take it personally. "It's not to everyone's liking, I know—"

"Are you kidding?" Del stuffed another bite into his mouth, promptly speared another piece with a plastic fork. "You made this from scratch?"

She nodded, feeling a blush of pride sweep up her cheeks.

"God, I haven't had anything this good since I was a kid at my grandmother's house." Then he gave her a smile, all goofy and wonderful and warm.

With a little cry, she ran from the room.

Chapter 4

What the hell?

Still chewing, Del stared in the direction Galen had fled. Great. Five minutes with the woman, she either throws up or runs away. Real boost for the old male ego.

Not that it mattered one way or the other what Galen Granata thought of him, especially since she was leaving in three days. Especially since he felt downright…unfinished next to her. No, she didn't exude the studied perfection of Maureen or Elizabeth, or even the casual stylishness of Nancy Braden, Elizabeth's best friend. But there was something about Galen's naturalness, her quiet reticence, that just knocked him for a loop whenever he saw her. She was, quite simply, flawless.

Del was, equally simply, not.

"What was that all about?"

He hadn't heard the kitchen door open, or seen Guy, armed with two cans of black olives, head in his direction. His head humming, Del turned to his step-brother-in-law. "Damned if I know. I complimented Galen on her contribution to the groaning board, and she lit out of here like I'd insulted her."

"Huh." Guy dumped the olives into the almost empty crystal dish, his layered, shoulder-length hair swishing over a bold, geometric-patterned sweater in shades of black, purple and bright blue. "Women are strange beasts, no doubt about it. Forget it, dog," he said to Einstein, who'd wandered into the room on the off-chance someone had called him to dinner. With a groan, the shaggy beast slunk out again, head and tail hanging. Guy set down the empty cans on the corner of the table, wiping his hands on his jeans. "Good-looking woman," he said, too casually.

Del shrugged, refusing to take the bait. "Yeah. I guess."

"Bet she doesn't think she is, either."

"I couldn't say."

Silence.

Guy rubbed his index finger under his lower lip, surveying the spread. "So. What'd she bring?"

Del bit back a smile at the way Guy had just backed down. For the moment, at least. "I don't know the real name. Pasta rolls, stuffed with cheese and ham. My grandmother used to make it when I was a kid. Go ahead—try one."

Guy picked up a piece, opened his mouth. Shut it again, his brow wrinkled. "What's the green stuff?"

"Spinach. Least, that's the way my grandmother made it."

Incredulous blue eyes met his. "And you *liked* it?"

"Hey—you ain't tasted spinach until you've tasted what an *Italian* can do with spinach."

Guy squinted. "I thought Cora said Granata was Galen's *married* name."

"Close enough."

Still, Guy took a cautious bite, chewing slowly at first, then more quickly, his expression changing from skeptical to "wow" within three seconds.

"Was I right or what? Good stuff, huh?"

Guy shoved in another piece. "Any woman who can do this to spinach..." Still chewing, he grabbed the cans and went back into the kitchen, leaving Del to finish the sentence any old way he pleased.

Her heart pounding painfully inside her chest, Galen ducked outside, hoping maybe a few breaths of fresh air would clear her head. She strode across the porch, down the steps, sinking onto the bottom one, her head clamped between her hands.

This had to stop.

Too many thoughts were stampeding through her brain for her to sort them all out, to make enough sense, even, of them to get control. She felt dizzy, off-balance, as if someone had tilted the floor underneath her feet. For heaven's sake, all Del had done was compliment her cooking and smile at her. Period. He wasn't flirting, coming on to her, or otherwise threatening her in any way. He probably wasn't even attracted to her. Not really. Not in the I'd-like-to-get-to-know-you-better sense, at least.

Heat seared her cheeks, again.

Okay, so it had been a while since a male-type person had even looked at her, let alone been nice to her. Other than the occasional bag boy at the Giant Eagle, maybe. And she was feeling a bit odd woman outish, in this house filled with people she didn't know. Refined, classy people. Oh, sure, Elizabeth and Guy were friendly 'n' that, and it wasn't like their house looked like a museum or anything. But even with four kids, from what she could tell, it still looked like something from one of those home decorating magazines. Like grown-ups lived there, too.

Galen hooked her hands around one knee, listening to the cacophony of children laughing and calling out to each other from the other side of the house. She knew she wasn't stupid. It wasn't that. But not having gone to college or pursued a career put her at a definite disadvantage. She simply didn't fit in with these people.

As much as she ached to be like them.

She frowned, thinking about that. She'd never envied anyone before, not that she could remember. Not even when the other girls in her class got to date or wear makeup and she couldn't. She guessed she'd always been one of those types who just accepted her lot in life. Her chin found its way into her palm as she let out a long, bewildered sigh. When had that changed? When had *she* changed? And what was it about the people inside that house she envied?

The answer came almost immediately: *confidence.*

She sat up straight, as if she'd been prodded. It wasn't their clothes or education or the material trappings of their lives, but the self-confidence they all radiated. They knew who they were, what they were about, what their purpose was in life. And it didn't matter, she realized, what that purpose was. Just that they *had* one. A purpose of their own choosing, whether it be family or career or whatever.

At that moment, Galen didn't know whether it had been family interference or just plain old-fashioned circumstances that had robbed her of the drive and focus all those people inside that house had in spades. But without it, she was face-less, a non-entity.

With it, she'd never have to run from a man's presence again, would she?

She got up from the steps, hugging herself as she walked toward the sound of the children's voices. The wind snatched at her hair, tugging it out of its clasp; she pushed it back as she watched the impromptu game of tag in front of her. A couple of the older children, particularly a tall, spiked-haired blond girl of about eighteen, kept watch over the toddlers while the middle-aged children raced away from whoever was "it," their voices shrill and clear. Galen recognized Elizabeth's and Guy's two boys in the pack, their shirts untucked from their pants, their faces flushed with cold and laughter. She folded her arms against her ribs, pushing back the pang of melancholy that still, no matter how hard she fought it, swept through her from time to time. She'd told herself, when Vinnie died, it was for the best they never had those babies they'd planned on.

But then, she'd at least have that purpose, wouldn't she?

Someone—a gangly boy with glasses, maybe fifteen or so—yelled out to one of Elizabeth's boys, blindly headed toward a little girl with white-blond hair, a doll of a child in a rust-colored jumper and white tights. Del's daughter, Galen real-ized, only a second before she also realized the child, who'd bent down to scratch the huge dog, now lying in the leaves, couldn't see that Elizabeth's boy had lost his balance and was about to land right on top of her.

"Hey!" Galen shouted, wishing she could remember the child's name. Leaves flew in all directions as she took off toward her, yelling "Watch out!" at the top of her lungs. She dove for the child, snatching her out of the way a split second before the boy tripped over the dog. Both of them tumbled into a pile of leaves, the little girl landing, her mouth open in shock, on top of Galen.

"Hey, sweetie," she said, more winded than anything else. "You almost got creamed. Didn't you hear us calling you?"

She noticed the child's gaze, riveted to her lips. Gently, Galen brushed back the little girl's wispy hair, revealing a large two-piece hearing aid wrapped around the tiny, delicate ear.

Del had seen what was about to happen from the side living room window, nearly going straight through the glass in his panic. How many times had he told her not to get so close to large groups of children when they were playing rough like that? She was so impossibly little, built like her mother...it wouldn't take much for a heavier kid to flatten her like a bug. He hit the side yard just in time to see Galen take that flying tackle, sweeping his daughter out of harm's way.

Seconds later, the child was in his arms. "You okay?" he signed, one-handed.

She nodded, that wicked grin pushing up her cheeks. "The lady caught me," she signed. She brushed the first two fingers of her right hand against the tip of her nose, twice. "Funny."

"Yeah." Del let his butt drop to the ground. "Hilarious." Wendy angled her head, not understanding. He echoed her "funny" sign, then scowled at her. "I thought I told to you to be careful playing around the other kids?"

She scowled back, pointing toward the far side of the yard. "They were over there," she signed. "I was being careful—"

"Really," Galen said, apparently picking up on the gist of Wendy's protest, "she wasn't in the thick of things." Del glanced over, his breath catching at the earnest expression in those clear blue-green eyes. Then she smiled, pushing a floating strand of hair from her face. "The thick of things found her."

"Yeah. They usually do," he muttered, then pivoted Wendy around to face Galen, hands on her slender waist. She looked back. "This is Galen," he said, finger spelling Galen's name. "Say 'thank you'."

Wendy turned around, touched her lips with the fingertips of her right hand, then extended her hand outward. "Thang you," she said slowly.

"You're welcome," Galen said, her eyes darting from Del to Wendy, then back again. She'd gotten to her knees, her sweater and hair—which had come loose from its clasp, twin sheets of copper against fair cheeks—embellished with bits of leaves. "What's your name?" she asked, pointing to Wendy, an instinctive sign that got the desired response.

"Wen-dy Fah-wan-dino," she said with a huge smile. She'd just learned to say her last name a couple of weeks ago, in fact, and the glow of accomplishment hadn't yet faded. Then she turned back to Del, whacking leaves off her bottom. "Can I go back and play?" she signed.

Del looked out at the raucous gang of kids hurtling themselves at each other with great abandon, then felt Wendy tug at his loose shirt. He looked down, wincing at the devilment in her dark brown eyes.

"I'll be careful," she signed, then touched her right index finger to her lips, opening the hand to bump her wrist against the top of her other hand. "Promise."

He let out a resigned sigh. "Hold on…" He reached up to check that both aids were securely seated, then sent her off with a pat on the behind.

"She's absolutely adorable," Galen said at his elbow. "And I bet Daddy's already plotting on how to keep the boys at bay."

For several seconds, all he could do was stare at Galen, unable to breathe, let alone move. His daughter's handicap was perfectly obvious—the hearing aids, the signing, the denasalized, almost mechanical speech. Yet, the first words out of this woman's mouth were to remark on how adorable his daughter was. But what had him momentarily unable to function was not so much the words—politeness, an unwillingness to hurt his feelings, could just as well have produced the comment—but the ingenuousness of her statement. The sincerity. Heaven knows, he and Wendy had met enough well-meaning people since her birth, people who'd say "What a pretty little girl" with that catch in their voice, smiling at Wendy with eyes full of pity. Or fear. Or embarrassed gratitude that their child wasn't "like that."

Not this time. He knew, as well as he knew his name, that Galen Granata had looked at his child and seen...a child. The child he loved. Not the child that made so many people uncomfortable or nervous.

"I had a deaf friend, growing up," Galen said quietly, looking back over the yard. "And the one thing she most hated was the way everyone always saw her as deaf first, a person second." She turned those impossibly turquoise eyes to him. "That stayed with me."

Del got to his feet, held out a hand to help Galen up, which, not surprisingly, she refused. "Did you learn to sign, then?"

Hugging herself, Galen shook her head. "Her parents wouldn't let her. She was being taught by the...Oral method, I think it was called. Actually, I think she picked up signing later, after she got out of school. But we lost touch soon after that. After I got married."

For a long minute, they both stood with their arms crossed, watching the racing, shrieking children. And he saw the longing in her face. If he had any sense, he wouldn't ask. Since he didn't, he did.

"You...don't have kids of your own?"

She flicked a glance in his direction, shook her head. "I can't have them," she said quietly. "Damaged goods and all that. Oh! Look—I think they're telling us the food's ready!"

She started toward the house; he grabbed her hand, twisting her back to him. "There's nothing damaged about you, Galen Granata. You got that?" There went that scared-doe look

again, intensified by the plain brownness of her outfit. Her
hand was smooth, but strong. A hand that rolled out pasta,
chopped ham. Brushed the hair from a little girl's eyes.

He longed to do the same for her, to touch that soft, shimmering mass floating around her shoulders, firestruck in the
shaft of late afternoon sunlight angling through the bare trees.
"You got that?" he repeated.

He saw the tears gather in the corners of her eyes, but she
nodded.

"Good." He gave her hand a brief, gentle squeeze. "Thank
you for coming to the rescue."

She slipped her hand from his, tucking it, with the other
one, against her waist. "It was nothing," she murmured, then
turned and walked quickly away.

Odd how, not a half-hour before, she'd been leery of being
with so many people she didn't know. Now she was grateful
for the crowd, for being one of a herd, swarming around the
feeding trough. Shyly, she introduced herself to various smiling middle-aged men in cabled pullovers and flannel shirts and
the occasional sport jacket and turtleneck, as well as to their
wool-skirted or denim-jumpered or designer-jeaned wives.
Most of them were Sanfords, she realized, as were the vast
majority of children. And other than Cora—and Del—she was
the only unattached person over eighteen there.

This person or that tried to draw her into conversation, but
since they all knew each other, talk quickly centered on what
this or that kid was doing, who got a new car or house, who
was expecting a new baby. They didn't mean to leave her out,
she knew. They just had a lot to catch up on. At one point,
she searched out Cora, who looked up, waving her over to the
handsome older couple at her side. The man's sharply-honed
features looked vaguely familiar, his hair that dark pewter
when black hair goes gray; he stood possessively close to a
small, fine-boned blonde who looked familiar, too. Galen
shook her head "no," however, indicating she'd meet up with
her friend later. Actually, after twenty minutes of being buried
in a dozen overlapping conversations, she'd had enough. Be-

sides, cutting turkey with the side of a plastic fork, standing up, was the pits.

She slithered through a knot of laughing Sanfords, filched a plastic knife from the table, then slithered back out to the far less populated entryway, settling with her plate on the next-to-bottom tread of the wide, carpeted stairway hugging one wall. She carefully set her cider-filled plastic "glass" between her and the wall, letting out a long, heartfelt sigh.

"Yeah, that's about my reaction, too."

Her head snapped up at the low voice, as her heart simultaneously did an erratic pool-shot number in her chest. She jabbed at a small pile of green beans, trying for nonchalant. "Amazing, the way we keep running into each other."

Balancing his own plate in one hand, Del awkwardly slid down onto the step beside her. But not too close, she noticed. Next to the banister. Leaving a good four feet between them. "And why do I get the feeling the phrase *like a bad penny* is in there somewhere?"

"That's not what I—"

"Joke, honey. Just a joke," Del said, a smile tugging at his lips.

"Oh. Yes." She glanced around. "Where's Wendy?"

"Couldn't pry her away from the other kids." He took a sip of the cider. Grimaced.

Galen couldn't help but smile. "There's beer out in the garage, I hear."

"Ah. I wondered."

He was watching her. She wished he wouldn't. Was flattered that he was. Well, unless she had marshmallow on her nose or something. She casually lifted her hand to her face to check.

Nope.

On a soft sigh—of relief? terror?—she poked at a chunk of sweet potato, then looked out toward the still-swarming dining room. "So," she managed over a suddenly trembling everything, "I'm here because of Cora. Obviously. From what I can tell, though, nearly everybody else is family. So how'd you wrangle an invitation?"

"Because I'm part of the everybody else."

Puzzled, she shook her head, a sweet potato hovering six inches from her mouth.

"I'm family, too. Elizabeth's mother married my father."

The couple with Cora! No wonder they both looked familiar. Then, on a soft gasp: "You're Elizabeth's *step*-brother?"

"Like Beauty and the Beast, huh?"

"No! No, not at all—oh. Another joke?"

Del chuckled around a bite of food. She watched, oddly fascinated, by the interplay of muscles framing his hollowed cheeks, his strong, angular jaw as he chewed. His hair, she noted, though still shaggy, gleamed like silk in the sunlight filtering through that cut-glass transom. She tore her gaze away, rubbing the fingers of her right hand against each other, as if wiping away crumbs. She wished he hadn't sat there. Wished she had the guts to just get up and leave. But that would be rude. Past rude. It would be mean. If the guy was being obnoxious, that would be one thing. Since he wasn't...

Well.

"Actually, though, we've only been connected for the last year and a half or so," she heard Del say. "Wasn't as if we were raised together or anything."

"Oh." Galen looked back down at her food. Del still stared. At her.

"You okay?" he asked gently, and she couldn't have said why such a simple, polite entreaty sent shivers of irritation skittering up her spine.

"Yes," she replied, more sharply than she intended, then sucked in a breath. "It's been a long time since I've been around this many people. Especially this many strangers. That's all."

"Hey, I can relate, believe me. But if you're gonna get stuck with a bunch of people you don't know from Adam, this is a pretty good group to get stuck with. Okay...skootch on over here, and I'll tell you who's who."

She froze. Del looked back at her. Gave her that off-kilter grin. "It's okay. I took a shower before we came."

"No...oh, no!" Without thinking, she reached out, laid a

hand on his arm, snatched it back immediately, then broke into nervous laughter. "It's not…that."

Del set his plate two steps up, then leaned against the banister, his head cocked. One long blue-jeaned leg stretched out onto the wood-planked floor. He'd partially buttoned the plaid shirt, which now lay in sensuous, haphazard folds across his chest and flat, hard stomach, accentuating the rise and fall of his muscles as he breathed. He exuded the easy, natural grace of a man fit from hard work, not from a gym. And a raw sexuality she didn't know existed outside of a novel. A sexuality that frightened her.

Fascinated her.

"Cora tells me you're a widow," he said quietly.

Eyes wide, she looked at him. Nodded.

"How long?"

"A little over three years."

"Happy marriage?"

Her face burned. She cleared her throat, drew her knees together. Fourteen years of marriage, and she couldn't remember a single time when she'd felt whatever it was she was feeling right now. Like she could set a lightbulb to glowing, just by touching it. "Sure."

Her gaze meandered to his hands. Strong hands, calloused and dexterous, the tops lightly dusted with dark brown hair, the nails short, squared off. Mortified at the direction her thoughts seemed bent on taking, she quickly looked away. Honestly—she was acting like a twelve-year-old sneaking peaks at *Cosmo* in the drug store, sure one of the Sisters from school was going to pop up from behind the rack of over-the-counter medications and discover "good" Galen's little secret.

Heavens! How long had her thoughts wandered? Then she heard, "Me, too. Did you know?"

She lifted her eyes to meet his, a little sad, a little…apologetic, she thought. "You, too?"

"My wife died four and a half years ago."

She was trapped in those rich, brown depths. Trapped and drowning and not caring. Caring too much, for a man she barely knew. No—she mentally shook her head. Not *for* him. *About* him. Big difference.

Knowing that did absolutely nothing to change the way her heart was stuttering at the pain, still tender, etched in his features.

"I'm sorry—"

"So was I," he said, cutting her off. Not wanting sympathy, she guessed. His honesty both startled and comforted her, somehow. He leaned forward, lacing his hands between his spread knees. "So. This may be a wild guess, but something tells me you haven't dated since then."

His presumption—not to mention his forwardness—should have annoyed her. His change of subject, thrown her. Instead, she realized his tactic for what it was—the effort to claw his way out of suddenly murky waters. That, she understood. A small smile tickled her mouth. "That obvious, huh?"

One side of his mouth lifted. "Uh, yeah."

She put her plate up as well, plucking a tiny crumb of something off her pant leg, dropping it onto the plate. "I had my grandmother to take care of."

A nod. "And...if you hadn't?"

Her smile grew, just a fraction. "And how is this your business?"

He shrugged. "It's not. So, would you have?"

Her answer hung, suspended like a spider on its strand of silk, for a long moment. "Probably not."

"Yeah. That's what I thought."

She decided not to press the issue. "What about you?"

"Nope. But then, I have my daughter."

"And...if you hadn't?"

Not ten feet away, in the room behind them, several people burst into laughter.

"If I hadn't had my daughter," Del said at last, his voice emotionless, his hand fisted tightly enough to make his knuckles white, "I'd probably still have my wife."

Galen flinched at the bitterness in Del's words. Flinched, and felt almost unbearably awkward. That little revelation, she suspected, had thrown him right back into those murky waters, a move he'd no doubt regret, if he wasn't already.

"You loved her very much, didn't you?"

After another long moment, he nodded. "Yeah. I did."

"Still do, I bet," Galen said softly.

His eyes darted to hers. Clearly, he hadn't expected her to say that. To understand.

She envied him. For what he'd had. For having found the kind of love that could leave a man looking like that, so long after his wife's death. "She was my life," he said simply, and she looked away to spare him the embarrassment of a stranger seeing him so shaken.

Until that moment, she hadn't fully realized how little she'd ever been let into anyone else's life before. Or at least, into anyone else's head. She'd been too young, she supposed, for her parents to share who they were, what they thought and dreamed and hoped and feared, with their daughter. Besides, how many parents did? Then there were her grandparents— oh, right. The only thing they communicated during her teen years was their constant disapproval. And their rigid, unrealistic expectations. And even Vinnie...her husband, for heaven's sake. How much had he revealed of himself to her?

How differently things might have turned out if he had.

Now this man, this...stranger, with a few words, opens himself up to her more than any other human being she'd ever known. It was, by far, the most intimate experience she'd ever had.

And she had no earthly idea what to do with it.

"Sorry," she heard Del whisper, his voice gruff, a man who didn't like apologizing, she guessed, because he didn't like getting himself into situations where he had to. She lifted her eyes again, meeting his, her heart pounding.

"For what?" The words scraped out of a throat so dry, the sides stuck together when she swallowed.

She saw him suck in a fast, deep breath, shake his head. "Nothing." Another breath, a ghost of a smile. "Nothing. Forget it."

And when she let herself, for the dozenth time, drift in those incredibly honest eyes, she thanked God she wasn't going to be around for more than a few days. Because she knew, on some level so deep and so pure the knowledge fairly hummed inside her, she could lose herself in those eyes.

In him.

And losing someone she hadn't yet found...well. How much sense would that make?

"So. You want to know who all these folks are?"

She could have told him that Cora had already made the introductions, cursory though they may have been. But she didn't. If letting Del fill her in helped to diffuse the tension sparking between them, what could it hurt, right? "Sure," she said, leaning forward, her chin cupped in her palm.

His grin as good as pushed her over.

Oh, shoot.

"Okay," Del said. "Look—over there? Next to the wing chair?"

She glanced over at the brunette with the impossibly wild hair, hunched over, her brow puckered as she listened to what a very little boy who looked just like her was trying to tell her. The tiny woman was nearly lost underneath a heavily embroidered thigh-length sweater over a long, coppery broomstick skirt. "You mean Nancy? Yeah, we met over the cranberry sauce. She's a scream."

Del chuckled. "She is that. And that's Rod, her husband, next to her—"

By contrast, Nancy's husband reeked of conservatism. Oxford shirt peeking over a navy crew neck sweater, gray cords, loafers. "Mmm, yes. Good-looking guy."

That got a look she found amusing. "Yeah, I suppose. Anyway, Nancy's Elizabeth's best friend. They worked together in some Realty agency in Detroit before Elizabeth moved back here to help out Maureen—my stepmother?—" she nodded "—in Maureen's agency. Except then Guy—Elizabeth's husband, only he wasn't her husband then—came to work in the same agency, and they fell in love and got married. You with me so far?"

She grinned. "I think so. And…Guy had three kids from a previous marriage?"

"Right. The pretty blonde over there is Ashli, and the two boys she's lording it over are Jake and Micah. She's twelve, they're—" he scrunched his mouth, thinking "—eight and six, something like that."

"The olive filchers. Met them, too. But I thought we were talking about Nancy?"

"Hold your horses. I'm getting there. Anyway, so then Elizabeth gets pregnant with the little girl trying to sit on the dog so Nancy moves here from Detroit to take Elizabeth's place at the agency. Only then *she* falls in love with Rod, who'd bought a house from Elizabeth out here when *they* were dating."

At that, Galen let out a hoot of laughter, not realizing she'd inched closer to Del. "Honestly. It sounds like a soap opera!"

She watched as Guy sneaked over behind his wife, slipping his arms around her waist and scaring her half to death. With his long hair, the earring, the garish sweater, he no more looked like the perfect match for the cool, pulled-together blonde than caviar on a Pop-Tart. Yet Galen had caught the looks between them, more than once that afternoon, as well as the nobody-else-is-in-the-room silent exchanges between Rod and Nancy, and she'd thought—

"Yeah," Del said. "Except I think we're looking at some pretty happy endings here."

Yes, exactly.

However, no way was she letting her thoughts wander down the Road to Regrets. Not even for even a second.

"So…do they have kids? Rod and Nancy?"

"Two teenagers—his—brought to the marriage, twins born about a year ago." He pointed them out: Nancy recognized the girl, Hannah, as the tall teen who'd been watching the babies outside, while her bespectacled brother Schuyler had sounded the alarm when Jake had nearly crashed into Wendy.

Another five minutes or so passed while they played their little parlor game, until Cora found them and read them the riot act for hiding out instead of socializing, then dragged Galen away to mingle.

Not long after, Galen was seated on the sofa, next to Elizabeth, when Del came in to say goodbye, a worn-out but happy Wendy in his arms. He cantilevered the little girl out to each person in turn—his father and stepmother, Elizabeth, Nancy, Cora—so she could dole out kisses, then swung her back up on his hip to leave. He'd no sooner turned around, though, when she signed something to him. He signed back; she nodded.

Del faced the sofa again, an odd, gentle expression on his face. "She wants to kiss you goodbye, too," he said to Galen.

A thrill shimmered through her, a jolt of joy almost dizzying in its strength and unexpectedness. Yes, there was bittersweetness, too, for things that would never be, but that was minor compared with the sheer *wonderfulness* of Wendy's request. Without thinking, Galen held out her arms.

With a huge smile, Wendy went into them.

She shut her eyes against the surge of happiness when the tiny arms wrapped around her neck, an impossibly soft cheek nestled against hers. The embrace lasted for only a second, the kiss a fraction of that, then she twisted around for her father to pick her back up.

This time, when her gaze bumped into Del's, the longing in his eyes nearly made her gasp aloud.

Chapter 5

Del wrapped up the sliced turkey—Elizabeth and Maureen had foisted off enough leftovers to last him a week—and wedged it back into the refrigerator between containers of sweet potatoes, green beans, stuffing and a special little package of spinach-stuffed pasta. Wendy had conked out an hour ago, her eyes drifting shut before he'd even signed half of *One Fish Two Fish Red Fish Blue Fish*. Dr. Seuss books were often difficult to sign, and required some pretty ingeniuous moves on his part, but Wendy loved the funny creatures and silly situations, so Del did his best. And he took heart that she was beginning to sign some of them back to him.

Just before she drifted off, though, she interrupted the story to talk about Galen, how pretty and nice she was, how she liked the way Galen smiled. How Galen didn't treat her like she was afraid of her, the way so many people did.

Del's chest had tightened with that one. He supposed it was too much to ask that Wendy not notice strangers' discomfort around her. If he could protect her from anything, it would be that.

He smoothed her hair off her face, smiling into half-mast

eyes. "You know a lot of people who don't act like they're afraid of you," he signed. "Like Aunt Nancy and Aunt Elizabeth."

She'd studied him for a long moment, as if trying to decide whether or not to broach the subject, before signing, "But they're already somebody else's mommy. I want one of my own."

Del was still rattled. And not simply because that was the first time Wendy had ever indicated she'd even *thought* about moms and the lack thereof in her life, but because, well, he was thinking the same thing. That here he was just beginning to consider getting back "out there" and bam! Enter one very nice woman, single and pretty, who immediately clicked with his daughter…

And who was going back to Pittsburgh in three days.

He slammed shut the refrigerator door, ambled over to the counter and the pecan pie just sitting there waiting for someone to cut into it. Del obliged, licking his fingers after slipping the wedge onto a plate, then lowered his weary, oversize form onto the kitchen chair. One of Guy's sisters-in-law had brought enough pies to open her own stinkin' bakery, for God's sake.

He wondered if Galen made pecan pie.

He wondered if the little green men had run off with his brain in the middle of the night.

Somehow, he swallowed the gooey sweet bite in his mouth, then sighed. Not in the middle of the night. This afternoon. When she hugged his daughter, then looked at him with that…that *look* on her face.

He scrubbed his with his palm, stuffed another bite of pie in his mouth.

A man could spend his whole life hoping to see genuine compassion like that in a woman's eyes. And understanding.

And he realized, with a kind of jolt, that Cyndi had never looked at him *quite* like that. But you know what was really weird? Up until today, he would have sworn she had.

Del let out a rueful laugh. Yeah, right. What he saw was

probably pity. Feeling sorry for the pathetic guy going all sappy about his dead wife.

God, she was so different from Cyndi. Galen really was demure. They did still make that model. Or maybe Galen was the last one left in stock, one of those people you'd call "sweet", and really mean it. That shyness of hers…it was refreshing. Appealing. Being involved with a woman like that would be a relief, wouldn't it? Nothing like the impetuous crazywoman he'd gotten tangled up with the first time—

Speaking of tangled up…out of nowhere—well, okay, not exactly nowhere—filtered images of bare, fair skin against rumpled sheets, entwined limbs, heavy breathing, those eyes locked with his as she…

He laughed. Loudly, since he knew Wendy couldn't hear him. Oh, Lord. Nothing like getting himself all hot and bothered and moony over a woman who—knock, knock?—wasn't going to be around. Besides which, if he was being completely honest and realistic and all that fun stuff, there was more than compassion and kindness in her eyes when she looked at him. There was also fear. As if his presence threatened her in some way.

Of course, it could be that he simply didn't ring her chimes and she was just being nice, because that's what sweet, demure women did. Took pity on maudlin bozos raising deaf children by themselves. Maybe what he really saw in her eyes was, "How on earth did I manage to attract this creep and I don't want to hurt his feelings since he's obviously pretty screwed up so I'll just sit here quietly and maybe he'll get bored and go away."

Yeah. That had to be it.

With a weighty sigh, he pushed himself up from the table, lumbering over to the sink to wash his plate. The curtains were pulled back; he caught a glimpse of himself in the night-blackened window over the sink. He lifted one dripping hand to his out-of-control hair, pulling a face. Hell. No wonder the woman looked at him the way she did. At the moment, he'd scare the crap out of Godzilla.

Just for the hell of it, maybe he'd go hunt down a barber tomorrow.

To Galen's shock, it was nearly noon when she finally dragged her carcass out of bed. She'd never slept past six-thirty the whole three years she'd been with Gran. She quickly showered, threw on a pair of jeans and a sweater, then hurried downstairs, the dog clicking at her heels, to find Cora had left a note.

"Went to run some errands," it said. "Be back around two or so."

Galen stretched so hard her spine popped, followed by a luxurious, lazy yawn. Rubbing her arms, she peered through Cora's living room window at the sunny day outside. Colder, though, she thought, judging by the hurried footsteps of the couple scurrying by. Not to mention their twelve layers of clothes. Still, there didn't seem to be any wind that she could tell, and the sky was a solid sheet of electric blue. She smiled at that, realizing she didn't have one single blessed thing to do. For anybody.

She thought she might pass out from the shock.

Feeling that funny off-balance thing again, she moseyed on back into the kitchen, fixed herself a couple pieces of toast and a glass of Minute Maid, then ate her late breakfast standing up, Baby sitting hopefully at her feet.

"Well, Baby, whaddya think I should do?"

The mop yawned, tiny pink tongue unfurling like a blow-tickler, then pranced around Galen's feet, begging for a bite of toast. "Here. Live," she said, tossing the beastlet the last corner, then figured, because the idea of staying inside gave her hives, she might as well take herself for a stroll.

Galen had been walking for about a half hour or so when she happened on what she realized was Spruce Lake's main drag. Maybe five blocks long with a small official looking building at one end, a park at the other, the thoroughfare had one stoplight and an assortment of quaint shops and stores she could tell had probably been there, in one form or another, since the town's inception. Several proprietors were putting up Christmas decorations—she found it comforting, somehow, that, unlike most places, Spruce Lake waited until *after* Thanksgiving, at least.

She walked slowly, her gloved hands fisted inside her coat pockets, savoring the early-season holiday excitement humming in the air. Strangers spoke to her—pleasantly—while goodies in old-fashioned paned windows enticed her. She felt at home here, she suddenly realized.

Like she belonged.

A children's bookstore snagged her attention, lured her inside, where she unbuttoned her coat with fingers stiffer than she'd realized. Smelling of heated wool and that unique, crisp scent of new books, the tiny store buzzed with whispers and giggles and the occasional snick of a page being turned as a million kids and their parents huddled at child-sized tables or in little secret nooks tucked between dozens of shelves teaming with thousands of volumes.

"May I help you?"

Startled, she turned to the smiling middle-aged woman a few feet away. But she shook her head, returning the smile with a fleeting one of her own. "Just browsing," she said, then added, "What a wonderful store!"

"Well, thank you!" the gray-haired woman said, glancing around the place with obvious pride. "Are you visiting?"

For just a moment, Galen regretted having to answer in the affirmative. "Yes. Just here for the weekend."

"Well, nice of you to drop in. If there's anything special you're looking for," the woman said as she drifted away, "just let me know."

Galen glanced again around the store, suddenly flooded with a longing for that "something special," although she had no idea what that might be. Deciding she might like to buy a book for Wendy, maybe for Elizabeth's kids as well—it had been a long time since she had an excuse to buy presents for children—she slipped off her coat, hugging it to her as she browsed. A half hour later, her selections made, she again met up with the cheery lady at the cash register.

"Find everything okay?" she asked, and Galen nodded in reply, knowing the woman was talking about books. But what she was really looking for, she finally realized, was *herself*.

And she had no idea where she might find *that*.

Galen's brain buzzed louder than ever by the time she left the bookstore. So many dreams, in that store, both in the books and in the children reading them. The air fairly vibrated with possibilities. With hope.

The lumpy red shopping bag bumped not unpleasantly against her leg as she walked, her brow furrowed. What *did* she want? What did she hope for? What was she supposed to be doing with her life?

"Okay, God," she muttered, casting her eyes heavenward. "A sign would be nice, right about now."

When, however, a few seconds passed and nothing clunked her over the head, she decided either God was being subtle, or He was trying to tell her she could jolly well figure this out on her own.

So she walked, and thought, chewing on the corner of her lip as she concentrated. Well, for one thing, she thought with a wry smile, it might be nice to finally decide what she wanted to be when she grew up. She had money, now, so that wasn't a problem. She'd been married, too, saw little point in going that route again. As for being in love…

Galen blew a stream of frosted air through her lips, coming to stop in front of a small jewelry store. *"Make her dreams come true this Christmas,"* encouraged a scripted sign peeking out from a dazzling display of diamond rings. She still had Vinnie's diamond, she mused. Somewhere. Maybe in the safe deposit box back home. She'd removed her rings after his death. She wasn't even really sure why.

As she had a hundred times since yesterday, she thought of Del, the look on his face when he mentioned his wife's passing.

She handily pushed the thought right back out. Tried to, anyway.

It would take one tough woman to withstand the love of a man like that. Yeah, she thought, resuming her walk. Withstand, like a house withstands a hurricane. Without that inner strength, that sense of personal accomplishment and destiny, a woman could easily find herself destroyed by a man's love.

Or very nearly.

She thought again of Elizabeth, Nancy, Maureen. Women secure in their own…completeness. Their own strengths and weaknesses and, yes, foibles, but at least they knew what those foibles were. Sure, they had husbands and children *and* careers, but she bet they knew who they were before they became mothers. Their children had stellar examples of what womanhood could be. *Should be.*

Galen was running just a wee bit behind in that department.

Her pace slowed, her frown deepened. She reminded herself of her apres-upchuck revelation out on the highway the other day. That, right now, she was a half person. A stunted adult yet to find out who the heck she was, what she was really capable of. That the last thing she needed was a relationship. With anyone. And that, of all the men she wasn't going to have a relationship with, Del would head the list. Except…

Except now she knew him a little better, and had met his daughter, and things suddenly didn't seem to be quite so cut-and-dry, did they? Ooooh, if only things were different. If *she* were different… Wendy clearly needed a mother, and Del needed…something. Backup, if nothing else, she thought with a little smile. And, let's be honest here: they were both lonely.

And being lonely was the worst reason for getting involved with someone. For her to get involved, at any rate.

Not when she was up to her eyeballs in his half person business.

Okay, so her body might not yet understand the grander purpose here, but since, far as she could tell, it only made noises when Del Farentino was in the vicinity, this shouldn't be any great problem. She'd probably never even see the man again.

A thought which shouldn't, by all rights, bother her one iota. And before she could figure out why it did, a sudden gust of wind spit dust in her eye. When, after a moment of blinking and tearing, she looked up to test whether the mote was gone or not, she noticed the For Sale sign in a streaked window across the street. Another few seconds of blinking, then her vision cleared enough to read the huge block letters marching over the windows: Lakeside Diner.

As if being led by the hand, she crossed to the other side of the street.

Cupping her hands around her face to block out the light, she leaned right up to the dirty window to peer inside. Standard diner decor, from what she could tell: a counter, booths, kitchen undoubtedly in back—

Galen backed away as if she'd been stung, her mouth falling open in a little gasp.

Oh. The *sign.*

"Well, I didn't think You'd take me literally," she said under her breath.

Well, why not? That's what she knew how to do, right? Run a restaurant? After all, she'd spent a lot of time at Granata's, both before her marriage, then once Vinnie had gotten so sick. Mama Granata might not have been so hot on the idea of her being around, but Galen had thought…well, no matter what she'd thought. Water under the bridge now. In any case, because of what she'd thought, she'd made it her business to learn everything about it she could, from bugging the bookkeeper about how the accounts were set up, to hanging around whenever Marco or Tony ordered from suppliers, to planting her fanny in on pricing discussions. And she knew food— Italian food—inside and out. Knew what people liked, how to blend the ordinary with the extraordinary to pull in all kinds of customers.

And thanks to her grandmother, she had the capital for start-up. She wouldn't even have to take out a loan—

"Galen?"

Fog-brained, she turned to see Elizabeth coming out of the hardware store just down the street, Ashli and the oldest boy— Jake?—in tow. Annoyance flashed through her, just for a second, at the interruption, but Elizabeth's bright, genuine smile somehow melted the prickles of resentment.

The blonde handed a pair of bulging plastic bags to the kids, told them to go put them in the Lexus parked at an angle in front of the store, then closed the few feet between them. "I was gonna call you at Cora's later, so this is great." Shivering a little, she hugged her coat collar closer to her neck. "We found a place to park *all* the kids tomorrow night, wondered if you might like to join some of us for a casual dinner at the Bradens'." She laughed. "And I do mean casual. After yesterday, I don't think anyone wants to cook again for a week!"

A flush of pleasure and trepidation, both, warmed Galen's cheeks. Elizabeth's invitation was tempting, it really was—what would it be like, to have friends again? People her own age, to laugh and joke with? But what would be the point, seeing as she was leaving the next day?

And what were the odds that Del wouldn't be part of the group?

So she smiled and shook her head. "It sounds great. Really. But I'd...planned on taking Cora out. As a, um, surprise."

Galen almost cringed at the genuine disappointment—and multitude of questions—in the green eyes, turning back toward the diner before Elizabeth could get the wind back in her sails.

"Oh. We'd really hoped for a chance to get to know you better..."

"Guess it won't be here, though," they said at the same time.

The pause was slightly too long. As Elizabeth sized up what was really going on, Galen surmised. But she bounced back into the conversation quickly enough for all that. "Shoot, this wasn't ever the kind of place you 'took' someone, although everybody ate here."

"It was popular, then?"

"Oh, Lord, yes. For years. The original owners retired though, oh, maybe two years ago? And their 'kids'—who were already well into middle-age—didn't want to spend what it would have taken to fix the place up." She shifted, crossing her arms, as her own kids came up behind her. The girl threaded an arm around Elizabeth's waist; Elizabeth hugged her back as she continued. "So they put it on the market, some time back. Kept it running for a while, then just gave up."

"And they couldn't find a buyer? I mean, if it was popular and all..."

"I know. Seems a shame. Nancy and I both—we work half weeks these days—have done everything we can to find a buyer for it. Not that we'd make much money on it, but because the street just isn't the same without a restaurant, you know? But no dice, for some reason. And honestly—anybody willing to make a go of it, as long as the food was good, would have no trouble getting customers. The diner was always packed, even in off hours. It's not as if there's a lot of competition. Well, except for fast-food places and Sam's Steak House out on the highway. And you wouldn't *believe* what they're asking for it now. Equipment and all."

"How much?" Galen asked before she even knew the words were on her tongue.

"Last I heard, less than fifty grand. Unbelievable, right? For a two-story brick building—there's a two-bedroom apartment over the restaurant. Not huge, but for two thousand square feet and change, not bad. Of course, whoever bought it would spend four times that much fixing it up, but I bet it wouldn't take long to turn a profit, once the place opened—"

"Mom," Jake whispered, his teeth chattering. He tugged at his mother's coat sleeve, leaning back toward the car. "It's *cold!*"

"Oh, right. It is a little brisk out here, isn't it? Okay, we're going." Laughing, she twisted back, a kid latched onto each hand. "Listen, I'm sorry you can't come to dinner, but I sure am glad we ran into each other. Next time you come visit, though—okay?"

Wasn't until they'd already gotten into the car that Galen remembered the books she'd bought for the kids, dangling from her frozen fingers. She started to call out, stopped herself, though she couldn't have said why. Well, Cora could pass them on, she supposed.

After Galen had left.

Almost as if someone tapped him on the shoulder, Del jerked up his head to look up at the clock at nine Sunday night. Right about when Galen's plane should be landing in Pittsburgh.

He pushed back from the kitchen table, where he'd been working up some figures for an estimate, twisting from side to side in an attempt to ease the tight muscles in his back. Wendy had been asleep for an hour already, so the only sounds in the apartment were the periodic whir of heat filtering through the vents, the wind's annoying whine outside. It was supposed to snow, they said.

He lifted a mug of tepid coffee to his lips, making a face. The kitchen chair grated across the tiled floor when he stood to put the cup in the microwave.

Two, three days, and he'd forget about her. A wry smile tugged at his mouth. If assorted females in his life would stop talking about her, he would.

The smile faded as the microwave dinged at him. He retrieved the coffee, wincing as he took a sip—now, natch, it was too hot. Salving his burned tongue against the roof of his mouth, he returned to the table, sank back into the chair.

Galen's leaving was *not* a lost opportunity, he told himself.

It was a blessing.

It was.

She wasn't sure whether it was the silence or the emptiness that hit her the hardest when she let herself into her grandmother's house Sunday night. Or the cold. Shivering, Galen scurried to the thermostat, letting out a chattering sigh when she heard the first-floor radiators begin their syncopated thunking and clanking, punctuated by an occasional *pssssst* of steam. She sprang a whining Baby from her carrier, who immediately hopped up onto Gran's woebegone armchair, regarding Galen with an enormous, accusing glare.

Speaking of puppy-dog eyes. Maybe now, back home, she'd stop remembering Del's. Stop hearing his voice, all low and sexy and…

Okay, so maybe this was going to take a day or two.

Still huddled in her coat, Galen turned on most of the downstairs lights, trying to dispel the gloom. Then she clicked on

Gran's old radio, set, as it had been for probably forty years, to Pittsburgh's preeminent easy-listening station. Galen walked away, twisted back. Strode over to the radio and twisted the dial until she hit a golden oldies station. The Bee Gees. Oh, Lord—she'd been in the seventh grade when *Saturday Night Fever* came out. Gran and Pop wouldn't let her go see it, of course. So Ellen Andretti's older sister snuck them in, one Saturday afternoon. Galen swallowed a laugh, remembering her heart-wedged-in-throat terror that Gran would call Ellen's and find out Galen wasn't there.

Coat flapping, she strutted and gyrated across the threadbare gold carpeting, figuring it was as good a way as any to warm up. She'd never been to a dance, not even her prom, since she couldn't very well show up with Vinnie, and she was hardly going to go with anyone else.

The dog inched farther back in the chair, whimpering.

"So I'm not Chita Rivera. Whaddya want from my life?" Unperturbed, Galen grabbed her bag, boogying up the stairs and into her bedroom, flipping on lights as she went. Bag deposited with a *whump* on the bed, she went right back out and into the bathroom across the hall, hitting the light switch. Yucka-ducka. The overhead light was even dimmer than she remembered, the tub more pock-marked, the tiles dingier.

She did Bette Davis in the mirror, spewing out "What a dump!" with enough force to spatter the mirror. A little yip— of agreement, she supposed—snagged her attention. Baby stood quivering cautiously in the doorway, apparently thinking it was better to risk being with the loony than being alone.

Alone.

Expelling a gust of air from her lungs, Galen sank onto the mauve plush toilet seat cover, patted her lap. With an expression of unbridled joy, the little dog scampered across the tiles to jump up on her lap. "I'm back. Now what?" She reached up, released her hair from its clip, tossing it with a clatter into a basket on the back of the sink. The gesture apparently merited consoling doggy kisses; Galen was too tired to protest. Or to move. So, here she was, plotting out the rest of her life, seated on the throne in her grandmother's house with this long-haired rat on her lap.

Fear rocketed through her veins.

Could she really run her own place? Did she really have the gumption to even try?

And was she going to let a little thing like sheer terror derail her from proving she wasn't an airhead?

Heck, no.

On a deep breath, Galen forked her hair back from her face, a couple tears escaping as she tried to line up her thoughts. Tried even harder to push Del Farentino from them. On that score, she wasn't doing s'hot, s'good.

Would a man like Del even understand where she was coming from? She'd grown up with men like that. Heck, once you discounted the surface differences, she'd married one, for heaven's sake. As had her grandmother. Men who believed their role was to take care of their wives. Men provided and sheltered; women cooked, raised the children, nurtured. Women didn't go out and open restaurants, for goodness' sake.

And why on earth did she keep dragging Del back into the picture?

Her brow scrunched, she stared at the dog snoozing on her lap. *Del isn't here.* Okay, got it. *Your imagination's run away from you.* Yeah, well, wouldn't be the first time. *This has nothing to do with Del, or any other man. This has to do with you.*

What you *want.*

She finally pushed herself up off her thinking spot, hauling the mangy beast with her as she went back into her bedroom. Well, she thought, slipping off her clothes, she'd asked for a sign, and she'd gotten it. After some sleep, she'd start making lists, figuring out what came next. But one thing she knew— she fished a flannel nightgown out of her bureau, slipped it over her head—she'd been cheated out of her rightful due one too many times; she wouldn't cheat herself out of it now. Nor was she about to let anybody get close enough to her to try to tell her what to do.

Or to make her doubt herself, ever again.

She crawled into the still-cold bed and lay down on her side, letting Baby skootch down under the covers to settle by her stomach. Light off, she wadded the old feather pillow underneath her cheek, attributing the sudden, vague sadness in her chest to exhaustion.

"So. What'd you think of Galen?" Elizabeth gave her hair three swift passes with the brush, then got up from her vanity to crawl into bed beside Guy. They'd turned down the heat an hour ago; she could feel her nipples tighten in the cold, knew they were plainly visible underneath her satin pj's.

Her gorgeous, naked husband lifted up the covers as she crawled in, slung his arm around her waist, his leg over hers. She tried to keep a straight face, pretending ignorance, but he was about as subtle as a brickbat.

Heh-heh.

"She's very nice," he said. "Kids asleep?"

"Mmm-hmm." Elizabeth twisted away to click off her bedside lamp, grinning as she felt Guy's hand slither down her hip. When she turned back, she could barely see him in the eerie green glow of his digital clock. "Only 'very nice'?"

Guy perched himself up on one elbow, his head cradled in his palm. "She lives in Pittsburgh, honeybunch."

"So? Nice people can't live in Pittsburgh?"

Guy chuckled, a low rumble that turned her to mush. Every time. She felt his hand move to her chest. A button popped open. Several crucial body parts began doing the happy dance.

"And Del lives here," he said.

"Who said anything—?"

His kiss shut her up for a second. Or five. "He's a big boy, sweetheart. He doesn't need you to find him a mate."

The happy dance had shifted into a fox trot. Elizabeth sifted her fingers through Guy's long hair, trailing one finger over the rim of his ear, tapping her fingernail on the gold stud in one lobe. "Did you see her with Wendy? She'd be perfect."

She felt his sigh brush her mouth. Then her neck. Oh, goody. He was moving south.

Another button gave way.

"You're terrible, you know that?" Guy whispered. Over her nipple.

She shuddered. "And you're undoing my buttons."

"A definite prerequisite to pushing them."

"Mmm. But you know," she said into her husband's hair, beginning to tremble as she anticipated where his mouth was going to land right about...now. She sighed. "Del really does need someone—"

"Liz?"

"Hm?"

"Shut up and put out."

She giggled.

Friday morning, December first, 7:37 a.m. Tiny face pinched into a glower, Wendy snatched the purple moonboots from Del's hand, hitched up her nightgown, and waded through an ocean of Beanie Babies and Barbies to dump them onto the floor of her closet. She turned to him, palms down, disgust crumpling her delicate mouth, flicking out both middle fingers. American Sign language for "hate."

This was getting *really* old. Already ten minutes late, Del squatted down to eye level with his daughter, who was clearly unimpressed with either his size or his position as an authority figure in her life.

"I told you, ladybug," he simultaneously signed and said, even though she didn't have her hearing aids on yet, "it snowed last night. You have to wear your boots." He stood, carefully maneuvered work-booted feet through the barrage of toys, plucked the discarded boots from the closet. Again, he stooped, regaining eye contact, then signed, "Please put these on. Now."

Sweatered arms crossed mutinously over some Disney icon or other.

"No," she said, clear as a bell.

Desperation kicked up Del's heart rate. And his signing fluency. "Wendy, I've got an appointment in forty-five minutes.

You've got to finish dressing.'' His right hand circled his chest. "Please?''

She tilted her head. Considering. Strangled by a purple hair elastic, a lopsided spray of white-blonde hair atop her head fluttered as she tapped one finger against her jaw. Hell. They hadn't even *discussed* hair yet. Let alone gone through the daily hearing aid trauma. Wendy hated wearing them. But the audiologist insisted if his daughter was ever to learn to talk— to communicate with the hearing world—they had to exploit whatever residual hearing she had. And that meant she had to wear her hearing aids.

And this was no time for him to be mulling over any of this. Right now, he had to get this kid shod, wired up and outta here. However, neither reason nor force worked worth diddly with his daughter. Just like her mother. Did what *she* wanted to do when *she* wanted to do it and consequences be damned.

He glanced at the clock by her bed. 7:41. He silently swore. Certain words were best left un-lip-read.

"Okay,'' he said, shoving his mop off his forehead, "what's it worth to you?''

He hadn't signed. Frowning, Wendy patted his hands. Del obliged.

She angled her head again, a spark of careful curiosity in her enormous brown eyes, then shuttered them with her long, dark lashes for the best effect. That's it: he was marrying her off the day she turned thirteen. He'd never survive her teenage years, that was for damn sure.

"Tacos,'' she signed.

Could've been worse. "Done. Now, *please* put your boots on, baby.''

Which she did—by herself!—while Del dashed around the tornado-stricken apartment pulling blinds and checking the coffee maker and frantically searching for Wendy's coat which he at last found peeking out from underneath his unmade bed, of all places. Slipping on his down vest over his lined flannel shirt, he dashed back to her room, helped her with her aids, then half tugged, half pushed her out the door and into his truck.

It wasn't until they were halfway down his street that he realized they never had done hair. That she hadn't noticed he took as a blessing from the Almighty. Del glanced over at Wendy, who seemed impossibly small this morning, sitting there with her hands neatly folded in her lap, her expression either vacant or serious, he wasn't sure. His cell phone buzzed; he saw Wendy's eyes dart to his face as he picked it up, knew she'd watch him carefully to pick up whatever she could of the conversation. She heard with her eyes, gleaning information from people's lips and facial expressions hearing people often overlooked. Although she missed the exact content of most conversations—even experienced lip-readers, he knew, rarely caught more than fifty percent of what was actually being said—her astute attention to body language and facial expressions made her far more perceptive than many of her hearing peers. She might not know what was being *said,* but she sure knew what was being *felt.*

He wondered just how much she'd picked up in the last few days. Since Galen's visit.

Since Galen's departure.

She was totally enchanted by the picture book Galen had given her, one of Tomie de Paola's fairy-tale volumes with his wonderful, rich illustrations. Then last night she'd informed him, "When Galen comes back, she can read this to me."

Del had actually felt his heart trip. "I don't think Galen is coming back," he'd signed.

Wendy had just given him this odd look, then signed, "Yes. She is."

Del had long since learned when to back down from an argument with his daughter. But he did point out that he'd "read" the book to her, several times.

Wendy shook her head. "I want Galen to."

"But Galen doesn't sign."

That had gotten a "so?" shrug. "Then I'll teach her," her hands said.

He'd had no idea what to say to that, so had simply left it. But the exchange had nagged him all night. Still did.

They'd pulled into the day care provider's driveway, Del realizing he'd only half heard Emma Saunders on the other end of the line, going on about his men tracking dirt over her clean kitchen floors. Why the woman insisted on washing her floor every day in the middle of a remodel was beyond him. However, his was not to reason why and all that. So he listened and commiserated and told her he'd make sure the guys swabbed the floor every evening before they left.

On a sigh, he disconnected the call, then explained enough of the conversation to Wendy to satisfy her curiosity. She nodded, leaving him to wonder if she'd really understood him or if she was just being polite. After a moment's struggle with the heavy truck door, she pushed it open, wriggling off the seat and prissily avoiding a puddle in the driveway.

Day care arrangements for the child of any single parent were complicated and expensive; for Wendy, they involved logistics of military-esque proportions. Several mornings a week, she attended Total Communication preschool classes at a local school for the Deaf, learning to sign, speech read and how to make the most of her residual hearing in order to learn to speak. Then there were the audiologist appointments, the hearing aid adjustments, the special speech therapist once a week and the tiny tot ballet class Wendy had begged to take. Otherwise, she was in a "normal" home day care setting with hearing children, run by a remarkable woman whose oldest son had been born deaf, too.

Del had been warned by some well-meaning "experts" that Wendy was apt to become confused unless they stuck to either an Oral or Manual method of communication. Far as he could tell, Wendy's drive to communicate in whatever way worked best at the moment had enabled her to keep the various methods straight in her head. She wasn't always successful, and there were certainly plenty of days she was often worn-out and frustrated. However, he gathered exhaustion and frustration were part and parcel of any teaching method, and Wendy was making progress. She had a large signing vocabulary and was even beginning to read. And most of the time, she seemed happy. That's all Del could wish for.

At least, up until two weeks ago, he couldn't have asked for more. Now, though…

Mrs. Battaglia, a vaguely middle-aged woman with tightly permed, very dyed black hair and a sweet smile, signed/spoke to Wendy, touching her lopsided, straggly ponytail. "What happened to your hair, sweetheart?"

Wendy's hand floated to her head. Del saw her frown, then sign, "Daddy forgot," throwing Del a look meant to cut him to the quick.

The caregiver clearly choked back a grin, then touched Wendy's shoulder to get her attention again. "Come on," her hands said. "We'll fix it. Then you can go help David and Justine with that puzzle they've been working on."

Wendy nodded, then turned back to Del, who'd already hunkered down in front of her. As she did every morning, she buried herself in his arms, a fragile thirty pounds to his two-hundred-ten. Some kinds of communication didn't need words, he thought as he cradled her to his chest, absorbing the scent of baby shampoo and fabric softener. Despite the circumstances that had brought her into his life—or maybe because of them—she was no less a miracle.

His daughter pulled out of his arms, signed, "I love you."

"I love you, too," he signed back, his throat tight as he watched her run off to play with the other kids. His life was already so full he barely had a moment to call his own.

Yet, since Galen's phantom appearance, it now also seemed pathetically empty.

Galen stood in line at the Giant Eagle, checkbook in hand. December 10th already. She blew a stream of air through her lips, then frowned. Two weeks, and she'd yet to find a property she could afford in a neighborhood the clientele she hoped to reach would set foot in. She knew she'd have to keep a fair amount of money aside while the business got established, so she couldn't shoot the whole wad on buying property and equipment.

And—why this had taken so long to hit her, she didn't know—how swift would it be to open an Italian restaurant in the same town as her husband's family?

Okay, so that place in Spruce Lake kept popping into her head. Fifty thou for the whole place? And Elizabeth had no reason to embellish about the traffic it might get. After all, she had no idea Galen was thinking of opening a restaurant. *Galen* hadn't even really known that's what she'd been thinking at that point. She could live in the apartment over it, and it was a very pretty little town 'n' that. And Cora was there.

As was Del.

So?

Yeah. So?

"Hey, Galen," the yellow-haired cashier crowed. "Ain't seen you for a while. How ya doone?"

"Fine," she said with a smile, keeping a sharp eye on the cash register as Mabel scanned things through. "Been busy."

"Yeah? Heard 'bout your grandma. You okay 'n' that?"

With a fleeting smile, Galen said she was.

"That's good, hon. Okay, that'll be fiddy-fi' thirteen."

Galen wrote out her check, handed it to Mabel. "Djew hear it was gonna snow later tonight?" the cashier asked. "An' me expectin' cupny tomorra, too." She shook her head, her turquoise eyeshadow glimmering in the stark light. "But dat's life, right? Airyago," she said, handing Galen her receipt. "You take care, hon."

The snow had already started by the time she got outside, the plastic bag handles biting mercilessly into her palms as she walked. Tiny, not-quite-sure flakes teased her nose and cheeks, melting the second they hit the pavement, just as tiny, not-quite-sure thoughts swirled in her brain.

Only those weren't melting.

She climbed the steps to her grandmother's house, sure her arms were at least six inches longer than they'd been fifteen minutes ago, dumping one of the bags on the porch to search for her key. Yeah, she knew she should have her key out before she hit the porch, but she'd been so muddled she'd forgotten. Besides, she was convinced old Mrs. Dupcek across the street stood guard behind her vertical blinds with a loaded shotgun. If not an Uzi. Anybody crazy enough to even think about breaking in would be Swiss cheese in a millisecond.

She shuffled through the house and into the kitchen, Baby clicking at her heels, clunking the bags up onto the counter. If she was going to open a restaurant, she'd better start working on some recipes.

If she was going to open a restaurant, she'd better figure out where the heck it was going to be.

Galen slipped off her coat, dropping it onto the back of a kitchen chair, then wiped suddenly sweaty palms on her jeans. Now, this was nuts, was what it was. She began pacing the linoleum floor, chewing her knuckle, Baby keeping her feet company. For all she knew, the place in Spruce Lake wasn't even available anymore. And all she had to go on was Elizabeth's idle comments. She hadn't done a lick of her own research into it, had no idea if the area would even support an Italian restaurant, hadn't even seen inside the place.

She stopped. Sighed heavily.

She also knew she'd run into a thousand dead ends here in Pittsburgh.

Baby whimpered when Galen took up the pacing routine again. So…so maybe she was supposed to do something else with the money. With her life. Not that she had a clue what that might be.

Once again, she came to a halt, this time leaning her palms on the sink, staring out into the blackness. The snow had picked up; large, sudsy flakes now slapped lazily against the window. "I know I'm really pushing it," she murmured, "but if You could manage just one more sign, I'd really, really appreciate it."

She barely had time to react to the lightning before a crack of thunder—in December!—rattled the windows. Her hand pressed to her thwomping heart, Galen sank onto a kitchen chair just in time to catch a squealing dog in her arms.

O-*kaaay*…

The phone rang. Galen stared at it. Nobody called her. Ever. She picked it up.

"Hey, baby—"

Cora.

"You were on my mind again, so I figured I'd call. What's up?"

Another rumble of thunder rolled through. Like a nudge.

Oh.

"A-as it happens," Galen said, somehow, over the terror constricting her breathing, "I need to ask you a favor."

"Oh?"

Nothing ventured, nothing gained, 'n' that. "Yeah. I, um, need Elizabeth Sanford's phone number."

Chapter 6

Elizabeth settled back against her sofa, plopping her slippered feet up onto the coffee table. "Now this is the way to trim a tree," she said to Del with a grin, nodding toward the cluster of kids all yakking at once at the base of the ten-foot-high, sweetly-scented Douglas fir in front of her picture window. And in the middle of the chaos stood Guy, halfheartedly trying to direct traffic, a chattering Chloe clinging drunkenly to his knees.

Elizabeth's entire house glowed with Mary Engelbreit Christmas cheer, all twinkling lights and pine boughs and bayberry candles. Christmas carol books fought for the best spot on the piano, while a fire popped and crackled in the fireplace. She'd even brought some of her crystal collection out of storage for the holidays, candybowls and candlesticks and what all, glittering from assorted spots well out of the reach of a toddler's hands. But somehow, maybe because there were still toys scattered everywhere and the furniture looked a little battle-scarred and this behemoth of a dog was waltzing through it all, nudging along a hamster in a plastic roly ball, the room didn't look "done". It just looked like home. The kind of home Del had thought he'd have, once upon a time—

Oh, hell. Not tonight. Not on top of everything else.

On a sigh, Del took a swig of hot chocolate. Although his stepsister wasn't averse to serving wine or beer at an adults-only affair, when the kids were around, all the beverages were definitely G-rated. He was getting used to it. And to her. She could be a little obsessive at times, but he could deal with that. The important thing was, she adored her stepniece, even going so far as to drag Guy to signing classes with her. While Del had a slew of cousins, he'd regretted—at times—not having a sibling. Maybe this blond winter maiden wasn't exactly what he'd had in mind, but she'd do.

"I take it tree trimming isn't your thing?" he said, his heart melting at the expression on his daughter's face when she was allowed to hang a glass angel on a lower branch.

Elizabeth laughed. Del caught Guy's glance, then the wink, at his wife. He took another sip of cocoa, battling down the pangs of envy and regret and sheer alone-ness that seemed to be multiplying like rabbits these days.

"Actually," she said, "I used to drive my parents crazy about the tree. If we had six of one particular ornament, I had to make sure they were placed equidistant from each other, that each icicle was individually hung from the branches, stuff like that. We always had a beautiful tree, but looking back on it, it was always a little...I don't know. Too-too," she conceded on a laugh.

She tucked up her feet, pulling her oversize white sweatshirt down over her legginged knees. The hamster ball *racka-racka'd* down the uncarpeted part of the hallway behind them; apparently bored, Einstein lumbered over and collapsed at Del's feet. "And I know myself all too well," Elizabeth added with a tiny nod, hugging her own mug of cocoa to her chest. "If I get within six feet of the tree, old habits will definitely rear their ugly heads. So I stay out of the way."

Del leaned back, watching Wendy signing to Ashli. The three kids had easily picked up the language, so there were lots of flying hands as well as giggles and vocal arguments too. Sometimes, two of the Sanford kids would continue signing to each other, even when Wendy wasn't part of the conversation. "And you don't go back later and rearrange one or two things?"

He slanted a glance in her direction, caught the blush. "Oh, maybe just…one or two."

He laughed, but even he caught the hollowness in the sound.

"Del?" When he looked over this time, he saw the faint crease etched between her brows. "What is it?"

She'd never give up until he told her. "Remember the Golden house I told you about?"

"Oh, yeah. The big one, out off the highway. They wanted to completely redo it, right?"

"Well, they picked another contractor."

"Oh, Del…I'm so sorry. Why?"

"I have no idea. I guess someone underbid me." The heel of his sneakered foot started tapping silently against the rug as he scrubbed the palm of his hand across his scratchy chin. "Three times, I was out to that house…"

"Their loss," Elizabeth said quietly, but with genuine concern.

"Yeah, well, that ain't gonna pay the bills."

"You must have other projects coming up, though."

"Piddly stuff," he said, shifting in his seat. "I mean, I'm sure things will pick up in the spring, but right now…" He let the sentence die.

"Then why, for God's sake, don't you let your father give you some leads?"

"We've been over this, Liz. You know why."

"Oh, don't give me—" she lowered her voice "—that nepotism crap. You're not starting out anymore. And one job from Hugh could triple your business. So is this stubbornness or pride?"

"I just need to succeed on my own, okay? Without my father's help."

Her mouth set, Elizabeth stared at him for a moment or two, then let out a long breath. And changed the subject.

"You'll never guess who called me today," she said, flicking something off her knee. He looked over, shrugged, ignoring the amusement hopping to and fro in those wicked green eyes. "Galen Granata."

His grip tightened around the mug's handle. After three weeks, he'd finally gotten to the point where he didn't think about her every ten seconds. Where he didn't wonder what she was doing. Where he didn't wake up, rock hard and frustrated, from an erotic dream in which she was the star attraction. In other words, he'd returned to being the same old boring, sexless slug he'd been for the past four years, and then Elizabeth has to go and bring things up. As it were. "Why?" slipped out before he even knew the word was there.

"She wants to buy the old Lakeside Diner."

"What?" His voice scooted up a notch. "Why?" he asked again.

"Because it seems she wants to open a restaurant."

He blinked. *"Here?"*

Elizabeth shrugged. "Well, actually, she'd thought she'd open one in Pittsburgh, but that doesn't seem to be working out. She'd seen the place when she was here before, and considering the price and all, she figured why not?"

Del just stared at his stepsister. "I take it she knows the shape it's in?"

"Generally, yes."

"What do you mean, generally? I did a walk-through with one of Maureen's clients, maybe two months ago? There's water damage from that forty-year-old roof that means some whole walls are going to have to be completely re-done, not to mention huge chunks of the ceiling over the eating area. The plumbing's shot, I'm sure the floorboards are rotted in some places underneath the linoleum and the wiring is flat-out dangerous. The potential buyer couldn't get out of there fast enough."

Elizabeth gave him a funny look. "Did you give a repair estimate to that client?"

"Yeah. A hundred grand, easily, not counting upgrading the fixtures and equipment."

"Hmm…" Elizabeth pursed her lips, seeming to take that

under advisement. "What if she did some of the work herself?"

He looked at her as if she'd truly lost it this time. "Excuse me?"

"To cut down on the repair costs."

Del combed a hand through his hair—which still needed that damned haircut—and let out a weak laugh. "She can't be that crazy. Besides, even if she shaved maybe ten grand off the repair costs, where's she gonna get that kind of money?"

"Seems her grandmother left her a large life insurance policy or something." Elizabeth waved her hand. "I don't know, we didn't go into details, since where a client gets his or her money is none of my business. But she wants me to put a bid on the place tomorrow. If the owners accept, she'll pay cash."

"For a place she hasn't even seen inside, just like that?"

"Well, yes."

Del bolted from the chair. Everybody at the tree stopped and stared at him; he waved them back to their task.

"Of all the lamebrained…You say she inherited this money from her grandmother? So, instead of investing at least some of it for the future, she's willing to throw the whole thing away on some whim? Good Lord, Liz—the woman looks like she'd jump if a mouse crossed her path. How on earth does she think she's going to run a business? Let alone a restaurant?"

Elizabeth stared at him for a second or two, her expression going from *amused* to *watch out,* then untangled herself from the sofa, grasping him by the arm and yanking him through the dining room into the kitchen. Maureen had warned him about getting his stepsister's dander up; unfortunately, he remembered it too late to do him any good.

"Now you listen here—" Against her flushed face, her green eyes glittered like faceted stones. "First off, buddy, it's her money to do with whatever she damn well pleases. Secondly, where do you get off assuming she's 'throwing it away'? Galen's husband was in the restaurant business; she was around it, even if peripherally, for nearly fifteen years. And she's a dynamite cook. She has every bit as much chance of making a go of this as anybody else, far as I can tell, and I get the feeling her shyness is due in large part to what people have done to her over the past several years. And thirdly, *brother* dear…'' One slender eyebrow lifted, as did the corner of her mouth. "Seems to me you're getting real hot under the collar about the doings of someone you barely even *know*."

She had him there. All he could do was stare at her, his heart hammering at the base of his throat. Why *did* he care? Galen Granata was nothing to him, and what she did with her money was, as Elizabeth said, her business…

"What do you mean," he said, her words having just sunk in, "'what people have done to her'?"

Elizabeth let out a sigh, shaking her head. "I don't know, exactly. Just from some things Cora said…" She looked up at him, her mouth quirked. "I gather this is the first shot the woman's had at making her own decisions in her entire life. But she's not a flake, Del, even if I do get the feeling she's scared to death. Just because it might seem as if she's going about things the hard way doesn't mean she hasn't thought this through. Not that *you'd* understand anything about doing things the hard way…"

Del grunted.

With a low laugh, Elizabeth folded her arms, angled her head at him. "Frankly, I think she's got a lot of guts."

Del narrowed his eyes at his stepsister for a moment, then turned and stalked to the kitchen door, every muscle in his back stiff as a two-by-four. Before pushing open the swinging door, he turned back, unable to decide, as she had said, why he gave a damn what Galen did, with her money or her life or anything. But he did, with a fierceness that frightened him.

"That's what some people said about Cyndi, too," he said softly. "And my mother."

Then he walked back out into the living room, feeling like a thunderstorm had just erupted in his brain.

Things took longer than Galen expected—as things inevitably did, she supposed—and it was nearly the middle of January before she officially became a resident of Spruce Lake.

She'd had to sell off or give away her grandmother's stuff, for one thing—there was no family silver, no precious china handed down over four generations, no priceless antiques worth lugging to Michigan—then fix up the house enough so the Realtor could at least show the place without being embarrassed. But sell it did, more quickly than either she or the agent had expected, so she had another nice chunk of change to stash in the bank. She sent some personal belongings on ahead to Cora's, opened a bank account via wire in Spruce Lake, and basically arrived to live with little more than she had when she'd spent the weekend, less than two months before. Except this time, she owned a decrepit—yes, she was fully aware of the condition of the place—storefront in the middle of town. And if things got bad, she had no "home" to go back *to*.

This was it.

And just as soon as she stopped feeling like a stake'd been rammed through her heart, she thought as she stuffed her stuff, including Baby's carrier, in Cora's car, she was sure she was going to enjoy the heck out of the situation.

"You okay, honey?" Cora asked as they pulled out of the airport's parking garage. "You don't look so good."

She cleared her throat. "I've decided I'm not a very good flier."

"You've flown less than a half dozen times in your entire life, baby."

"There's a reason for that."

Cora chuckled, pulled out onto the highway. A recent snowfall had flocked the scenery like something out of a Sierra Club calendar, the ground and trees glistening in their icy coats against a breathtaking sky.

"It's so pretty," Galen breathed. Beside her, Cora *hmmphed.*

"You act like you've never seen snow before."

"Only in Pittsburgh. Snow in the city is pretty for about ten minutes."

"Well, honey, snow out here ain't nothing to wax rhapsodic about, either. Yeah, I suppose it stays pretty longer, but it's a pain in the butt, no matter how you look at it. Especially if you're trying to drive in it.''

Galen sucked in a sharp breath.

Cora's eyes darted to her face, back to the highway. "You sure you okay?"

"You just reminded me. I haven't driven in three years."

Another eye-dart. "You're kidding?"

"Nope. Gran didn't have a car, I couldn't afford one, so I didn't bother. We used taxis or public transportation to get wherever we needed to."

A moment passed. "Three years since you've driven, huh?"

"Mmm-hmm."

Cora's throaty chuckle gave her away. "Bet that's not the only thing you haven't done in a while."

Galen's face flamed. "Cora, honestly! It's only been—"

"Three years, baby. We already established that. Oh, for goodness' sake, honey—nobody'd get on your case now. I mean, if you were to find someone."

A wry smile tugged at Galen's mouth. "*Nobody* is right. However…" Folding her arms against her chest, she fixed her gaze out the window, figuring she might as well lay down some ground rules, right now, because it wasn't as if she couldn't see where this conversation was headed. "The idea of hitching myself to someone who probably *would* care—as in, interfere—does not appeal. At all."

Cora did more hmmphing. "This may come as a shock, baby, but it was your grandmother who died. Not you."

"Precisely. Which is why, Cora—and anyone else you might speak to who might happen to be interested—for the first time in my life, I am a free woman. F-R-E-E. I've spent my entire life answering to other people. Doing for other people. Doing what other people expected me *to* do. The last thing I need, or want, is some man messing about with my head, giving me 'advice,' telling me a pack of lies…"

She jerked her head away, hoping against hope Cora hadn't heard her. Of course, that was a pipe dream and she knew it.

To her surprise, though, several seconds passed without so much as a *hmmph*. Then Cora said, softly, "They ain't all like that, honey. Men, I'm talking about. Sure, maybe the good ones aren't that easy to find, but they're out there—"

"Cora?"

"Yeah, baby?"

Galen slumped down in her seat, thinking maybe if she closed her eyes, both the nausea and Cora would disappear. "Suppose someone offered you, say…I don't know." She opened one eye. "Chocolate cream pie?"

"You got my attention now, girl. Keep going."

"So say somebody offers you a chocolate cream pie—a really, really good chocolate cream pie, with real whipped cream topping and everything—but you just ate two pieces of chocolate cream pie not a half hour ago, and the thought of even another bite is making you ill—"

"Then I'd keep it for later."

"Nooo, you can't keep it for later, because it's a magic chocolate cream pie and it'll spoil if it's not eaten right away. Would you just play along, already?"

Cora sighed. "You're breaking my heart, but go on."

"The point is, it doesn't matter how good it is—you can't use it, see, because you've had all the chocolate cream pie you could possibly eat already." She looked at the side of Cora's face, hopefully.

"Uh-huh. So what you're saying is, even though the chocolate cream pie you're so full of is that inferior, worthless, plastic freezer case stuff that goes on sale three for five dollars, you couldn't find even an inch of room for something made with real whipped cream?"

Galen squirmed, fixing her eyes straight ahead. "Who said anything about the first chocolate cream pie being inferior and worthless?"

Cora let out a loud laugh. "Honey, you're full of something all right, but it *sure* ain't chocolate cream pie."

Now it was Galen's turn to *hmmph.*

"Besides," Cora said, reasonably. "Men keep. Pies don't."

Galen decided to quit while she was behind.

An hour later, she and the dog and the paltry few belongings she hadn't already shipped on ahead stood in a heap in the middle of Cora's entryway as Cora flapped back out her door to return to work. She stopped, hand on doorknob, to tell Galen the blue towels were hers, anything in the kitchen was fair game and Elizabeth had left the keys to the restaurant in an envelope which Cora thought she'd left either on top of the desk in the den or maybe in that what-all box under the phone in the kitchen. And then she was gone.

Galen stood for a full minute with her hand pressed to her stomach, breathing slowly so she wouldn't hyperventilate and keel over. Then, when she was reasonably sure she was going to stay vertical, she let the dog outside to piddle, lugged all her stuff to Cora's guest room, came back down to fix herself a peanut butter and jelly sandwich and a glass of skim milk, then decided to go searching for those keys. Which turned out to be neither in the what-all box or on Cora's desk, but in plain view on Cora's coffee table.

The thrill that zinged through her when she held them in her hand...well. It was something. Certainly enough to elbow aside the panic that tried to choke her every time she realized what she'd just done. But then, wasn't that what *thrill* was all about? Excitement and terror, all balled up together?

A minute later, after she let the dog back in and washed up her two dishes, she was on her way downtown, not minding the cold or the snow or the wind. Not minding anything at all. And when, simultaneously achy and numb, she pushed open the door to *her* restaurant, she simply stood with her gloved hands pressed to her stinging cheeks and laughed and laughed and laughed.

Oh, it was indeed a mess. It was absolutely the most run-down, pitiful place she'd ever seen. The joint made her grandmother's house look like a castle in comparison. The ceiling sagged and the plaster was stained and there was more duct tape than vinyl on the cranberry-colored booth seats. The black-and-red tiled floor was so scuffed and scarred, the checkerboard pattern wasn't even clear anymore. And it was, without a doubt, the most beautiful building she'd ever seen in her entire life.

"Bit chilly to be leaving the door open, doncha think?"

She whirled around, blinking over a shimmer of tears, to see Del and Wendy standing in the doorway, one huge and one tiny form silhouetted in the stark afternoon light. And at that moment, she didn't even care that she wasn't supposed to feel a jolt of delight at seeing him again, that her first impulse was to run over and throw her arms around Del's neck.

But even if, at the moment, she didn't care, she certainly wasn't about to act on that impulse, which she was sure was more about this sorry old building than it was about Del. So instead she held out her arms to Wendy, who eagerly ran into them. And as she swept the child up into a hug, it hit her—hard—that if she thought she'd just avoided unnecessary complications, she couldn't have been more wrong.

Especially when she saw the look on Del's face when she gently lowered his daughter back to the floor. His hair was even stragglier than when she'd seen it last, and he was covered with plaster dust and mud, but she saw nothing, really, save the gentle, aching gratitude in those puppy-dog eyes.

Galen slipped off her knit cap, tucking her hair behind her ear as she stuffed the cap into her coat pocket. "I didn't figure, since there isn't any heat, it would make much difference. It's just as cold inside as it is out."

"Good point."

They stood awkwardly for several seconds, then both spoke at once.

"What are you—?"

"I saw the door open—"

Nervous laughter. Galen gestured at him. "You first."

One side of Del's mouth hitched up, his breath frosting in front of his face. Although, the way the sun was slicing across the front of the diner through the bank of street-facing windows, it really didn't feel all that cold. "Wendy has private speech lessons with a woman who just lives a few blocks away. I was driving past to take her back to day care, when I noticed the open door." He hooked his thumbs into his pants pockets, shoving the vest out of the way, smiling that cattywompus smile and looking about as dangerous as the Easter Bunny.

Which was precisely why he *was* so dangerous.

And if she had any sense, she wouldn't even be considering hiring him, especially since she'd already decided she wanted to do some of the work herself, which meant they'd be thrown together probably a lot more than was good for newly liberated thirty-five-year-old women with an agenda that had *remain celibate* scrawled in great big capital letters at the top of the list.

But she already knew how good he was at what he did, having seen his work at Cora's, for one thing. And that his little company needed the business. She also knew, when she made this decision, to buy this place, to move here, she'd have to deal with this man, one way or the other. Spruce Lake was a small town, and her best friend here was indelibly linked to people who were indelibly linked to Del. Yes, she'd thrown herself into the deep end, but if she didn't drown, she'd sure know how to swim by the end of all this.

If she could withstand her attraction to Del Farentino, if she could see this man every day, work beside him, listen to that voice and inhale that rich scent, and not collapse into a puddle of hormonal mush, then she would have proven something to herself far more valuable, even, than the challenge of running her own business: that she didn't need a man to feel complete. That she didn't have to let the deadly combination of emotions and physical yearnings dictate who she was and what she wanted from life.

That she could resist the temptation to fall into the same trap that had cut her grandmother, and Galen herself, off at the knees.

She'd been led here, she realized, to do far more than open a restaurant: she'd been led here to prove she could resist temptation.

She only hoped she was up to the challenge.

Quickly, Galen looked away, touching Wendy's head to get her attention. The little girl was warmly dressed in a turtleneck, long thick sweater, down vest like her dad's and heavy tights, all in shades of purple. "And how did your lesson go today?" she asked, speaking directly into her deep brown eyes.

"Good," Wendy said back, slowly and clearly, a huge grin on her face.

Galen grinned back and clapped; Wendy giggled, then signed something to her father.

"Sure, go ahead. You can't hurt anything," he said as he signed. "Just be careful."

With that, Wendy drifted off to investigate, her Barbie sneakers thumping up little poofs of dust from the tiled floor.

"Well. What do you think?" he asked.

She could hear the derision in his voice. The well-meant you've-lost-it censure. Tough. It would take a lot more than Del Farentino's macho disapproval to wipe out the giddy joy swirling through her veins. Let alone her sheer determination to make this work. Galen swept out her arms, feeling like one enormous smile. "It's bee-yoo-ti-ful!" she said, laughing.

"It's a wreck."

Although her spirit still soared, her arms fell to her sides with a slap. "Of course it is. Why do you think I got it so cheap?" She sidled over to the counter, hauling herself up onto a patched stool to peer over the counter. Nothing unusual—a griddle, shelves, a sink. Nooks and crannies that had probably housed clean and dirty glasses, crockery cups and dishes. Glass-enclosed cabinets where slices of homemade pie had once tempted customers into spending a couple more dollars, stuffing themselves just a little more—

"You're looking at months of work. Not to mention big bucks."

She sighed, then spun around, bracing her elbows on the counter's edge, steeling herself against the concern pouring forth from those eyes. She nearly lost her breath, right then, when it slammed into her that his concern was not only genuine, but genuinely *for her.* Not about how what she did might reflect on him in some way. He was really, truly worried that she'd gotten in over her head and would regret it.

For a moment, the realization that this man who knew her

so little would care so much shook her to the core. And she didn't quite know how to catalogue this revelation, let alone what to do with it. "I suppose I am," she finally said. "But I knew full well what I was getting into when I bought this place. Uh-uh-uh, you can just wipe that 'yeah, right' smirk off your face, Del Farentino—I did. I know it needs work. And I know it's going to take time and money and I'll probably find myself using words I've never used in my life, but…it's mine, Del." She slapped one hand to her chest, both to make a point and to reprimand her erratically thumping heart. "Totally, completely mine. Other than my clothes, a book or two and an occasional lipstick, I've never, ever had a single solitary thing that belonged to me and nobody else."

He looked flummoxed. "Ever?"

"Ever." She waited for this to sink in. "So. If this turns out to be a complete bomb, at least it will be *my* bomb."

Arms crossed, Del leaned back against a booth table a few feet away. Part of him found her enthusiasm refreshing, if not energizing; most of him, however, simply thought she was out of her gourd. "Eighty percent of new businesses fold within the first two years. Did you know that?"

She measured him for a second, her gaze steady and clear. And wary. Extraordinarily wary. "Yes."

"And that doesn't worry you?"

"Of course it does. But that's not going to stop me."

"You could lose everything."

"Only what I never had before," she said with a shrug, then sighed, looking out toward the street, her chin lifted. Proud. Resolute. When she returned her attention to him, her mouth was set in that way he recognized all too well. He'd seen it countless times before, from his mother, his wife. His daughter. That "I'm-gonna-do-it-my-way-anyway-so-you're-wasting-your-breath look.

This was not the same woman he'd held while she puked all over I-94, or the one who'd run out of Elizabeth's dining room when he complimented her spinach rolls. He wasn't sure who this gal was, and he was even less sure, because it made no sense, why he somehow thought he liked this one better.

Crazy.

"If this works," she said, "and you better believe if it doesn't, it won't be because I didn't give it everything I've got—then I'll know I took a chance that panned out. If it doesn't—and I'm well aware of the thousand and one things that can go wrong, things out of my control that might mean the whole thing will blow up in my face—I'll be no worse off than I was before. I don't have anyone dependent on me, after all. I'll survive. But I'd never be able to live with myself if I didn't at least *try*."

Again, he heard the determination. And the courage. He also heard a wistfulness in her admission that she was, as far as family went, completely alone in the world. Del had always had relatives coming out of his ears. He couldn't imagine not having *anyone*.

And perhaps it was that realization, of how alone she was, that caused his protective instinct to kick in even stronger. He realized the feeling was akin to the way he felt about Wendy, a cross between wanting her to succeed and not wanting to see her get hurt in the process, a feeling that led to far too many sleepless nights. But he had no choice with Wendy: she was his daughter; worrying about her was part of the job description. He wasn't responsible for Galen. He wasn't involved with Galen. Or her project. It was none of his business what she did or didn't do with her life, or her money, or anything. He didn't *have* to care. If he was smart, he wouldn't.

Yeah, well.

"You really know how to run a restaurant?"

After a second, she nodded in that crisp, brisk way she had. "Yes. I do. Thought I was going to, in fact—" The sentence ground to a halt, as if she realized she was about to reveal more than she'd intended. Instead, she offered him a little smile, softened by something almost apologetic in her expression. "I know this is a huge risk, Del," she said quietly. "And I know I might fail. But if I do, it won't be because I don't know what I'm doing, even if it might seem that way to you."

She hopped off the bench, heading toward the kitchen. "Now, if you don't mind, I'm gonna go take a tour of *my* building."

He decided to stay, if for no other reason than to be on hand in case she needed rescuing from a pile of rubble. Okay, so maybe that was an exaggeration—the building wasn't in imminent danger of collapse, even if most of the stuff inside it had passed *decayed* years ago. So he and Wendy tromped up the stairs behind Galen to the second-floor apartment, Wendy just as wide-eyed as Galen. Occasionally the child would poke at him to get his attention so she could sign a question to him, which he'd answer as best he could. Yes, the building belonged to Galen. Yes, she was going to open a restaurant. Yes, like that one they went to in Detroit a month ago, but probably with different food.

"Galen is really staying?" she signed.

He nodded his right hand up and down. "Yes."

Wendy clapped her hands, a broad smile lighting up her face. "I told you she'd come back," she signed. "I told you!"

Del just felt…muddled.

As they reached the second-floor landing, Del caught himself frowning at Galen's heavily-clothed form, wondering what it was about this woman that was affecting him so strongly. Then he thought of the earnestness in Galen's expression when she'd told him she'd never had anything of her own before, her unspoken plea for his understanding.

And the plea had gotten him. But good. That she'd reached her mid-thirties with nothing of her own seemed nearly too preposterous to be believed. Nor was it as if he didn't completely understand her need to try to leave her mark on the world, to be in charge of her own destiny. Like Elizabeth said, he could easily be working with his father, designing Hugh's developments, or at least overseeing their construction. But then, what would he have proven to himself? This way, if he succeeded, at least he'd earned every scrap of that success completely on his own.

However, Del had gone into his own business with his eyes wide open. He had years of working construction with his uncle Frank in Chicago under his belt, plus his architectural engineering degree, *and* a whole lot of business courses, before he even thought about going out on his own. At least he knew what he was getting into. *Really* knew.

He doubted the same could be said for the pretty, bright-eyed redhead scowling at the peeling linoleum in the tiny upstairs kitchen. She pushed up the faucet, which fell off in her hand.

At least he hadn't bought some building virtually sight unseen.

Galen stared at the broken faucet for a moment, then let it thunk onto the scarred gold-flecked counter.

"Good thing the water's off," Del said mildly, his arms crossed.

"Which reminds me," she said, clearly undaunted as she left the kitchen, walking into the infinitesimally small second bedroom to peer into the closet, such as it was. "I should probably see about getting the utilities hooked back up."

"Just the electric," Del said. "No point doing water or gas until all the pipes have been checked. And, uh, fixed."

She glanced at him, brows knit. "Oh, yes. Elizabeth mentioned you'd done a preliminary inspection for another client. Is it really that bad?"

"Worse."

That got a sigh. "Thanks." Her soap-and-shampoo fragrance drifted over him like a breath as she passed him on her way back into the living room, where Wendy was sitting cross-legged on the filthy floor, flipping through the pages of a stack of ancient *Ladies' Home Journals*. Del walked slowly around the perimeter of the room, hands in his vest pockets, occasionally stooping to inspect a dark splotch on the floor. Twin shafts of white winter sunshine knifed through the dust motes in what could very well be a nice room, once all the old wallpaper was stripped and the dark molding painted white or something—

"When can you start?"

Del stopped dead in his tracks. Squinted at her back. "What?"

She turned, gesticulating like a slightly annoyed schoolteacher who doesn't understand why her statement should require more explanation. "What's your work schedule like? So you can start getting this place in order? I mean, you'd probably have to do the plumbing first, then the electricity? I'd like to move into the apartment as soon as possible—"

Del's hands shot up by his shoulders. "Whoa, lady—hold on. It doesn't work that way."

She blinked. "What doesn't?"

"You just don't go hiring the first contractor you meet. You get bids, compare them, decide who's going to give you the biggest bang for your buck."

She crossed her arms, her head tilted. "So, you think someone else might underbid you?"

Del thought of the Golden project he'd lost last month, felt his jaw tighten. "It's been known to happen."

"But...I assume you use only quality materials? And guarantee the work will be done right the first time?"

"Well, yes, but—"

"So even if you charge a little more, that's probably because you don't cut corners, right?"

He jammed his hand through his hair, then laughed, the sound pinging off the walls in the virtually empty room. "That's what I keep telling potential clients, but they don't all seem to see it that way."

"Well, there's no accounting for shortsightedness, is there?" she said quietly, gesturing to Wendy that they were leaving. His heart did a slow, moderately painful turn in his chest as his daughter beamed at the crazy lady, trustingly put her tiny hand in hers. As they all trooped back down the narrow stairs connecting to the kitchen, Galen turned back and said, her voice reverberating in the musty-smelling stairwell, "Now why would I waste my time and energy, as well as other contractors' time and energy, getting bids when I know you won't pull a fast one on me?"

They all tumbled out into the kitchen, Del hanging a little behind. "And what makes you so all-fired sure I won't?"

"Because there's no less than a half-dozen people in this town who'd skin you alive if you did," she said simply, then levered herself on top of a prep table in the middle of the kitchen coated with a half-inch of dust. "Or don't you need the job?"

She'd gotten him again. Damn. "I'd be lying if I said otherwise."

"Then it would appear we have what some might see as a mutually advantageous situation here, huh?"

Del felt his mouth thin. He hooked one elbow on top of a rack of some kind, settling against it with his hands laced in front of his chest. "And since this is the first time you've seen the place, you don't even have a plan yet. *Huh?*"

He'd derailed her. Maybe only momentarily—certainly only momentarily—but he caught the flicker of doubt in her eyes.

"A plan?"

"Drawings. Something that tells me what you've got in mind. I can't just start in without knowing where I'm headed—"

"So you'll do it?"

He huffed a sigh. "I didn't say that. And until I see some plans, or at least some drawings, sketches—*something*—I'm not saying anything. Got it?" He nodded toward the table, not giving her a chance to reply. "You realize your butt is now covered in dust?"

"I imagine my…rear end will see a lot more than a little dust in the next several months. Which is the other reason I want to hire you."

Took a good five seconds before Del found his voice. "Excuse me?"

"I want to do a lot of the grunt work myself, and you'll let me, right?"

Another five seconds, and enough brain cells shifted so it finally clicked what she was saying. Elizabeth had been right, then. She *was* that crazy. "What makes you think that?"

She laughed. She had a nice laugh, when she let it out. Natural sounding, not too loud or high. The kind of laugh that makes everybody else in the room smile, wondering what's so funny.

The kind of laugh that got soft-touch guys like Del in real trouble.

"Oh, come on, Del. I'm sure I can swing a sledgehammer and pull up old tiles 'n' that as well as anybody. We could both save some money that way." Most of her hair had worked its way out of the clip; she reached up, unclipped it, clipped it back. "And since you're so worried about my fiscal stake in all this..."

"You are absolutely, positively, out of your mind," he said.

Her grin told him she didn't take offense.

"I can live with that."

"Galen, you have no idea what you're saying. None. This is hard, backbreaking work. Whatever you've been doing before, I somehow doubt it was anything physical enough to get you into the kind of shape you'd need to be in to do this. Three swings of a sledgehammer, honey, and every muscle in your back and arms is going to give you hell, believe me."

The grin faded. "Then I'll get in shape. But this is my place, and I fully intend to do as much of the work myself as I can. I don't know beans about plumbing or electricity, I'll give you that, but I'm sure I can learn to plaster and refinish and paint. A few sore muscles will be more than worth the knowledge that, when I open this place in June, my own sweat, and probably blood, will be worked into the floorboards."

"Don't forget tears," Del added dryly.

"That goes without saying."

Then it hit him. "You think this place will be ready by *June?* You really do have a screw loose!"

"You know, if I didn't know better, I'd swear you were trying to tell me something." She hopped down from the table, swiping in the general vicinity of her fanny. "But when would *you* be more likely to drive into town to try out a new restaurant? When it's eighty degrees, or in the middle of a blizzard?"

He had to hand it to her: she might be inexperienced, but he couldn't fault her logic. Well, except about her buying the place to begin with, but that was something else again.

"You've seen the basement, I take it?" she now said.

He shifted, following her to the door, signaling to Wendy who'd been drawing pictures on all the dusty surfaces. "Yep. Just as charming as the rest of the place."

She opened the cellar door, peering into the darkness. "You think there might be rats?"

"Oh, I'd bet my life on it."

She shuddered, but she clomped down the stairs anyway. Del shook his head and followed.

Three tiny windows along the back wall washed the space in thick charcoal light, but it was enough to see the furnace and hot water heater—the furnace might make it through another season, Del figured, but not the heater—a bunch of boxes stacked along one wall and a whole boatload of wooden shelves that looked as though they might have stored contraband goods during the Civil War. Oh, and there were a few barrels and boxes with the old yellow Civil Defense logo on them, too. Oh, yeah. In the event of a nuclear holocaust, this would definitely be his first choice of where to eventually starve to death. There were, however and at least, no rodents in evidence.

Which might have something to do with the tiny cries he heard from a darkened corner. Del unhooked the small flashlight he always carried from his belt and clicked it on, swinging it in the direction of the sound.

"Yeah, I heard it, too," Galen whispered, her breath closer to his skin than was probably good for anybody, least of all a man who hadn't had sex in nearly five years. But it was Wendy, alerted by the sudden sharp arc of the beam, who found the booty first. By the time Galen and Del got to the mother cat and three tiny kittens, curled on an old wadded up burlap sack behind more boxes of God-knew-what, Wendy had already bonded. She'd been begging him for a kitten for a year now, but since he was determined she couldn't have a pet until she could take proper care of it, he'd put her off. She turned to him, her hands going a mile a minute. "Sweet cats," she signed, yanking her fingers out from underneath her nose, like cat whiskers, four times to indicate four cats. "Can we keep them?" Her right hand circled her heart. "Please?"

Galen chuckled, crouching down, her hands laced over her knees. How anyone could still smell this good in a musty old basement was beyond him. Not to mention grossly unfair. "Even I could figure that one out," she said, her attention now riveted on this new problem. "She asked to keep one."

"Not quite. She asked to keep all of them."

"Oh. That could be a problem."

"You're telling me?"

"Well, somebody has to keep them or they'll all starve. Mama can't keep feeding them if she's not eating herself." Galen glanced around, her brow crinkled. "How on earth did she get in, I wonder?"

Del scanned the windows with the flashlight beam. "Over there, I bet. The middle window's broken." He returned the beam to the corner to discover his daughter had planted her what-used-to-be-clean bottom right smack on the cruddy floor. "Oh, Wendy," he moaned, not even bothering to sign.

That got another low laugh—Del decided he liked those, quite a bit—then a sigh. "The poor thing must be so cold!"

How did he know where this was headed? "She is wearing fur, after all. Besides, being in here is better than being outside, I imagine."

"True. But still." Galen stood, her sneakers scratching against the gritty cement floor, pawing through the boxes until she found an empty one. "This will do, I think, to carry mama and her babies in."

Del didn't even sigh. "And just where do you think you're taking them?"

"Well, to Cora's, I suppose."

"In?"

She batted her eyes. "Your truck?"

Del's knees popped as he straightened up. "Of course." Wendy caught the movement out of the corner of her eye, looked up expectantly. Hopefully. "We're taking the kitties to Cora's house," he signed.

Her hands fisted, right over left, in front of her. "I get one?"

Oh, brother.

Galen was busy with her box and no help whatsoever.

Del decided it was too dark to answer.

As if she understood the nice lady with the soothing voice was the best thing that had ever happened to her, Mama Cat let Galen move her and the babies into the box. Galen locked up, and a few minutes later they were all snug in his truck, heading to Cora's.

"Every little girl needs a kitten," Galen said after a minute, looking straight ahead.

Startled, Del looked down at Wendy between them, who was too busy making grumpy faces to even try to pay attention to what they were saying.

"I suppose you had one by this age, huh?"

The silence was telling. "My father said he was allergic," she said quietly, "so I never got one, even though he was rarely home. Then my grandparents always had dogs, my husband hated them and then I was back with my grandmother. By then, I'd lost interest."

"Or so you'd thought."

She glanced at him, then gave a little shrug.

"You have a dog," Del pointed out.

Galen smiled. "Which this cat outweighs by at least four pounds. This is not a problem."

He pulled up in front of Cora's house, cut the engine. "For the cat, maybe."

Laughter sputtered from her lips, bringing a hand to her mouth and color to her cheeks. And memories twisted around his heart, memories of another woman's laughter, another woman who'd laugh at his silly jokes.

Another woman who had no problem with taking risks.

Odd, how it had never occurred to him before this…but had he married Cyndi because she reminded him so much of his mother?

Was he doomed to be attracted to women who had more guts than sense?

"Del?"

Shaken, he looked over to run headlong into a pair of curious eyes gone gray in the darkness. ''What's up?'' she said softly.

Del gave a quick jerk of his head, knuckled his right temple. ''Nothing,'' he replied, equally softly, allowing a smile for his eagle-eyed daughter. ''Just tired, I guess.''

Just wondering why I'm thinking about things I thought I'd let go of. Things I thought couldn't hurt me anymore.

Pushing out the thoughts, he got out of the truck, signing to Wendy to stay put, he'd just be a minute, then helped Galen gather up her box of felines.

She took them from him, though, cooing and clucking at the beasts like they were her babies, for heaven's sake...and he remembered she couldn't have babies. And if any woman should have had kids, it would have been this one. Fate could sure be one mean sucker, that was for damn sure.

One strand of her hair had escaped from underneath her knit cap; it curved around her jaw, flirting with her mouth as she whispered reassurances to the cats. Without thinking, his gaze latched onto that lock of hair, teasing Galen's lips, and he thought about the sorts of things normal adult men think about, about kissing and touching and being close. About pretty redheads who had no idea, he was sure, just how pretty they were, or the way they smelled, how their smiles warmed up a man's insides like a cup of hot chocolate after shoveling snow.

Oh, yeah. Things would be a helluva lot easier if she hadn't come back.

He could tell the piece of hair was beginning to annoy her. With his gloved hand, he gently lifted it off her face, tucking it underneath the hat.

Their gazes sort of bumped into each other; she flashed one of those smiles at him. ''Thanks,'' she murmured, but her bravado of not moments before evaporated like a burst of steam from a teakettle, and he'd bet his last dollar she was blushing.

And none too pleased that she was.

His voice had grown too thick to ease past his throat, although he couldn't have said why. So he simply did one of those shrugging/nodding things.

She nodded back, then turned and trudged up the steps, flinching when Cora flung open the door. The smell of something fried and undoubtedly not on the American Heart Association's A list shimmied out from around the imposing woman, dressed in a pair of black slacks and a gold sweater large enough to house Del, Wendy and Galen combined. Wiping her hands on a dish towel, Cora peered into the box, then pulled back, frowning at Galen.

"As hostess gifts go, I'd've preferred a box of chocolates."

"We found them in the basement at the diner," Galen said breathlessly, pushing Cora slightly to the side so she could get in. "I couldn't just leave them."

"Oh, Lord. Another one."

"Another what?" Galen asked from behind her.

"Just like Nancy Braden. Woman went to the pound to get a kitten, came back with every cat they had in the place." With a heavy, resigned sigh, Cora turned her attention to Del, still standing at the bottom of the porch steps. "So what are you doing down there? And where's that baby girl of yours?"

"Out in the truck. I was just the delivery boy."

"Huh. Well, go on and get her, child, before she freezes half to death."

"Uh, no, it's kind of late…I need to get on home and start dinner—"

"Now why would you do that when I've got a whole mess of fried chicken in here, just waiting for someone to enjoy it? So go on, now—you go get the baby and bring her on in here."

Fully expecting to be obeyed—and with good reason—Cora flounced back inside, revealing a catless Galen standing a few feet inside the entryway, her hand at her throat.

Uh-oh. His guess was Cora had just unwittingly gotten back at somebody for bringing a boxful of cats into her house.

Big-time.

Chapter 7

If it hadn't been for Cora's non-stop monologue through dinner, there wouldn't've been any conversation at all, Del mused as he took the dripping dish from the close-lipped woman on his right. Which, he mused some more, was what you got when the other three people at the table included a ticked-off deaf child—who had not reacted well to Del's finally admitting he really didn't think the time was right yet for her to have a kitten—and a pair of adults who had no idea what to make of this weird trembly non-thing going on between them.

Galen wasn't angry, he didn't think, as much as...well, if he knew the answer to that one, he wouldn't be standing here with a frown locking his forehead muscles, now would he? As soon as they'd finished eating, Cora had commandeered his daughter for a quick trip to the grocery store to buy some cat food for this animal she insisted was only here temporarily—having already given the far-too-thin beast a can of Chicken of the Sea—leaving the kitchen chores to Del and Galen. And it wasn't as if Galen didn't say *anything*, but her verbal offerings were meager. Like the crumbs left on the fried chicken platter.

Just like that first day, in his truck. Lord above, he'd never seen anyone who ran hot and cold the way Galen did. You'd never know this was the same woman who a few hours before had been bubbling away, giddy and giggly over her very own collection of ripped vinyl and stained ceilings.

But then, he remembered, the wariness had still been there, in her eyes, in the way she took great care not to get too close unless she couldn't help it. As long as she was on her turf, as long as they were talking about her project, she could laugh and talk and even make jokes, because that was just…stuff. But here, having dinner, even though it was Cora's idea and this was Cora's house, was clearly getting waaaay too personal for Miss Galen.

Not that Del didn't understand—he could use a shot of that stress-activated deodorant himself, right about now—but he thought maybe he was handling it better than Galen. Maybe.

God, there was nothing stickier than two people who were attracted to each other when neither of them knew what to do about it. But if they were going to work together—and, yes, he'd take the job because a) he needed the money and b) he needed the money—then somebody had better do something or they'd both expire from holding their breath around each other.

"You think I'm being hardheaded about not letting Wendy have a kitten, don't you?"

Her gaze darted to his, immediately away. "Maybe a little," she said, the slightest smile playing around her mouth. She lifted one shoulder, vainly attempting to push back that once-again-escaped hank of hair; Del reached out to smooth it behind her ear, but she recoiled. Then frowned, like she was trying to decide why she'd done that. "In any case—" she rinsed off a handful of silverware, rattled it into the basket in the drainer "—she's welcome to come over anytime and play with them." Galen plunked the last dish in the drainer, then let out the now-sudsless dishwater. "You want some coffee?"

Del wiped that last dish and put it away, hung the dishtowel through the loop attached to the cabinet door underneath the sink, then leaned against the counter, his arms crossed. When he hadn't responded after a few seconds, Galen finally looked over at him. "Do you want—?" she began again, but he held up one hand.

"What I want," he said softly, "is for you to tell me what's rattling you so much."

Her eyes went wide, her cheeks apple red. Then she laughed, an odd, hollow sound that was only about ten percent amusement. Shaking her head, she opened the refrigerator to pull out a can of coffee. "What on earth makes you think I'm rattled?" she asked, promptly dropping the coffee can, which neatly rolled to Del's feet.

He picked it up, handed it back to her. "Call it…a remarkably developed insight into the human psyche."

Galen snatched the can from him, thunked it onto the counter. "I'm just tired," she said, echoing his earlier excuse. "In all the excitement about seeing the restaurant for the first time, my body forgot I got up at 5 a.m. to finish packing." She spooned coffee into the filter, shoved the basket shut.

She was obviously near tears, and he had no idea why. Not really. Clearly, she didn't want him to touch her—that was one signal that wasn't in the least bit ambiguous—yet he'd never felt the urge to touch a woman more. Heavens knows, there had been women in his life, pre-Cyndi, who simply hadn't liked him, or who'd had someone else or whatever, but they usually had no trouble just coming out and telling him to back off. This was different. *Galen* was different. She was reacting like…like…

Like Wendy did when she wanted something really, really badly but knew she'd catch hell if she so much as reached for it.

"Galen?"

He saw her fight for control, then turn to him. Her hand, however, was shaking; she realized it, clamped it into a fist.

"I don't know what, if anything, is going on here," he said gently. "Between us. I mean, I'll be the first to admit, I'm so out of practice, I'm probably imagining things. And if I am, just ignore this whole conversation, okay? But all I can tell you is, I'm no threat to you."

Color washed up her neck, suffusing her face. "I know that."

"No. I don't think you do." It took everything he had in him not to reach out, take her hand. "So let me just say a couple things, here. Get this out in the open. Then maybe we can just go on with our lives without this…whatever it is hanging over us, okay?"

She didn't move. Didn't say go. Didn't say stop.

Del took a deep breath and dived in.

"I don't believe in crowding a woman. Or I should say, I didn't, before I was married. There hasn't been anyone since, but I doubt my philosophy has changed. Even though I think you're very nice and extremely pretty, I'm not going to put the moves on you, for two reasons: first, because I think we'd kill each other as a couple, and second, because it's clear there's some real heavy stuff going on inside that lovely head of yours that has nothing to do with me. I may be a plain kind of guy, but I like to think I'm a couple notches up the evolutionary ladder from your average beer-guzzling couch potato who thinks a woman's place is in his kitchen, fixing him snacks that are going to eventually kill him anyway. I can be friends with or work with a woman without thinking of her in sexual terms." He allowed a grin. "Or, if I do, I can at least keep my trap shut about it. And my hands to myself."

Her blush deepened, but he caught the faint smile tilting the corners of her mouth.

"I guess what I'm saying is, you're safe with me, Galen, okay? What's *not* safe—" he leaned against the counter, his hands braced alongside his hips "—is the flock of matchmaking females who are going to do their level best to get us together, starting with Cora but God knows not limited to her."

Galen made a funny little noise in her throat, then lifted one hand to the back of her neck. "Yeah. I kinda gathered that. Maybe that's what…" She hesitated, shaking her head, then turned to him, meeting his gaze. "Thank you," she said, giving a short, crisp nod. "I'm afraid…" She sucked in a deep breath, letting it out on a thin stream of air. "I was sixteen when I met Vinnie, Del. Eighteen when I married him. He wasn't just my only lover, but my only *boyfriend*. I've never even been kissed by anyone else. I frankly—'' she laughed, shaking her head, embarrassed ''—don't know what to do with men. Or how to act around them. Which is bad enough, I suppose. But there's more...oh! The coffee's ready. Want some?''

He almost cursed the coffeemaker, but smiled anyway. ''Sure.''

She fixed them both cups, then sat back down at the solid wood kitchen table in the middle of Cora's kitchen. After dumping in three teaspoons of sugar and a dollop of fat-free milk, she continued, her lashes fanned over her cheeks as she studied the swirling coffee in her cup. ''You remember how I said the restaurant is the first thing I've ever had that's completely my own?''

Del swallowed, nodded.

''Well, this is the first time I've ever had my own life, too. The first time I'm completely free to come and go as I please, without being answerable to anybody. I know you think I'm several sandwiches short of a picnic for doing what I'm doing, but the challenge is more than my seeing if I can get this restaurant up and running. It's...oh, I don't even know if I can put it into words. It's my chance to find out who the woman is who wants to do this crazy thing. And since that's something I can only do alone anyway...'' She skimmed one short-nailed finger around the brim, then lifted one shoulder.

''No men,'' he said.

''No men,'' she echoed, doing that shoulder-lift thing again.

Del found the gesture a sad one, to tell the truth. Like, somehow, Galen thought she was being punished for something and her having to work out some life-problem on her own was her penance. But he didn't doubt her conviction about needing to be on her own. And it gave him a convenient excuse to keep his distance, too. He really couldn't go through this again, dealing with another headstrong woman. And somehow, because of the circumstances behind this particular woman's drive to do things her own way, she would probably be the worst of the lot. Not that he ever expected to find someone—or, in truth, wanted someone—with no backbone, no mind of her own, but neither was he in the mood for the horn-locking sessions that would inevitably arise with this one.

There had to be something between *demure* and *reckless*. Didn't there?

So. Now he knew where they stood, he could just forget about it. Her.

Them.

Whew.

So he lifted his cup, saluting her, mentally telling the pang of disappointment vicing his heart to go take a hike.

"Understood," he said, which got a small, but very relieved, smile.

Galen realized Del was very right about one thing: absolutely nothing was going to happen with this project until she had some sort of drawings or ideas or could at least tell him what she wanted. The trouble was, though, she couldn't draw worth squat. Oh, she'd gone over and measured everything and gridded it all out, but she had to admit, after several used-up newsprint drawing pads and a week of tearing out her hair she had no idea what she was doing.

This was not putting her in a wonderful frame of mind. And it was in this not wonderful frame of mind that she opened Cora's front door late one afternoon while Cora was still at work to find Nancy Braden on her doorstep, her thin arms strangling a ten pound bag of what looked like very ritzy cat food.

"Oooh," the brunette said, shifting the bag of food to one arm to frown at Galen over her sunglasses. "This is not a happy person in front of me."

Galen quirked her mouth. "You could say that."

"Look, if this is a bad time, I can just leave this—" Nancy shoved the bag of food into Galen's arms, then craned her neck to peek inside, obviously looking for the cats "— and maybe come back later?"

Like that was going to work. "You wanna see the babies?" Galen asked.

"Could I?" Nancy lit up like a Christmas tree. Or maybe, in her case, a menorah. "Cora told me about them," she said, shucking off her down coat as she swooped inside. She was simply enough dressed in a red angora tunic and black leggings, but on her tiny, slender frame, and with that full mane of deep brown curly hair, her exotically dark eyes, the effect was somehow dramatic. Galen didn't think she'd ever looked dramatic in her life. Galen wasn't sure she ever *could* look dramatic. "You found them in the diner's basement?"

"Yep." Galen led the way into a small sunroom off the kitchen, where the southern exposure kept the temperature cozy all day. "I decided it was a sign of some kind, although I'm not yet sure what." The kittens' eyes had just opened a couple days before, but they were still little more than balls of fluff with tiny, pointed tails. The mother, a long-haired tortoiseshell, was beginning to fill out, as were her babies—a ginger tabby, an all black with white nose and feet, and a black-and-white spot. Their basket, a padded, hooded number Cora had brought back from PetSmart, declaring the box far too tacky, sat up on a low platform Cora had strong-armed Del into making so the poor things wouldn't have that nasty draft blowing over them, you know. And keeping assiduous guard from her perch on a perfectly situated wicker chair with a thick, floral cushion, lay Baby, nose pointed, ears sporadically twitching.

"Oh, God," Nancy breathed, dropping to her knees, "aren't you just the most gorgeous things!" She held out one hand with perfectly painted, tapered nails to Mama, who sniffed, then angled her neck for Nancy to scratch her chin.

Galen knelt down beside her, palms on thighs. "I have no idea what I'm going to do with them. I'll keep Mama, and I'm pretty sure Cora would kill anyone who tried to take the ginger tabby, but about the other two..."

Nancy flapped her hand. "Don't give it another thought. I'll take the black one, and give the black-and-white spot to Wendy for her birthday."

Galen laughed. "Del will kill you."

"Del will get over it."

"And I thought Cora said you already had a lot of cats?"

"Seven," Nancy said, carefully lifting the little black one from the nest. "But I never had a kitten." She cooed and clucked at the itty bitty thing, then slyly chuckled. "And *my* birthday's coming up, too."

"And your husband wouldn't mind? If you brought in another cat?"

Nancy gave her a funny look. "No. Why would he? For one thing, it's not like one more would make any difference. And it's just a cat, for God's sake. Now, something larger…like, say, another child—" her mouth spread into a mischievous grin "—that, we'd discuss. But not a kitten."

The phone rang; Galen excused herself to take the call, telling Cora's daughter Lynette—who was due to have a baby any second—she expected Cora in around five-thirty. While she was on the phone in the living room, however, she noticed Nancy had found her way into the dining room and was having a gander at Galen's latest botched attempt to get her ideas down on paper.

Her heart fell to somewhere around her ankles.

She untangled herself from Lynette—who took after her mother in the gabbing department—and inched into the dining room.

"I'm no artist," she said, worrying the neckline of her sweater.

Nancy looked up, not even embarrassed at having been caught snooping. She tapped one fingernail on one of the drawings. "A fountain?"

Heat flooding her face, Galen stepped closer. "I was just sort of trying to see what I came up with. They're pretty dumb, some of them—"

Nancy looked at her as if she'd begun speaking in another language. "These aren't dumb at all," she said softly, an odd catch to her voice. "They're very good, in fact." She looked down again at the drawings, slowly moving them around, her mouth quirked up on one side. "I really like the idea of changing the windows to arches, and all the panes. It's very old-world. Charming.''

Galen hadn't expected the compliment, especially from such a sophisticated source. Pleasure, accompanied by a wave of relief, coursed through her. "Thank you," she said quietly.

Nancy glanced at her, back at the drawings. "So. Who told you you were dumb?"

Galen started. "What?"

Those dark, generous eyes met hers. "You heard me."

Shaken, Galen clasped her hands in front of her, both ashamed and oddly relieved when she felt the sting of tears. "My grandfather, mostly. But how—?"

"In my case, it was my mother," Nancy said, then came around the table, her arms crossed. "No matter how hard I tried, I could never do anything right. She called it being protective, but she went way beyond the call of duty when it came to me. So you might say I recognize the signs."

Galen hugged herself. "What happened?"

"For one thing, although it took thirty-four years, I finally grew up. Wised up. Realized, so what? So I couldn't get my mother's approval? Sure, I still wanted it, but I didn't need it. I was okay, you know? Whether Belle Shapiro saw that or not. Although I have to give Rod some credit for my con-sciousness-raising." She smiled, a soft smile somewhat at odds with what Galen had already decided was the woman's naturally aggressive personality. "He was the one who finally shook me awake, made me see I really *was* just fine. And that I was worthy of being loved and appreciated, just as I was."

Then Nancy walked back to the drawings. "I…kinda have a vested interest in what you do with the diner," she said.

"Oh?"

She nodded. "Mmm. See, Rod's a great cook, and thought maybe, at one time, he'd like to open a restaurant, too. We talked about his buying the diner when it first went on the market—or, more accurately, I tried to convince him to give it a go—but he eventually decided against it because he wanted to spend time with our children. His and ours. Once I was really, truly convinced he was making a choice based on what was best for *him*, not just *us*, I backed off. But I guess I hoped that whoever did eventually buy the place did it because of a dream. That maybe…'' Her olive skin darkened. ''Oh, this sounds silly—Rod tells me motherhood has made me almost unbearably sentimental, but what the hell—that Rod's dream might be realized for someone else.''

Stunned was far too weak a word to describe Galen's reaction. ''I…I don't know what to say.''

Nancy shook her head. ''Just make it happen.''

That got a sigh. ''Well, that could be a problem at this stage. Del said he wouldn't even consider taking on the project until he saw some plans or drawings or something.''

''What were those all over your dining table?''

''The scribblings of a madwoman?''

Nancy laughed. ''Del's worked with worse, believe me. Not to mention less. When he worked on our house, my stepdaughter Hannah and I would stand and tell him what we wanted, pointing and waving our hands around a lot, and Del would go away and come back with drawings and plans and things and then he'd work his magic and ta-da! It would happen.''

''You mean…Del can do the plans?''

''Well, of course Del can do the plans! The man's got a master's degree in architectural engineering. Which of course just drives his father to distraction, that his only son seems hell-bent on doing things the hard way with this construction company of his, when he could be working alongside Hugh and actually making some money. No one's quite been able to figure that one out. But one reason the man's so good is that he can not only take on a project practically from scratch—or chicken scratch, as the case may be—but he can spot problems in other people's drawings in a flash. So tell him what you want. I guarantee, he can make it work. Oh, hell—I've got to get home. Hannah's got a basketball game tonight and she'll have five fits if she thinks I'm gonna miss it.''

Suddenly moving at the speed of light, the tiny woman zoomed to the front of the house, grabbing her coat and purse and opening the door. But as she did, she stopped, the breeze from outside teasing the million and one curls suspended around her slender face. "By the way—you decided what you're gonna call the restaurant?"

Galen shook her head. "Nothing's come to me yet. I, uh...well, I've kinda been relying on signs to tell me what to do, you know? So I'm hoping I'll get one about this, too."

"How about your own name?"

She laughed. "Granata's is already a famous restaurant in Pittsburgh. And somehow Volcek's Ristorante Italiano doesn't exactly cut it."

"Hmm. You could be right. Well, I'm sure you'll think of something." Suddenly, Nancy leaned over, her arm around Galen's neck, and gave her a quick hug. "We're glad you're here," she said, only to dash off before Galen could ask her what, exactly, she meant by that.

"Now, why do you suppose Del didn't tell Galen right off he could do her working drawings for her?" Nancy asked Rod, grabbing sixteen-month-old Kelsey and plopping her up onto the changing table to get her jammies on. At the other end of the room, Rod tussled with a giggling Quinn, Kelsey's twin brother, trying to match limbs to corresponding openings in a red blanket sleeper. From down the hall, clashing CD's fought it out from Hannah's and Schuy's rooms, punctuated by the occasional, "Turn that down, dweeb!"

Nancy zipped up Kelsey's sleeper, then drew her up into her arms for a hug. God, she'd waited a long time for this. But damned if it wasn't worth every agonizing, frustrating, lonely minute it had taken to get here.

"Maybe he wanted to make sure she had her ideas in order first?" Rod said over their son's infectious laughter, flying him into his crib as Nancy did the same to Kelsey on her side of the room. "And maybe that brain of yours is wandering into territory that's none of its business?"

Nancy made a face at him as they passed each other to give kisses to the other's baby. A thousand "nite-nites" duly dispensed, Rod slipped his arm around Nancy's shoulders as they left the room, waiting for a moment to make sure the babies stayed quiet. Then, hands linked, they walked down to the family room, collapsing onto the sofa in front of the fireplace.

"She'd be perfect for him," she said.

"You don't know that. So stay out of it."

Unfazed, Nancy snuggled up to her husband, watching the fire writhe and leap in front of her. "She could use a little sprucing up, though, don't you think?"

Rod's chuckle tickled her ear. "Okay, I'm probably going to regret saying this, but…"

She hoisted herself up, frowning. "But what?"

"But if the way Del was looking at Galen at Thanksgiving was any indication, I don't think *he* thinks she needs a drop of 'sprucing up', as you put it."

With a smug little grin of her own, Nancy snuggled back against her husband's chest. Just wait until she told Elizabeth *this*.

Chapter 8

"This ain't gonna come cheap," Del said, leafing through her sketches. They weren't pretty, but they were remarkably clear. Basically, they'd have to gut the entire restaurant area and start over, if they did everything she wanted.

Elizabeth had told him that Nancy had told him how uneasy Galen had been about showing him her rough sketches. And Elizabeth had said that Nancy had said he should fawn over them, a little. That, he could do. No problem.

The problem came with ignoring what Elizabeth hadn't said but he knew she wanted to say, and undoubtedly would say, very soon.

And God help him if he ran into Nancy anytime in the next century.

Of course, what he hadn't had the nerve to tell all these well-meaning meddlers was the single most important thing that anybody *had* said about this whole business, which was that Galen wasn't interested.

He'd mulled that over, too, a lot more than he would've thought necessary. And after a week, he still hadn't decided

PLAY "LUCKY 7" AND GET
THREE FREE GIFTS!

HOW TO PLAY:

1. With a coin, carefully scratch off the silver box at the right. Then check the claim cha
see what we have for you — **2 FREE BOOKS** and a gift — **ALL YOURS! ALL FREE!**

2. Send back this card and you'll receive two brand-new Silhouette Intimate Mome
novels. These books have a cover price of $4.50 each in the U.S. and $5.25 each in Can
but they are yours to keep absolutely free.

3. There's no catch. You're ur
no obligation to buy anything.
charge nothing — ZERO
your first shipment. And you c
have to make any minimum nun
of purchases — not even one!

4. The fact is thousands of readers enjoy receiving their books by mail from the Silhou
Reader Service.™ They enjoy the convenience of home delivery... they like getting the I
new novels at discount prices, BEFORE they're available in stores... and they love their *H
to Heart* newsletter featuring author news, horoscopes, recipes, book reviews and much m

5. We hope that after receiving your free books you'll want to remain a subscriber.
the choice is yours — to continue or cancel, any time at all! So why not take us up on
invitation, with no risk of any kind. You'll be glad you did!

YOURS FREE!

PLAY LUCKY 7 FOR THIS EXCITING FREE GIFT!

*THIS SURPRISE
MYSTERY GIFT
COULD BE
YOURS FREE WHEN
YOU PLAY*
LUCKY 7!

Visit us online at
www.eHarlequin.com

The Silhouette Reader Service™ —Here's how it works:

If offer card is missing write to: Silhouette Reader Service, 3010 Walden Ave., P.O. Box 1867, Buffalo, NY 14240-1867

BUSINESS REPLY MAIL
FIRST-CLASS MAIL   PERMIT NO. 717   BUFFALO, NY

POSTAGE WILL BE PAID BY ADDRESSEE

SILHOUETTE READER SERVICE
3010 WALDEN AVE
PO BOX 1867
BUFFALO NY 14240-9952

NO POSTAGE
NECESSARY
IF MAILED
IN THE
UNITED STATES

whether her flat-out "leave me alone" disappointed or relieved him.

She bugged him and fascinated him and annoyed the living daylights out of him and she clearly had way more baggage than a perpetually broke, perpetually busy, single father of a smart, sassy, deaf, four-year-old needed to even think about dealing with. Unfortunately, it was the fascinating part he couldn't seem to shake loose.

Like a wad of gum stuck to your shoe.

They sat, at seven-thirty in the morning, in the cold, at one of the booths, the sketches sprawled between them, cups of steaming coffee at their elbows. Galen's idea. Because, she'd said, he might not understand what she meant unless she could show him on site. He'd left Wendy with Elizabeth, who'd said she'd be happy to drop her off at Mrs. Battaglia's on her way in to take Chloe to Gymboree, and to be sure to say "hi" to Galen for her. So he'd done that much, at least, taken aback at her genuinely surprised expression. As if she couldn't quite believe anyone would care enough to send a casual greeting.

He'd also told her, without having to lie, that her sketches were enough for him to work with.

Okay, he told her he was very impressed.

Then he watched nervousness and skepticism leave the stage just long enough for delight to make a guest appearance. The woman downright *glowed.*

When the hell was the last time somebody gave this woman a compliment? What would she do if he did? A personal one?

"Just answer me one thing," she said, her forearms crossed on the table in front of her, her mouth pinched as she frowned at the drawings. Then she lifted her eyes to his, shadowed by those thick lashes. "Why didn't you tell me you could do the working drawings for me to begin with?"

Because I'd hoped you'd find someone else.

He took a swig of coffee, hitching his shoulders. Lowering his gaze. "Because you didn't ask. So I figured you already had somebody else."

"Why would you figure that?"

He shrugged again. Let her come to her own conclusions.

The eastern sun was just really getting cranked up at that hour, limning the gentle lines of Galen's face a rosy peach, delineating each freckle, setting a dozen staticky strands of hair afire. She wore it loose today, although the front and sides were caught up with clear plastic combs, one over each ear. As usual, she was dressed in the baggiest thing she could find, in this case what looked like a man's navy sweatshirt over a white turtleneck. As usual, Del was struck by how it didn't matter what she wore. Not to him, at least.

He'd bet his life she wore Fruit of the Loom panties. Full cut. White. No trim. And bras to match. And why, one might ask, was he thinking about Galen Granata's drawers?

She was giving him a funny look. Like she knew.

Couldn't have been more than forty-five, fifty degrees inside, and his cheeks burned.

She cleared her throat, that hand floating up to tug at the turtleneck. Ah. She was blushing, too.

You know, the more he thought about this, the more this was obviously a really, really bad idea. Not that he was going to renege on his promise to steer clear, but as long as she kept blushing like that and looking all vulnerable like that and he kept obsessing about her underwear …

And just wait until the sap started running in the spring.

Finally, somebody said something. Galen, in fact. "I do have a budget."

"Glad to hear it."

"Yes. Well. I'll admit, I don't know how much things cost, so could we, uh, just kinda pretend I've got all the money in the world and can do anything I want, then trim from there?"

Del took a long, slow sip of scalding hot coffee, actually relishing the long, slow burn searing between his ribs. "How about I tell you you're looking at three hundred grand, easy, and save myself about twenty hours worth of drawings?"

She went very white. "Oh, dear."

"Yeah. I figured your eyes were a little bigger than your pocketbook."

She hauled in an enormous breath, except that circus tent she wore was so huge, he didn't even get the benefit of watching her breasts rise and fall. Intuition told him she had them, somewhere in there. Shame she kept them sequestered away like that all the time.

And maybe two, three cups of coffee down the road, he'd snap to and realize what a slimeball he was. How would he feel, knowing some guy was thinking about *Wendy's* breasts, huh? Well, when she got them. Which he gathered could happen anytime after the next six or seven years.

He suddenly felt ill.

"I can afford about half that," Galen said, her hands folded in front of her.

What? Oh. Right.

"Can I get anything even close to what I want for that?"

Those eyes. God. They were worse than Wendy's. Except Wendy was a born manipulator. This woman wasn't. Which is what made those eyes even more treacherous. Especially as he could *see* her eyes.

With a weighty sigh, Del hooked his elbow on the back of the boothseat and twisted around, letting his gaze rake slowly, professionally, over the space. His torso still angled away, he looked back, resting his other elbow on the table, his chin caught in the palm of his hand. "We can do a lot for a hundred fifty grand," he said, knowing he was, somehow, going to regret this. "Not everything you want, but I think we can probably get the look you're aiming for."

"So I can rip out the booths?"

"Uh…no."

"I really, really want new booths."

"Then you can't stucco the walls."

A neat little crease settled securely between her brows.

"Besides, faux painting would be cheaper, anyway," he pointed out. "Or we could go for exposed brick, if the wall's thick enough."

"Hmm." Lip caught between her teeth, she shuffled through the sketches. "How about I rip out the middles ones, recovering the ones along the windows?"

"That might work. You thinking of putting tables in the center?"

She nodded.

Del gazed out over the area, his lips pursed. "Yeah. That'd be nice."

When he turned back, he saw renovation lust sparkling in her eyes. "Recessed lighting?" she asked.

"Track might be cheaper. We'll see."

"Mullioned windows?"

"Single sheet. Fake mullions." At her pout, he added, "The customers will never know, believe me."

She sighed. "Flagstone entry?"

"Tile."

"Bronze lighting fixtures?"

"Iodized iron. You'll love it."

Another sigh. Then she came to the last sketch, jabbing her finger at the crude drawing in the center of the page. "And this?"

Del lifted his chin to see the drawing better. "A fountain I can give you. Complete with naked cherubs with water coming out of their—"

"Those are *fish,* Mr. Farentino," she said, tight-lipped.

Somehow, he suppressed the chuckle, but it was making his eyes water. Then she drew in a very long breath. "Okay. What's next?"

"I do plans and we start ripping out stuff."

"But what about the money?"

Weird, the way she had of sounding efficient and out of her depth at the same time. The difference between theory and practice, he guessed. "Once we agree on the plans, get them approved, then I draw up an estimate. We do some tweaking until everybody's happy, then I send you a contract. Then you give me a deposit, based on the estimate."

But she was shaking her head. "I understand that. No, what I mean is, how do I know you won't go over my budget?"

Now it was his turn to be surprised. "Because I give you my word?"

She shook her head again, then rummaged in that boxcar of hers she called a purse for a pen and paper, pushed it over to him. "In writing, please."

"It'll be in the contract, for heaven's sake—"

"If I'm going to let your crew start ripping this place apart, I want to know, before a single nail is removed, that I can count on you, Mr. Farentino."

He could argue the point, but somehow, he figured it was just easier to do what she wanted. Then it struck him, what she was doing: she was trying to convince him she wasn't a space cadet. Small wonder, considering the way he'd come down so hard on the idea to begin with. With a sigh, he scribbled his assurance and signed it, but couldn't resist adding, "But what's with the 'Mr. Farentino' business?"

She snatched the piece of paper from his hand, scanned it, then let the purse swallow it back up. "Just a little something to remind both of us that this is a business arrangement. That's all."

Now, that puzzled him for a minute. Why on earth did she feel the need to go formal, all of a sudden? Mulling this one over, he shrugged, gathered the sketches so he could begin translating them into working drawings, then made his way to the door, when it hit him what had probably caused the wall to suddenly come up.

What had caused him to think she could read *his* mind earlier.

"*Ms.* Granata?" He waited until she looked up, then hooked his hand on his hip, figuring her eyes would follow. Which they did. "They're black, in case you were wondering. Low cut. Nothing fancy, but they get the job done."

Then he left, sure the temperature in the diner must've risen at least ten degrees, just from the heat generated from that magnificent blush.

She wanted to die. Just crawl into a deep, dark hole and never come out again. Was she really that transparent?

Or were his skivvies?

"Jeez-o-man, Galen," she muttered, "cut it out!" Except she knew that thanks to a certain someone's indiscreet clairvoyance, now all she was going to be able to think about for the rest of the day was Del Farentino's butt.

She supposed there could be worse images to have stuck in one's head.

She giggled. A little one, soft and short. Then another, tickling its way up through her chest, followed by another, and yet another, until she was laughing so hard she thought she'd wet her pants, laughing hard enough to make her muscles hurt and her eyes water. The look on his face...

And the look that must have been on hers...

Laughter roared up from the soles of her feet, leaving her breathless and helpless and boneless, a rag of a woman, all alone, laughing her head off. Then, suddenly, she was weeping, with as much gusto as she'd been laughing not a minute before. She sobbed and choked, crying as if this was the only chance she'd have to cry, ever again. The odd thing was though, she really had no idea why she was crying, since she hadn't been feeling particularly sad.

Or maybe, she thought as she ransacked her tote bag for a tissue, she'd been sad for so long she no longer recognized it.

Galen stilled, nose to tissue, letting this revelation wash over her, understanding replacing hysterics.

Criminy. It was true. When was the last time she'd been absolutely, completely happy? The closest she'd come, she realized, was when she'd walked in here a week ago, seen this poor shoddy place for the first time.

Pitiful.

She honked and wiped and sniffed, then let out a long shaky, soul-deep sigh. And felt the corners of her mouth lift. It'd felt good to laugh like that. And cry, too. Kinda scary though, to think all it took to set her off was some smart-aleck comment from a man she'd vowed not to let past her emotional security system.

Well. She hauled herself to her feet, wending her way to the back and up the stairs to the second floor. Nothing like a good cleaning session to banish wayward thoughts. And when it came to this man she'd just hired to work alongside her for the next several months, her thoughts seemed as determined as a herd of wild mustangs to break out of the little tidy corral of logic and propriety she'd set up.

Pushing up her sweatshirt sleeves, she shoved a plastic bucket underneath the kitchen sink faucet—now fixed, thanks to Mr. Hinkle down the street who owned the hardware store and had said, far as he knew, the plumbing should be decent enough for her to do some cleaning, water just needed to be turned on, was all, and that the broken faucet probably wouldn't take more'n two shakes to fix, which turned out to be true, too—watching the Simple Green froth up nicely in the stream of water pounding the bottom of the bucket. Her little explosion had left her feeling strangely lighter. Lighter, and…cleaner, somehow.

Like what these disgusting kitchen cabinets were going to be when she finished with them.

She hauled over the collapsible step stool she'd probably paid too much for at Hinkle's, but since she didn't have a car—the purchase of which was rapidly approaching the top of her to-do list—she couldn't get to Wal-Mart or Target or any place like that, and she already felt like she was putting Cora out enough as it was. Besides, Mr. Hinkle had thrown in the Simple Green and a pair of gloves for free. Because he was glad someone finally bought the diner, he said.

Good thing, considering the energy she was about to expend. From the next-to-top step, she attacked the soffit, caked with so much grease and stringy dirt and bug bits, the sponge turned black—and crusty—after one swipe. Yuck. Perhaps it was just as well the light fighting its way through the filthy window was as weak and diffused as it was.

It had worried him, Mr. Hinkle had said, seeing the place sit there empty month after month, what people might think. That Main Street was dead, if the diner couldn't make it. Oh, he'd said with a wave of his hand, he and the other merchants could tell folks the diner's owners didn't quit because they didn't have the business, but because they didn't want to do it anymore. But you know how people are. Always thinking the worst. Before you know it, he'd said, someone else would leave for one reason or another, then there'd be two places vacant, and where would it lead, huh? Like letting one tooth, then another, decay. Pretty soon, there'd be nothing left.

She climbed down, dumped the blackened water into the sink, got fresh, climbed back up. Only—she twisted around, counted—nine cabinets to go.

Underneath her sweatshirt, sweat meandered down her back. She scrubbed even harder, a woman hell-bent on banishing the dirt demons.

And perhaps some others as well. The ones that crowded her fragmented sleep, doing their level best to undermine her determination.

Loneliness.

Doubt.

Fear.

She briefly shut her eyes, sucked in a quick breath, opened them. Continued with her task.

The bookseller and the florist and the jewelry store owner had all pretty much echoed Mr. Hinkle's sentiments, the lot of them clearly relieved and grateful to see that blasted For Sale sign gone. They all wished her tremendous success, they'd said. And from them, she'd already gotten recommendations for butchers and greengrocers, paper and linen suppliers. The lovely woman from the bookstore was getting a new computer, did Galen want hers with the accounting software already on it? And the florist said she'd give Galen a courtesy discount if she wanted to use fresh flowers on the tables. And the best thing was the baker down the street said he'd be thrilled to supply all her fresh-baked Italian bread and breadsticks—

Oh! Oh, my goodness…these people, they were all *counting* on her to make it, weren't they? Not just for her own sake, but for theirs as well.

Frowning, she scrubbed more slowly. First, Nancy asks her to do this for Rod. Then, she comes to find out all these people are thinking of her project as some sort of salvation for their beloved community.

Well. Was there some bigger plan unfolding here, or what?

And here Del thought she was nuts. Impractical. Illogical. Well, they said that about Christopher Columbus, too. Galileo. Air travel.

Honestly, she thought, screwing up her mouth as she tackled a particularly stubborn smudge on a door, what on earth did it matter what Del Farentino thought, anyway? He was just the contractor.

A contractor who wore black skivvies.

She scrubbed harder.

The drawings were going more quickly than Del had expected. In large part, he supposed, because Galen Granata, it turned out, was a bit of a noodge. A nice noodge, a nervous noodge, but a noodge nonetheless. Oh, she'd left him alone for the first couple of days—no surprise, considering the way they'd parted—but by day three, the calls had started coming. "Just checking to see how we're doing," she'd say, and he could see her tuck her hair behind her ear, lift her hand to her throat. Now they were up to Day Five, and he could tell she was getting anxious to get things moving.

The renovations, at least.

That was worth a rueful grin as he leaned back, the drafting stool groaning a bit in protest. He rented a small office in the building where his father had his headquarters—his single concession to mixing their relationship with business—large enough for a desk, some files, a drafting table and a computer. He also had a laptop he worked on at home, but he didn't like bringing work home much. Wendy needed as much of him as he could afford to give....

His brow crumpled, thinking of Wendy, who'd pitched yet another fit about nothing this morning, making him late, making him crazy. Worrying the crap out of him. Mrs. Battaglia said it was because of Wendy's increasing awareness of her difference. That she couldn't do some things other kids took for granted.

Elizabeth said it was just hormones, doing a little pre-pre-game warm-up.

Terrific.

It wasn't fair, ya know? So he meets this lovely woman who adores Wendy—and she, her—but said lovely woman has some kind of bug up her butt about needing her "space" or whatever the hell she was going on about. Not that Del begrudged Galen for needing whatever it was she needed. It was just the timing of things that was rotten, was all.

She would've been ideal.

His gaze fell to the drawings.

More or less. If she hadn't turned out to be so hardheaded, anyway.

Del glanced at his watch—forty-five minutes, yet, before he had to pick Wendy up from school, take her back to Mrs. Battaglia's—then resumed translating Galen's helter-skelter sketch to something workable. Orderly.

No, he could *not* smell her on the paper.

She was a contradiction, all right. Impulsive yet cautious, kindhearted but on her terms. A passionate nature buried under a passel of insecurities.

Guy had told him—casually, of course—Elizabeth had been a lot like that. Needing to be in control, to call the shots. All because she was afraid, of losing, of being hurt, of not being good enough.

Del's frown deepened as something almost like recognition twisted in his heart. What was Galen afraid of? Of being hurt? Of losing, again?

Of not being good enough?

Galen, we were talking about. Not…Del.

And his daughter—was her sudden orneriness due to her fear, too, that she might not be good enough? That she was somehow incomplete?

A heavy sigh pushed from his lungs as he pressed two fingers into his throbbing temple. God knows, he had enough to deal with, figuring his daughter out. The last thing he needed was to be worrying about a woman who had made herself off-limits.

Who made him look at himself too damn closely.

His cell phone burped on the table. With another sigh, he picked it up. Elizabeth, as usual, was halfway through the first sentence before he got out "Hello?"

"I promised Galen I'd take her car shopping but Chloe

threw up twice this afternoon so I'm not about to leave her with a sitter. Can you take her?''

"Elizabeth? It's about this job I have? And my daughter? And the fact I'm supposed to have dinner with my dad and Maureen tonight?''

"This shouldn't take too long, promise. And I can get Nance to pick Wendy up, if that's a problem.''

He knew this conversation had "exercise in futility" written all over it, but you know macho pride. "So why can't Nancy take Galen?''

"Because she's got to take Schuyler to some science fair dealie or something, so she said she'd just take Wendy with her and the babies.''

"She's going to take a deaf four-year-old and sixteen-month-old twins to a science fair? Where on earth's Rod?''

"He went with Hannah to an out-of-town basketball game. And Guy's showing houses until six, so don't ask. Galen's at Cora's, expecting me about three-thirty. And don't forget to call Mrs. Battaglia to tell her Nancy's picking up Wendy.''

The phone burped again into silence. He stared at it, waiting until the first wave of doom crested, before jabbing the caregiver's number into it.

The front door flew open; she'd grabbed her purse and had all but smacked right into his chest before she realized—

"You're not Elizabeth,'' she said, stumbling backwards.

Del managed a tired smile. He'd caught a whiff of pretty-smelling soap, clinging to that clear, freckled-kissed skin. "You noticed.''

Her cheeks went all rosy, framed by shiny, slippery, tea-colored hair, held back by a thin velvet band that accentuated her prominent cheekbones. She wore a heavy, brick-colored turtleneck, jeans, a tweed jacket which she now hugged closed, as if trying to hold herself together, as well. The wariness was right there, boy. It fairly shimmered off of her, right along with the flowery soap. "Yeah,'' she said. "You're not blond.''

That got a weak chuckle. "Chloe came down with some

crud or other. So Liz asked me if, um, I wouldn't mind taking you car shopping.''

"You?"

For some reason, her incredulity irked him. Then he saw her glance at his truck, which looked, he had to admit, like he'd tried to outrun a herd of elephants and failed. "It was a great truck when it was new," he said, irked again at the tinge of indignation in his voice. "It still is. Most vehicles with that much mileage on it would have rolled over and died years ago. So if I hadn't done a good job to begin with…"

Pure pity darted from her eyes, only to immediately change to something else. He knew this something else, all too well.

"You really want to do this?"

"No." Her brows shot up. More curious than hurt, he thought.

"Why not?"

He was tired and his head ached and the chili dog he'd had for lunch was giving him a fit and he really wasn't in the mood for any of this. "Because this is too personal. I mean, considering the way you feel and all, right? Working on your restaurant's one thing. That's business. This…isn't.''

Confusion, and that damned wariness, swirled in her eyes. "So why're you here?"

"Because if you want to get a car today, I'm your only option. And my brain's too fried to work on those damn drawings of yours anymore right now, anyway."

She angled her head, still clutching that jacket closed. "Elizabeth didn't give you a chance to say 'no', did she?"

"Something like that, yeah."

Then he saw the hurt. "Look, I don't have to get a car this very second." She stepped back inside, grabbed the door to shut it. "I'm sure you have better things to do, so I'll just arrange with someone else to do this another time."

Damn! Clutz-mouth, Nancy called him. With good reason. Somehow, though, it hadn't occurred to him Galen'd care. What with her not wanting to get too personal and all, y'know?

He grabbed the door to keep it from shutting, which brought

him at least a foot past comfort zone. Close enough to really smell her. To see tears glistening in her eyes. "Galen, hey— I'm sorry, okay? This hadn't exactly been a stellar day, but since I'm already here, you might as well take advantage of not only my scintillating company, but the luxury transportation—"

The tears blossomed, threatening to spill. "They're trying to fix us up, Del!"

On a sigh, he lowered his chin, bracing his hand on the doorjamb as he peered up at her from underneath his brows. "I told you that, remember?"

No smile. In fact, her arms were folded so tightly across her ribs, he wasn't sure how she was breathing. "If there's one thing I really, really hate, it's being manipulated," she said, almost more to herself. "Not to mention pitied. You don't want to do this. You already admitted as much. So you really think I'm gonna buy that you just changed your mind?"

"It's been known to happen." If anything, everything got tighter. Del let out a heavy whoosh of air from his lungs. "Galen, look—haven't you ever not felt like doing something, but once you got into it, you actually had a good time? Or at least, you didn't die or anything?"

That actually got a sliver of a smile. "Like going to the dentist?"

"Not the example I would've chosen, but whatever rocks your boat. Sure."

For a very scary few seconds, he thought she was going to either cry or lean her head against his chest. Or both. Scary, because he didn't want her to. Even scarier, because he did. Because he wanted to hug her, and be hugged back. Because he hated seeing anyone as tormented as this women was. Because, maybe, by making this woman feel better, even for a moment, he'd get a moment's surcease from his own problems.

"If you're sure," she finally said.

He ached to stroke her cheek. He didn't. "Galen?"

After a moment, she looked up.

"You really want to go buy a car, don't you?"

After another moment, she nodded.

"Then let's go."

Pride and need fought it out in her eyes for a couple seconds before she said, "On one condition."

"What?"

"You keep your mouth shut."

The laugh escaped before he knew it was coming. "Then what's the point of my taking you?"

"Because I can't walk to the dealerships. I'm serious, Del…this is something I have to do for *me*. On my own. No interference, well-meaning or otherwise."

Here we go again. Miss Gotta-Do-It-My-Way. Still, he wondered if she heard the tremor in her voice, could feel the twin spots of color in her cheeks. Something in her eyes twisted around his heart, reminding him of Wendy when she wanted so badly to do something she wasn't at all sure she *could* do. He crossed his arms. "You want me to stay in the truck?"

Oh, if she only knew how transparent she was, how every emotion that even flirted with that complex brain of hers blazed like a flare in those deep blue-green eyes. It was like watching the ball spinning on a roulette wheel, wondering where it was going to land.

"No," she finally said, brushing a stray hair off her cheek. "You can come. You just can't talk."

Then she swooped past him down the walk, yanked open the passenger side door to his truck and climbed in. Shaking his head, Del had no choice but to follow suit.

Wasn't until they'd been on the road for several minutes that he noticed she had her purse in a death grip. She sat forward, straining against the seat belt, her lips a little more than a thin, colorless line, while a pulse jumped in her temple. Any fool could tell her nerves were brittle as antique glass.

"Galen?"

She jumped. Wide, terrified eyes met his. "What?"

Under normal circumstances, with a normal woman, he'd reach over, take her hand, give her a little reassuring squeeze. But nothing about this—or her—was normal. "You're going green on me again. You okay?"

She nodded. Once. Sharply.

Del slowly shook his head, figured there was little point in pursuing the issue. "Okay. You know where you want to go?"

A sudden flurry of activity caught his attention. He glanced over to see her wrestling a wad of printed papers out of the boxcar. She nervously straightened them out, her lower lip caught between her teeth. "Um...okay," she said after clearing her throat. "What...what I'm looking for is a used minivan, maybe a year or two old. So any place that has a good selection, I suppose."

"Well, that limits us to about a dozen dealerships, easy."

"Yeah?"

She sounded pleased. Now confused, he spared her a quick look, noticed a little of the tension in her face seemed to have eased up. At least she wasn't green anymore. "Yeah." With one hand, he steered the truck onto the highway. "Let's start with Miller's. They're the biggest."

"Are they...reputable?"

He chuckled. "You don't do this very often, do you? Shop for cars?"

"There's an understatement."

"Well, considering most people would rather undergo an appendectomy without anesthesia than go car shopping..."

She let out a huge sigh. "So I've heard." The papers rattled back into the purse. "Okay," she said, as if steeling herself. "Okay. We'll do Miller's, then." One hand found its way to her mouth; she started chewing on a nail, realized what she was doing, snatched the hand away. Those dual splotches of red on her cheekbones flamed hotter; she kept clearing her throat a lot.

Del forced his gaze out the windshield, feeling his brow knot. Hell—the minute those salesmen sensed her nervousness, she was a goner. And this had nothing to do with smarts. This had to do with experience. Moxy. Guts.

Which Galen might have if she could keep from puking them up everytime she got shaky. Yeah, he knew what she was trying to do, and it wasn't as if he didn't admire her for it, up to a point. But when you're talking big bucks, this is no time to pull a pride number. He knew how to negotiate, how to deal with these sharks. He could get her a good deal...if she'd let him talk.

He glanced over to see her pop a stick of gum into her mouth, begin to chew so fast he could barely see her jaw moving.

Hell. She was gonna end up fish food.

They pulled into the lot, strung with the requisite multicolored plastic flags snapping in the stiff winter breeze. At least it was winter—dealers were usually more keen to move a car for a little less when there weren't a hundred summer-crazed potential buyers sniffing around it. If Galen knew how to use that to her advantage, that is.

She removed the gum, stuck it back in its wrapper, stuffed the wrapper in the outside pocket of her purse. Then she hauled in a deep breath and was gone.

Man. The woman could *move*. Del scrambled from the truck and hurried to catch up, groaning when he saw the salesman slinking over to her. Overfed, overeager, his cheap dress pants wind-plastered around skinny legs poking out from underneath a hunter green parka. From ten feet away, the guy's suck-up grin brought the hairs on Del's neck to immediate attention. The wind was brutal; Del huddled inside his vest, stuffing his hands in his pockets. How Galen wasn't freezing in that little sweater and jacket...

That clingy little sweater and open jacket.

Breasts. Oh, Lord, Mama, she had 'em. Just as he'd suspected. But to finally meet them, after all this time...well. It fair took his breath away. Not that she was thrusting them about or anything. And it wasn't like the sweater was all that tight, because it really wasn't. But it was tight enough.

Sure was a good thing it was cold as it was, that's all he could say.

"Minivans? Oh, sure..." Spying Del's approach, Old Snake Eyes dragged his gaze away from some spot vaguely between Galen's jacket lapels, his grin broadening. Breasts were nice and all, the grin said, but they didn't buy cars. "The lady says she's looking for a minivan?'' The salesman's gaze slithered to Del's truck, then back to Del. ''As a trade-in for the truck?''

''Excuse me? Marv, isn't it?'' Galen said, clutching her purse. Her knuckles were still white, Del noticed, and her voice still soft, but the words were clear and take-no-guff strong. ''You mind directing your comments to me, seeing as I'm the one buying the car?'' And with that, she turned on her loafered heel and headed to the back of the lot and the row of minivans glistening in the late afternoon sun.

Marv and Del followed in her wake. Del was grinning. Marv wasn't.

The next fifteen minutes proved extremely enlightening. Galen slowly surveyed each van, not a glimmer of expression on her features, asking the occasional question about engine size, braking system, safety features. Whenever Marv attempted to talk up one vehicle over the other, she held up one hand, silencing him.

Del hung back, hand to mouth, and just watched, fascinated. The basket-case female who'd been about to jump out of her skin in his truck had metamorphosed into a killer negotiator. Who'dathunkit?

More minutes ticked by. The sun slipped behind a cloud, slicing a good ten degrees off the temperature. Marv was beginning to subtly dance from foot to foot. ''So, you want to take one of these for a test drive or what?'' he said, trying not to let his teeth chatter.

Galen turned to him. Squinted. Nodded. ''Okay, sure. How about…the beige one there—'' she pointed ''—the silvery blue number at the end of the row, and, mmm, maybe that red one over there?''

She glanced at Del, frowning at him when he raised his eyebrow. The red one—a two-year-old Windstar—was a good five grand more expensive than the other two. Marv shuffled away to get the keys, a little relieved grin of near victory loosening some very tense facial muscles.

Del leaned against the hood of a pretty little pickup he wouldn't mind taking for a whirl himself. ''Somebody looks like she's having fun.''

"God knows, I'm trying."

Ah. Still nervous. "You want me to come with you?"

Now, why wasn't he surprised when she shook her head? "Nope."

He kept a straight face when she lurched out of the parking lot in the beige van, squealing the brakes when she turned onto the street. Marv looked a little pale.

"You know how it is when it's not your car," Del said mildly.

"Uh, yeah, sure." Marv flipped up the collar of his parka. "You want to come inside, get a cup of coffee or somethin'?"

"Nah." Del tucked his hands in his jeans pockets, strolling around the pretty little pickup like he was interested. Maybe he couldn't talk, but she didn't tell him he couldn't help her out by freezing her salesman's butt off.

"She's really something," Marv said. Del figured it wasn't exactly a compliment.

"Mind of her own," Del replied.

Marv gave a not-amused half laugh. "Wife?"

"Uh-uh."

"Girlfriend, then?"

The devil made him do it. "No. My attorney."

"Huh," Marv said, looking more unhappy by the minute.

And who also wasn't swift enough to question why an attorney would be buying a *used* anything.

Twice more, vans with Galen behind the wheel disappeared, reappeared, each time a little more smoothly than previously. At last, the red van popped back into view. Galen gracefully eased it back onto the lot, then got out, a frown neatly creasing her brow. She made a great show of walking back and forth between the three cars, every muscle in her face a study in concentration. Then she turned and calmly said, "Knock five thousand off the red one, and I'll give you a check for the whole amount right now."

Del nearly dropped his jaw. Marv did. "Whoa, lady— you're asking me to slice a huge chunk off that baby, you know? I mean, the other two are already in your price range—"

"But this one has the features I want. And it's still under factory warranty." She actually blinked.

Marv fumbled for another minute, then shook his head. "We might be able to shave a thousand off the price...but five?" He shook his head, thrusting out his lower lip. But he was shivering, Del noticed.

To Del's amazement, Galen simply shrugged. "Oh, okay. If you can't, you can't." She turned to Del. "Well, come on. How many other lots did you say there were around here—?"

Marv snapped to like a dog hearing his food dish rattle. "On second thought, maybe...I could go check with my boss, see how we can juggle the figures."

Galen gave him a brilliant smile. "Oh, could you? Well, I suppose we could hang around for a few more minutes..."

Marv loped off to the office.

Del gently elbowed her in the arm. "Hey. You're a natural."

But Galen wouldn't look at him, except to offer him a brief smile. And the sweetest blush he'd ever seen.

Two minutes later, ole Marv reappeared with the fabulous news that his boss okay'd chopping the price by two grand, and that was a steal for a car only two years old. And only 20,000 miles on it? Nobody could beat that—

Galen sighed, shook her head and began to walk away.

"Okay, three grand off, but that's as low as we can go. You're killing me here as it is—"

Galen slowly turned around, all sweetness and disbelief. "Maybe you didn't hear me, Marv. Five off, or I walk."

"You'll never find a car like this at that price, anywhere."

She tilted her head at him. "You don't know that for sure, do you?"

Marv looked like he'd just been poleaxed.

"Besides," she continued, her voice soft as a kitten's belly, "I know you've got that car jacked way up over Blue Book, *and* I know you probably didn't give the former owner squat in trade-in. So the way I figure it, I'm still offering you a nice bit of change over book, and you guys get the whole wad, in cash, today.'' She checked her watch. "In fact, if you hurry, you could probably still find someone at the bank to verify funds. But, if you're not interested…" She shrugged, a sweet little lift of her shoulders that somehow stretched the sweater in all the right places.

This time, Marv held up one of his hands. "I'll…be right back."

A half hour later, the lady had herself a car.

And that, Del thought, was that, as he headed back to his truck, after watching Galen climb behind the wheel of her brand-new minivan and head off into the sunset.

Except ten blocks from the dealership, he saw a candy apple red minivan parked in a Long John Silver's lot, the redhead at the wheel sobbing her heart out.

Chapter 9

He nearly did a wheelie turning the truck around, arrowing it into the empty spot beside Galen. He got out, saw her jump when he slammed shut his own door, then madly swipe at her face as he marched around to her side, gesturing to her to lower the window.

She did, but she clearly didn't like it. Fair-skinned redheads were not pretty when they cried, he decided. Their skin went kaflooey and their noses lit up like Rudolph's and he couldn't remember the last time a woman had made his heart ache like this. Among other parts of his body.

"Y-you weren't supposed to see this," she said.

"Yeah, I figured that. You wanna explain?"

"Oh, Del," she said on a rush, her hands clamped to the wheel. "The minute I saw this one, being red and all, I just thought I had to have it, which was a really dumb, emotional, female reaction, wasn't it?" Not waiting for an answer—which he wouldn't have given if his life depended on it—she kept going. "So I asked all the questions the consumer magazines say you're supposed to, and then I made a deal...with, um, God. I decided, if I could get Marv to come down on the price, then this car was meant to be mine. And if I couldn't, well, then it wasn't. But I did it! I just went in there and bluffed my way through, and it actually worked!''

She scrubbed again at her face; Del remembered he'd put a clean handkerchief in his pocket that morning. He fished it out, handed it to her.

"Wasn't like you were cheating or anything, though," he pointed out. "I mean, everything you said was true. They did overprice the car—"

"I know, I know, but that's not the point. The point is—" she took a deep breath "—I didn't back down. The point is, I successfully negotiated a grown-up transaction all on my own!"

He wondered if she had the slightest idea how sexy he found her childlike reaction. He wondered if he had the slightest idea why he did. "You could have started with something simpler, you know. Like paying your electric bill. Worked your way up to car-buying."

"But now, see—" she hooked one hand over the door, her eyes sparkling "—think how much easier all that other stuff will be!" She twisted back in her seat, planting her hands once again on the steering wheel, grinning so broadly her cheeks had to ache. "I'm hot stuff, huh?" she said, and he had to laugh.

"Yeah, honey," he said softly as she raised the window again, waving to him as she backed out of the parking space, "you're hot stuff, all right."

Then he stood in the dusky cold for probably a full minute before returning to his truck, climbing in.

Galen Granata was one of the gutsiest women he'd ever known. Not because she'd just done something thousands of people do every day, but because *she* had just done something thousands of other people do every day. She'd been scared out of her wits, but she'd plowed through the fear. And triumphed. There was something far more than mere bullheadedness at work here, he realized. Something far more precious.

Something his daughter could sure use in her life.

Among other people living at his address.

His head fell forward onto his arm, folded on top of the steering wheel. Would somebody please, please explain to him why the more independent and strong-willed Galen became, the more he found himself attracted to her?

Various and sundry relatives on Del's father's side had always told him how much Del looked like Hugh at the same age. If the pattern held, Del supposed he at least wouldn't be breaking mirrors at sixty. Or swelling the pocketbooks of stockholders in the company that made Rogaine. With his still-trim body, his full head of silver hair framing classic Mediterranean features, Hugh Farentino still had the power to cause females from thirteen on to sidle up to him with enormous, "pick-me" smiles.

But he'd only "picked" twice: Del's mother Sofia, a dark-haired beauty who'd died when Del was twelve; and Elizabeth's mother, Maureen, a go-get-'em blonde who epitomized the word "tasteful". And who made her stepson's life marginally more peaceful by distracting Hugh from what had been, before their marriage, his near-constant harping about Del's life choices.

Now he only harped occasionally. Like whenever he saw him. Which might not have been as often as it was except that Wendy and her grandfather absolutely adored each other. And considering Hugh and Maureen were the only grandparents Wendy had, Cyndi's parents having both died before their marriage, a little harping was a small price to pay to hear his daughter's giggles when Papa Hugh gave her horsie rides around the yard, or to watch her eyes grow wide with delight as her grandfather—who'd begun taking signing classes from the moment he learned she was deaf—"told" her a story.

Del leaned his aching head against the back of the white satin-striped sofa in Maureen's living room, praying, however pointlessly, that his father would please, please, stay off his case tonight. Maureen and Wendy were holed up in the kitchen, Maureen yammering away a mile a minute, from what he could tell. His eyes shut, Del heard a grunting sigh as Hugh sank into the light blue striped club chair to his left, the ice from his one-a-day, pre-dinner highball rattling in his glass.

Sprung from solid working-class stock, Hugh and his siblings had all grown up in a blue-collar Chicago suburb, each one in turn working for their father's built-from-nothing construction company. Del gathered that money had been tight and luxuries few for his father and uncles, and they'd all struggled to give their own children a better life. Hugh had opted early on not to go into construction, but to be one of the people who hired people like his father. That his only son seemed hell-bent on reverting to his roots was simply incomprehensible to a man who'd spent his whole adult life rising above them.

"You look like hell," Hugh said, bringing a wry smile to Del's lips.

"Thanks."

"Headache?"

"Mmm."

Silence. Respectful, Del decided. As opposed to strained. From three rooms away, he could hear his daughter's giggles. Then: "How're those drawings coming? For Galen's restaurant?"

Del pointed to his head.

"Complicated?"

"Yep. But I'm not talking about the drawings."

And what in God's name had possessed him to say that?

He dared to sneak a peak, hoping against hope his father hadn't picked up on his comment. Somehow, from the bemused expression on the older man's face, Del didn't think that hope had a chance in hell.

Hugh took a sip of his drink, then nearly knocked Del clear into the following week with his next comment.

"For once," he said, his mouth twitching into a grin, "I'm not going to even ask what you meant by that. You got yourself into this—" he lifted the drink, as if in a toast "—you figure it out."

"There's nothing to figure out," Del said, too quickly, feeling his ears warm.

"No, no. Of course not," Hugh parried, equally quickly.

"If she just wasn't so hell-bent on doing everything the hard way…"

Hugh chuckled. "Not that you would know anything about that, I don't suppose."

Well, he'd set himself up for that one, hadn't he? Rubbing the back of his neck, Del muttered, "It's not the same."

"It never is, is it, when it's someone else?"

Another long spate of silence followed, broken only by the laughter drifting out from the kitchen and muffled sounds of wind-tossed evergreens battering the house. Del knew what was coming. It always did. And even though he really did understand the offers were always made out of concern and love, he found them no less irritating.

"Got a new project coming up, just outside Ann Arbor," Hugh said.

"Good for you."

Hugh didn't react. "On the small side. New strip mall, but upscale. Trendy nostalgic, if you know what I mean. Would be perfect for you—"

"No."

His father just stared at him, those dark eyes unflinching. Del had never heard his father raise his voice, or lose control. Still, even at thirty-six, Del hated making his father angry. But not enough to do the one thing to avoid it.

"You have something against strip malls?"

Del lifted one hand. "Dad. Don't. Look—could we just fast forward through this conversation? Thanks for the offer, I really appreciate it, I know you don't understand why I don't want to accept your handout, yadayadayada…"

Jaw set, Hugh rose from his chair. "You're just as hard-headed as your mother," he said quietly, before slowly walking from the room.

The barb hurt, as it always did. Especially because Del couldn't refute the accusation. His mother had been one of the most stubborn women he'd ever known. And then Del had managed to marry a woman just like her, in that respect, at least. And now, God help him, his daughter seemed destined to follow in both her grandmother's and mother's footsteps.

A shudder streaked up his spine. He shut his eyes again, against the pain, and fear, and dread that haunted him every day, more than anyone knew.

But it wasn't the same, Del's determination to succeed on his own merits, without a leg up from his father. He was stubborn, maybe, he'd concede to that. But Del wasn't unreasonable. Or incautious.

Lost in thought, he hadn't even realized Maureen had called him to dinner until her hand, light on his shoulder, startled him out of his reverie.

She sighed, understanding glimmering in her amber eyes. Even for a casual dinner, she was elegantly dressed—off-white cashmere sweater set, beige wool skirt—but for all her fastidiousness, just like her daughter, Maureen was as genuine as they came. "He did it again, didn't he?"

"Who? What?"

"Your father. Bugged you."

Del stood, looking *way* down at his stepmother. "It's his mission in life," he said with a half smile.

She linked her arm through his, as if he needed guidance to find her dining room. Hugh had moved into Maureen's tidy little Cape Cod cottage after their marriage, the house where Elizabeth had grown up, and Maureen had gamely—and without a single word of complaint—accommodated anything Hugh had wanted to bring in, the result of which was that the occasional piece of dark leather furniture popped out of Maureen's pastels like a rhinoceros in the middle of Swan Lake. She obviously cared more about making her husband happy than whether or not her house was worthy of a spread in House Beautiful. Del admired that. He admired her. Even though he knew she was every bit as bad as his father when it came to dispensing advice.

"Parents do that, you know," she said softly, patting his arm. "Interfere. Worry. Deep down, I think he's actually very proud of you."

Del snorted. "Oh, right. For what? Getting myself in hock without anyone's help?"

They stood for a moment in the doorway to the dining room, watching Hugh help Wendy light the candles. "For being such a wonderful father, for one thing. Taking Wendy's deafness in stride, for making your life work around her. And even, though he'd never admit it, for keeping your head above water with the business these past three years." Maureen gave his arm a squeeze. "Of course he wants to make things easier for you, Del. Of course he worries. He loves you. And he does want nothing more—or less—than for you to be happy. It just gets him that he thinks he can see a less fraught way for you to achieve that goal, that's all. And—" She hesitated.

"What?"

Kindness glittered in her eyes. "Your father spent a long time being lonely, Del, after your mother died. A long time blaming himself, refusing to believe he deserved a second shot at happiness. You know how long we dated before he got up the nerve to ask me to marry him. He doesn't want to see that happen to you, honey. He doesn't want you to avoid becoming involved with another woman because you don't have enough money or you're not sure how it would work with Wendy or whatever other excuse you'll make for yourself."

Del drew himself up, shaking his head. "Elizabeth's been talking, huh?"

Maureen squeezed his arm. Smiled. "Galen seems like a lovely girl."

"Yes, she is. She's also not available."

"She told you this?"

"Yep."

"And you're just going to let it go at that?"

Del let out a sigh. "Even if she was interested, which she's not, did it ever occur to you that maybe she's not for me?"

Maureen squinted up at him. "And did it ever occur to you that you're a lousy liar?"

And with that, she drifted in to join her husband and grand-daughter.

* * *

"No!"

Clear, perfectly enunciated and shouted at the top of her lungs, the word rang through the apartment as Wendy threw her nightgown across the living room floor, then took off for the kitchen, shrieking with laughter.

"Not funny, little girl," Del lobbed back, taking off after her, not caring whether she could hear him or not. Still wound up from dinner and all the attention she'd received from her overindulgent grandparents, Wendy was not in the least bit interested in going to bed. Judging from what he'd seen of Elizabeth and Nancy's attempts at dealing with small, unreasonable children, he knew the battles royal he had every night—and every morning—with his daughter were, unfortunately, normal. But reasoning with a strong-willed four-year-old was hard enough when the child could hear; the added communication difficulties just made the challenge all that much greater.

Giggling, she led him on a merry chase around the kitchen table, then hauled off down the hall and into the bathroom, locking the door behind her.

Del sighed, more in exasperation than concern, since the lock was one of those easily picked open from the other side with anything skinny and straight. Still, "Open the door! Now!" had popped right out of his mouth before he remembered.

After nearly five years, he still slipped occasionally. In his zeal to make as normal a life as possible for his daughter, he sometimes forgot she wasn't, as far as the rest of the world went.

Although his head had stopped hurting, Maureen's spaghetti sauce was rebelling in his stomach. And he had to bring those damn drawings home, since he'd lost time with Galen this afternoon, and if he didn't get them done tonight, he'd end up behind on another project due next week. Was it too much to ask for this sweet, lovely child to simply go to sleep already?

He knocked on the door, knowing she could feel it.

"Who...is...id?" he heard from the other side. Then more giggles.

"Open the...oh, hell." He felt along the top of the door for the long nail he kept there for just this purpose, unlocked the door to find his nearly naked little girl standing in the sink, calmly festooning the mirror with shaving cream. Del stormed over, grabbed the can from her hands, the child from the sink, then looked to see what she'd done.

Completely unfazed by her father's obvious annoyance, Wendy pointed to her handiwork from her perch on Del's left hip. "Wendy," she said carefully, then pointed to herself. "Me." Then she signed, "Good girl."

All the steam went right of him. Sinking onto the toilet seat, Del pulled his baby onto his lap, dragging a towel off a nearby rack to wrap around her goose-bumpy shoulders.

He'd been trying to teach her to write her name for months. Her teachers said there was no reason why she couldn't, but she simply didn't appear to want to. Until tonight.

And what hit him, right then, as he sat in his bathroom with his daughter safely tucked against his chest, was how much he ached to have someone to share this moment with. This small triumph over fate and odds and childish willfulness. Then he smiled, wryly and sadly, at the irony that the only woman he could think of offhand who would somehow really, truly understand the significance of what had just happened was the one woman least likely to volunteer for the job.

Wendy patted his face to get his attention. "I want to go see the kitties," she signed. "Galen and Cora said it was okay. Can we go tomorrow?" She circled her heart, "please", and gave him her most winsome smile.

The only way he'd been able to get her home that night they'd taken the cats to Cora's was by promising her they'd go see the beasts from time to time. He'd avoided it until now—as he had her pleas to take one of the kittens when it got old enough—and had thought maybe she'd forgotten. One of these days, maybe before she turned thirty, he was gonna catch on: small, bright children don't forget *anything*.

"I don't know," he signed. "I'm real busy right now."

Ah, hell. There went the tears.

Del sighed. Wendy wanted to see the kitties. Del didn't want to see Galen any more than was absolutely necessary. Which of those was more important?

He dared to glance at his daughter's face. Realized she wasn't pitching a fit. "We'll have to check with Cora and Galen," he signed.

Which Wendy took as a "yes", judging from the big kiss she planted on his cheek before snuggling up against him.

Why was it, everytime he vowed to stay away from the woman, fate seemed hell-bent on throwing them together?

That thought had no sooner limped through when he realized Wendy had grown very heavy on his lap; peering down, he saw she'd conked out. No pajamas, teeth unbrushed and hair still done, she was dead to the world.

Great.

Well, hair and teeth could be skipped, but she'd freeze to death without her jammies. Holding his breath, he oh-so-carefully stood, smiling a little when she snuggled closer against him, tiptoed down the hall, one-handedly grabbed another nightie from her top drawer, and somehow got the thing on her without her waking up. It was enough to renew his faith in God. For the moment, anyway.

After he tucked her in, Del stood at Wendy's doorway a long moment, watching her sleep, his thoughts all a-jumble in his head. Maybe his father was right. Maybe he was just being stubborn, refusing to take the opportunities his father kept offering him, when those opportunities could possibly lead to better things for Wendy, a larger house, an income sufficient to support a family, maybe get married again, have a couple more kids.

But Galen can't have kids.

"Not the sharpest tool in the shed tonight, are you, Farentino?" he muttered to himself as he dragged out the portable drafting table he kept in his bedroom, setting it up on the kitchen table. The sooner he got these drawings done, the sooner he could start on this project, finish this project, not have to deal with Galen and her goofy ideas and the way she unhinged him whenever she did that thing she did with her eyes. Blinked, that was it. She had the sexiest damn blink he'd ever seen, but don't ask him to explain why. It just was.

He pushed his shaggy hair out of his eyes, muttering when it fell right back. Since getting to a barber never quite seemed to be in the cards, he'd taken to hacking at it himself from time to time, but he hadn't even done that in a while. At this rate, it was gonna be longer than stepbrother-in-law's…

And why was it, everytime he thought of Elizabeth and Guy, he felt…cheated?

He refocused on the drawings. Yeah, the sooner this blasted project was done, the sooner he could stop wondering about the haunted, sad look in Galen's eyes that was always there, even when she laughed.

Pencil poised, Del looked up, straight at the pile of dishes on the counter from at least two days which he probably wouldn't wash until at least tomorrow. Night. And as he did, his heart tightened in his chest, making breathing damned difficult.

It wasn't up to him, he realized, to dispel that haunted look. To make her happy on anything but a professional level. Because—listen carefully, Del—*she doesn't want you to.*

So, you see? The sooner he was done with this, the sooner he could stop thinking of her declaration that she wasn't the least bit interested in a relationship as some sort of personal challenge. That he'd stop wondering what was behind the declaration, what was really going on underneath all that fragrant, tea-colored hair.

Then maybe he'd start getting some sleep again.

He thought of Wendy's request to go see the kitties.

Then again, maybe not.

Galen still wasn't quite sure how this happened.

She stood in Cora's kitchen, scissors poised, one hand tangled in the luxurious mass otherwise known as Del's hair. Del sat backwards in front of her, his long jeans-clad legs sprawled halfway to the other side of the room, a towel draped over his shoulders, waiting for her to re-humanize him, he'd said.

They'd just come over to see the kitties because Wendy had begged—Del said—so Galen had said sure, come on over about six, she'd be there.

They were only going to stay a few minutes. Except, somehow, since she was elbow deep in recipe-trying anyway, she'd invited them to stay for dinner. Just to help her decide, that's all.

And then Wendy had gone back to play with the cats again and fallen asleep on the sunroom floor, and she was sleeping so peacefully…well, they could hardly move her, could they? So Galen had covered her in the afghan from the sofa and put a pillow under her head, and then she and Del had gotten to talking—about the restaurant and stuff, nothing too dangerous—and Del kept pushing his hair off his face and finally, Galen couldn't stand it anymore. His hair.

So she'd offered to cut it for him, since she'd done it all the time for her grandfather because he was too cheap to go to the barber's and her grandmother flat-out refused to listen to his guff.

And Del had actually agreed.

They were both doing a good job of pretending there was nothing buzzing between them, she thought. Respectful of each other, she thought.

Full of it, she thought.

She picked up the first lock of hair and cut a good two inches off of it.

"Now, you sure you know what you're doing?" Del asked.

"Yes," she said calmly, snipping off the next hunk, not admitting just how long it really had been since she'd done this. "But in any case, too late now."

Del sort of grunted.

The house was so quiet, the silence was almost like a third person in the room. Cora's daughter had had her baby last night, so she'd flown out to San Francisco this morning. Every other living thing in the house besides them was asleep, they couldn't agree on a radio station—he wanted rock, but she was in the mood for classical—so the only sounds were their breathing and the snip, snip, snip of the scissors. Almost peaceful, really.

Until Del asked about Vinnie.

She couldn't decide whether she did or didn't want to talk about her husband. Or how much she should say. Could say. But refusing to talk about him...well, that didn't seem right, either. Although she hadn't. Talked about him. Not to her grandmother or Cora or anyone else. Mistakes were hard to own up to, she supposed. But she figured the basics weren't exactly classified information, like how they'd met 'n' that, how he'd been fourteen years her senior.

Of course, Del wasn't about to leave it there.

"You really got married at eighteen?" he asked, watching her in the hand mirror she'd given him to keep tabs so she didn't scalp him or anything.

"Yeah," she said quietly. "And I wouldn't recommend it."

"Too young?"

"And stupid." She caught Del's glower at her in the mirror. "Inexperienced, then."

"He mistreated you?"

She hesitated for a moment, then shook her head, stepping around to trim over his ears. Not a lot. Just enough so's you could see he *had* ears. A couple gray hairs suddenly appeared, as if they'd been hiding. "Not that anyone would notice," she said. "Turn back around," she added when Del twisted to look up at her. "You're messing me up—"

Fury had turned his eyes black. "He knocked you around?"

For a moment, his concern—*that much concern*—made a grab for her heart like a kid a pop fly in the sandlot. She neatly dodged it. "No, Del, never," she said softly, laying her hand on his shoulder. Lifting it almost immediately. "And yes, I swear it. Now turn back around."

Only when he did, when she didn't have to look at him, did she continue. Snipping away at his hair, watching it fall to the floor, as she snipped away at the memories, the secrets, she'd carried inside her for so many years.

"It's hard to explain," she said, eyeing her next cut, "because in his eyes, he wasn't mistreating me at all. In fact, I wouldn't have put it that way, either. Not at first. I was too much in love, for one thing. And, at first glance, Vinnie was everything my grandfather wasn't." She combed where she'd just cut, trimmed a little. His hair was so wavy, there was little she could do to ruin it. Thank God.

"And that was—?"

"Overbearing." *Snip.* "Dictatorial." *Snip.* "Suffocating." She told him about all the restrictions Papa had placed on her, how she saw in Vinnie a savior, of sorts. "Vinnie seemed so sweet, so concerned about me, what I wanted. He didn't dare give me gifts at first—how would I have explained them?— but he always had a smile for me, a kind word. And he was respectful. Always. He wasn't at all like the boys in the neighborhood." She smiled, a little. "The very boys Papa wouldn't let me go out with. And for good reason."

She saw the wicked grin in the mirror. "Boys like me, huh?"

Ignoring him, she frowned at a particularly stubborn spot, her facial muscles relaxing when it finally cooperated. "Then Vinnie started talking about wanting to marry me, how he and I would be perfect together. That I was perfect, just the way I was." For just a second, she remembered. Not just the words, but how they'd made her feel. How much she'd wanted to believe them. "And after we got married, Vinnie was very generous. He treated me like gold. Bought me a house and a car, would take me shopping, picking out all these expensive clothes for me, and jewelry. Even the perfume he wanted me to wear. He took care of me, Del. Took care of everything *for* me." Tears bit at her eyes as the memories refocused. "To this day, I believe he loved me. As much as he might have a prize mare, in fact."

There. She'd never said it aloud. But that was it, wasn't it? All she'd really been worth.

Del shifted to look up at her, his mouth drawn. "And then you never had kids," he said quietly, understanding.

"Nope," she said over the knot in her throat. "But not for lack of trying. By the time I was twenty-five, I'd had four miscarriages. While other women my age were going to college, starting their careers, I spent half my time in doctors' offices being tested and fussed over, nobody able to figure out why this perfectly healthy woman couldn't do the one thing her husband had married her to do—give him children.''

She laughed, the sound sharp in the heavy silence in Cora's kitchen. "Sounds like something out of a Victorian novel, doesn't it? In any case, I got pregnant a fifth time. When I made it past the sixth week, we were so sure this one would take. Except it turned out to be a tubal pregnancy. One they barely caught in time.''

She moved to the other side, carefully cutting away over his other ear, willing the pain to remain dulled, powerless to rock her as it once had. "After that, I said *no more*. Even if I could have stood it physically, I couldn't go through the emotional trauma again. See, maybe Vinnie married me for my childbearing potential, but I wanted those babies, Del. With my whole heart. My husband might have been annoyed each time I miscarried, but *I* was heartbroken. In any case, the one tube was shot, anyway, so I just asked them to tie off the other one, too. Because of the likelihood I'd have another tubal pregnancy—and the first one nearly killed me—Vinnie's objections were overridden.''

She paused, aware that, in the mirror, Del's eyes were fastened on her face. She slipped to the back, began the final trimming. "Vinnie barely talked to me for months," she said.

She saw Del's shoulders tense. "Because you wanted to save your life?"

"I'd like to think it was because he was just horribly disappointed, you know? And he didn't know how to handle it. Men like him..." She shrugged. "They're not real big with getting in touch with their inner child 'n' that, I guess. Anyway," she said on a tight sigh, "then he got sick.''

"And you became his nursemaid.''

The disgust in Del's voice was plain enough, but Galen didn't really think it was aimed at her. And if it was...well. She couldn't do anything about what Del Farentino thought about decisions she'd made all those years ago, now could she? "I was still very young. And all I wanted—really wanted—was for someone to love me. Care about me, you know? Vinnie was all I had, Del. Or so I thought. And suddenly, I was about to lose even that.

"In any case, divorce had never been an option. Not for him at all, and not for me, either. Not really. Young or not, I was still old enough to know what I was doing, if not what I was getting into. If there were lessons to be learned, I figured I might as well learn 'em right where I was, instead of turning tail and running like some scared child. And once he got sick... The family had never exactly taken me to their bosom to begin with, not being Italian. I wasn't about to give them more ammunition by walking out on their baby boy when he was dying."

A pause. "You didn't want them to hate you?"

She managed a half smile. "Can you blame me?" she said softly.

She was cutting air at this point, having actually finished the haircut some time ago. But it was safer, pretending to still be working, than having to face Del.

"So you knew from the beginning it was terminal?" he asked.

"Not at the beginning, no. But within a year, yeah. We knew. Amazing what knowing you're going to die does to a person's conscience, I guess. Even though it actually took nearly six years to happen. Vinnie finally came clean about why he'd married me—because I was good, old-fashioned, malleable. Although he never admitted to the last part; I kinda figured that one out on my own. He didn't want some liberated, smart-mouth woman giving him grief, he'd said. He'd seen what his brothers went through with their wives. And for the most part, I'd lived up to his expectations. Played my role just the way he'd written it. All except for the giving him five sons part, anyway. And he was going to reward my loyalty, he said, after he died. In gratitude for my not leaving him, not making him look like a fool to his family. He was going to leave me his share of the restaurant."

Del frowned. "So what happened?"

"I honestly don't know. I saw the original will, but I guess he thought...better of it. Who knows? He left it instead to his three brothers. I was stunned. And frankly, I felt betrayed. There was a note, along with the will. In it, Vinnie said he'd decided it was better *for me* if he just left me the car and the house and the life insurance. That trying to run his part of the business would be too hard. That I'd see, eventually, that he'd done the right thing.'' Tears bit at her eyes; she blinked them back, but one popped out anyway, racing down her cheek.

"I'd loved him, Del. Maybe my love was immature and incorrectly placed or what-have-you, but I did love him. And what really hurt, still hurts to this day, is that after taking it on myself to learn the restaurant business backward and forward—despite the battles royal I had with his mother which he never knew about—not to mention taking care of him through his entire illness, he still felt he had to protect me from the potential stress of being a partner in the business. Because, he said, he loved me too much to let me take those kinds of risks—''

"Galen—''

"And then, to top it off, his medical bills ate up every crying dime of the life insurance, the proceeds from selling the house, the car, the jewelry he'd given me. I had nothing.''

Except the experience to keep me from making the same mistake twice.

"Which is why I went to live with my grandmother. At least, at the beginning. I had nowhere else to go. Then, when I realized how much she needed me...'' She shrugged.

Del twisted around, grabbing her hand to bring her in front of him. "Hell, honey. No wonder you want this so badly.''

She felt so much strength in that grasp. And gentleness. Tingles of need she didn't dare acknowledge swirled through her, pleasant and frightening all at once. The sense of loss when she removed her hand from his nearly derailed her.

"Not because I had a lifelong dream of running a restaurant, though,'' she said, tucking her arms against her ribs, forcing herself back on track. "Vinnie robbed me of far more than that. He robbed me of *me*. I went into that marriage incomplete, a partially formed creature whose wings weren't even dry yet. And I came out of it crippled, my wings deformed from never even having had the chance to spread.''

No matter what, she could not tear herself away from those eyes.

"And…?"

"No, to answer your question," she said softly. "They're nowhere near healed yet."

Chapter 10

Her openness had rocked him to the core. *Please understand,* her eyes begged. *Please support what I have to do.*

He broke the connection, lifting a shaking hand to his hair. "Done?"

He gave her the second or two she needed to recoup. "What? Oh, yes…let me just…" She unwrapped the towel, gently brushed the stray loose hairs from his shoulders, the air between them laced with tiny, brittle chips of tension, like ice crystals you can feel more than see.

Del stood, regarded her for a moment, then walked down the hall to where Cora had hung a wood-framed mirror over a small table by the front door.

"Hey—this is great," he said, angling his head from side to side, then turning, the small mirror in hand, to check out the back. There was still plenty of hair, but at least now he didn't look like a throwback. Or a bum. Galen silently came out of the kitchen, her arms linked together in front of her. He tossed her a smile. "Listen—if the restaurant doesn't pan out, you can always turn it into a barber shop."

She didn't smile back. Del sighed. "Just kidding, honey."

He closed the space between them, thought twice, laid a hand on her shoulder anyway to give her a quick squeeze. "It really does look great. Thanks."

Now she gave him a half smile. "You're welcome. It does look pretty good, doesn't it?"

"The guys won't recognize me."

She gave a short laugh, drifted into the living room, then on out into the sunroom, which of course hadn't been sunny for several hours. She squatted beside Wendy, still sawing logs on the carpeted floor. Baby, blissfully plastered against the child's legs on top of the afghan, lifted her head and wriggled, ears back against her head, tongue flicking in and out like a lizard's, in sheer joy that someone had noticed her.

"I really need to get her home," Del said, kneeling next to his daughter. But Galen put up a hand, stopping him.

"Not yet. She's fine."

"She'll wake up all stiff."

Galen laughed softly. "No. *We'd* wake up stiff. Kids are made of Silly Putty, I've decided. They just mold to whatever surface they're on."

"But isn't there a draft—?"

Galen twisted her head, amusement twitching at her mouth. But her gaze was dead serious. "Stop trying to protect her so much, for goodness' sake. She's a lot tougher than you think she is."

Del knew where this was headed. "She's only four, Galen. She's my daughter. And I'm well aware of how tough she is. She lets me know in no uncertain terms several times a day. I'm also well aware that she doesn't understand her limitations, sometimes—"

"Then let her discover those limitations on her own, Del." He saw tears shimmering in her eyes. "Because that's the only way she'll ever learn how to compensate for them. Or overcome them." She stood, her arms still crossed, a single tear streaking down her cheek. She irritably swiped at it.

Del shifted toward her; she leaned away, shaking her head. She was miserable. And angry. Though not, he knew, with him. Or her even her husband. Uh-uh. The frustration rolling off of her in palpable waves was directed completely inward.

Galen Granata was absolutely furious with herself.

And the only person who could forgive her for whatever it was she thought she'd done, was her.

"It really is late," he said gently, yearning to touch her, to at least let her know somebody gave a damn. But she'd probably deck him if he tried. "If I don't get her in bed, she'll be awake until three." He knelt down before Galen could say anything else, scooped his daughter up into his arms. "So trust me. The only person I'm trying to protect right now is myself."

She hovered silently, at a safe distance, as he sat on the sofa, carefully inserting tiny limbs into coat sleeves. Wendy was dead weight against his chest as he stood, walked to the door. Galen scooted in front of him to let him out.

"Thanks again for the haircut," he said, whispering even though Wendy couldn't hear him. "Dinner, too."

That got a small smile. "You're welcome."

He paused, shifting the sweet-smelling sack of rocks in his arms. Smiled. "Honey, I gotta tell you—your cooking's gonna really knock some socks off."

"Oh, Del...you don't have to..."

"What? Tell you the truth?"

She touched her throat, embarrassment shining in her eyes in the porch light. "Thank you," she whispered, and he nodded.

He turned, started down the steps into the silent, icy darkness, then twisted back, his words floating on clouds of white vapor. "Look, chalk this up to macho pride or whatever, but I just think you should know, for the record? Not all men are like Vinnie. Or your grandfather. Okay? And one more thing, since I'm on a roll here—you don't have to stick your hand in a flame to prove to the world you're not afraid of fire, either."

Then without waiting for a retort, he continued down the stairs to tuck his daughter into the truck, to take her home, to get her to bed, to make sure she was safe. Because taking care of the people he loved was what he did, dammit.

Even if he didn't always do such a hot job of it.

Three weeks after first laying sponge to cabinets, Galen moved into her apartment, Del having assured her—after lighting in to her about turning on the water before he'd checked the plumbing and she was damned lucky a pipe hadn't given way and who gave a damn what Mr. Hinkle said—she probably wouldn't freeze, flood, be electrocuted or die in the middle of the night from a gas leak. He did make noises about was she absolutely sure she should be living all alone down here when it was so deserted at night, but she pointed out that, actually, the whole block on this side was backed by other yards from other houses, and she felt perfectly safe. As safe as she'd ever felt alone in her grandmother's house in Pittsburgh, for heaven's sake.

And she felt far safer alone, in the middle of the night, than she did when Del was here, that was for sure.

She grabbed the same sweatshirt and jeans she'd worn the day before from the floor by her bed, wriggled into them.

Fortunately, he wasn't. Around all that much. According to Elizabeth, who periodically showed up to ooh and ahh, Del had gotten really busy these last few weeks. So he only stopped by once or twice a day to check in with Mike, the job foreman, often missing her, since she was out a lot trolling for suppliers and what all. And when they did speak, he was...well, not cool, exactly, as much as careful. Giving her space. Just like she'd wanted.

Emotionally, at least. About everything else, he was in her face even more than ever, with his "you can'ts" and "you shouldn'ts" and the ever-popular "I think you're making a huge mistake".

For a nice guy, he sure could be a real pain in the neck.

And for someone determined to keep the guy from getting to her, she was doing one lousy job, wasn't she?

She tramped barefoot into the bathroom, with its brand-new

shiny shower curtain splashed with huge, bright, tropical fish, ran a comb through the hair, clipped it back as usual.

And saw, as she had a million times since, the way he'd looked at her the night she'd given him a haircut. She couldn't even describe it, really. Like…like what she thought, and felt, and wanted, mattered. Like he respected her. He might not agree with nine-tenths of her decisions, but he didn't out of hand dismiss them, either.

She let out a sigh. Didn't it just figure? If she'd been actively looking for a man, what were the chances of meeting someone like Del? But since she wasn't, since she was in no way, shape, or form interested in forming any sort of permanent alliance with any sort of male, there he was.

Honestly.

She headed back into the bedroom for her shoes, shaking her head at the cat and dog curled up together in the middle of her double bed, while the kittens, who couldn't yet negotiate the bed, scampered around on the newly refinished floor.

Which she'd done herself, thank you very much. Nearly ran over her foot at least a dozen times, and there were a couple gouges here and there, but she could always cover those up with scatter rugs.

Del had called her crazy. Del called her that a lot. She was beginning to think of it as a term of endearment, actually. Well, if they'd been…you know. In some sort of relationship that called for things like terms of endearment.

Now in the kitchen, she was raising the cheap miniblind in the window to let the sunshine splash exuberantly across the narrow room, then grabbed a carton of OJ out of the fridge, grinning at her freshly painted, zonk red kitchen walls. Del had only shaken his head at that one, but she could still see ''crazy'' in the way the corners of his mouth turned down.

Maybe she shouldn't think too hard about his mouth.

She poured herself a glass of juice, popped two pieces of whole wheat bread into the toaster—found for two bucks at a yard sale, and she'd known it worked before she bought it because she insisted the seller let her plug it in and test it— watched a couple minutes of the *Today* show on the 13-inch black-and-white TV she'd found last week. Touched her hair, idly wondered if she could wear hers like Katie Couric's.

Toast ready, she carried it and the juice out to the light-flooded living room. Buttery walls. White sheer curtains. An old armchair, badly needing to be recovered, slouched near the radiator, next to a slightly crooked swing-arm lamp. A smallish oriental rug, worn and faded with memories, sat at a jaunty angle in the center of the room. A small hutch hugged the wall opposite the chair, waiting to be filled.

That was it. And Galen loved it.

The Hens, as Del inelegantly referred to his stepsister and her cohorts, had tried their level best to foist off all sorts of furniture 'n' that on her, but Galen insisted she wanted to pick out every single thing in the apartment by herself, even though that meant starting out with what Elizabeth kindly referred to as an Oriental minimalist look. And since she was hardly going to spend much on the apartment with the restaurant swallowing so much of her capital, she'd become a devout yard sale junkie.

For the restaurant, she'd found wonderful old chairs and funny little tables, or what was left of someone's mother's best china or crystal or flatware. For herself, there was the funky iron headboard, a handpainted bedside table, the hutch, the rug. And after the car ordeal, shoot—she could dicker with the best of 'em. It was exhilarating, being able to buy whatever she wanted. Almost enough to compensate for not having anyone to share it with, once she got it here. Well, other than the beasts, but like they could care, right?

She frowned, plucked a kitten off her leg and headed downstairs.

The guys—and one woman—had been at work since eight. To cut costs, most of the changes would be cosmetic, rather than structural, since repairs alone had already claimed a good-size chunk of her stash. But Del assured her she'd still get what she wanted.

Del assured her a lot. Almost as much as he called her crazy.

She had, just as she'd threatened, helped to tear out old fixtures and knock down sodden ceilings and strip the tacky wallpaper from the customer restrooms. And yes, she'd gotten so sore a couple times she could barely move the next day. Not that she'd ever tell Del. This morning, he'd told her she could tackle the old floor tiles.

Oh, goody.

She wondered if he was here, until she heard his voice, over hammers and saws and horrible whirring noises she still hadn't gotten used to. He was laughing at something, the sound deep, warm, delicious. Her heart thunking in her chest, Galen picked her way through the maze that would eventually be her restaurant, inhaling the scent of sawdust and newly installed plasterboard and a couple of men who should probably consider changing their work clothes a little more often. As if he sensed her presence, Del turned before she'd gotten within twenty feet of him, his smile instantly fading.

"Dammit, Galen—where's your hard hat?"

Every noise stopped, every head turned in her direction.

For the first time, she didn't blush because she was embarrassed, but because she was ticked. "I didn't figure," she shot back, "since all the work was going on *below* my head, I needed it."

"Well, you figured wrong. I don't take chances on my sites, lady. Now go get your hat." And with that, he turned back to whatever it was he'd been doing.

She felt like she'd been slapped. Okay, yeah, she knew his workman's comp insurance rates were astronomically high, which is why he demanded absolute obedience to safety rules. But she hadn't realized she'd need a hard hat to scrape tile from the floor, especially as the major overhead work was complete. So, fine, she was in the wrong. That didn't mean he had to treat her like a child!

And why on earth was she overreacting like this?

Uh-oh.

She turned and stomped back through the kitchen, up the stairs, into her apartment. Not because she was throwing a hissy fit or because she was feeling petulant, but because she just realized she was totally screwed up. That this dumb, stupid, idiotic plan of hers was royally backfiring, because the more she was around Del, the more attracted to him she was becoming. The more she liked him.

The more she...she...

Wanted him?

Oh, *crud.*

She locked the door behind her, leaning against it, her heart pounding in her ears...*stoo-pid, stoo-pid, stoo-pid...*

She was lusting after the man.

The knock right on the other side of her head brought a good-size yelp. Followed by a flat, weary request to open the damn door, for God's sake.

So she did. She didn't want to, but then he really would think she was acting like a child. And that time, he'd have reason.

Leaning against the doorframe, Del lifted one hand, palm up. "What? You mad because I got after you?"

He looked exhausted. His hair was clean, but that was almost all you could say for it, since in three weeks it had reverted to shaggy again. And he hadn't shaved. Maybe he was growing a beard. He'd look good with a beard. Sexier.

Like this man needed to look sexier.

"No," she finally said when she realized he was giving her a really odd look. Then she realized what she was doing. What she was letting him do to her. "Yes," she said, noting the raised eyebrow. "I got mad. Because you could've simply asked me to put the hard hat on, instead of...instead of..."

Del crossed his arms, pure confusion in his eyes. "Instead of what, Galen? That *is* what I did. Ask you to put on the hat."

She didn't mean to fly off the handle. She didn't. And even as she felt her face go red, heard her voice tremble, she knew her words weren't directed at Del. Not really. "No. No, it wasn't. You didn't have to shout, 'Where's your hard hat?' clear across the room so everybody would turn and look at me. You didn't have to embarrass me. You didn't have to treat me like I didn't have any sense."

One side of his mouth hitched. "You don't."

But today, she didn't find his teasing funny. At all.

"Yes, I do," she said, annoyed as all get-out to feel her eyes sting. "I'm not a little kid. I haven't been a little kid for more than twenty years. If I screw up, I screw up, but that's not because I'm stupid..." Then suddenly, she wasn't so sure of that anymore. She looked up into Del's face, realizing there was no way to keep the tears from falling. "Or am I? Am I so hardheaded, as you're so quick to tell me every chance you get, because I'm too dumb to know any better?"

Then she saw the horror flash in his eyes, just for a second, before he pulled her into his arms, tucking her against that too-good-to-be-true chest. He swore, gently, into her hair, then let out a long sigh. "Cripes, Galen, I forget sometimes...I'm sorry, babe. No, you're not dumb. Not by a long shot. Yes, I think you go about things the hard way, but hell, I do that myself. Although I have to admit, sometimes I wonder how smart I am. But not you. Not you."

Oh, yes...she'd caught the "babe." She should protest. Go all feminist 'n' that. He was being macho and sexist and why wasn't she mad, or something?

She let her stinging eyes drift closed, not saying anything because (a) she had no idea what that might be, and (b) she was enjoying the moment. And she had a sneaking suspicion Del was enjoying it, too. And that, with very little provocation on either of their parts, they could both go on enjoying the moment for, say, the rest of the day?

Her eyes popped open. Jiminy Christmas! What *was* she thinking?

Psst—I think the word you're looking for is—

Shut up! Shut up, shut up, shut UP!

"Just for the record," she heard him murmur into her hair, "I'd've done the same thing to any member of my crew who walked onto a site without a hard hat, okay? I wasn't singling you out."

She lifted her face then, pulling back just far enough to see into his eyes.

But what if I want you to single me out?

She was smart enough to keep that thought to herself. Too.

Then Del traced a knuckle down her cheek. That was it.

Just the one simple, sweet gesture. And she felt the tremble clear to her soul.

So did he, she was sure.

"Oh, Galen," he said on a breath that brushed her lips, her cheek. "You're playing with fire, and you don't even know it." He looked away for a second, then back into her eyes, and her lips parted, yearning for a kiss she had no right to want. But, oh, how she did. Del smiled, sadly. "Uh-uh, babe—"

Twice! She really shouldn't let him get away with—

"—I am *not* going to kiss you."

What?

"Much as I want to, much as I'm sure we'd both enjoy it, I won't play that game. I'm way too old to be necking with a girl in the stairwell. Especially one who has bigger fish to fry than jumping in the sack with her horny contractor."

Galen's eyes went wide with shock. "Who said anything about—?"

He let her go. She felt dizzy. Slightly ill. Abandoned.

Protected.

He was already to the top of the stairs, one hand on the banister. Tightly. "You don't always need words to communicate, you know. Wendy taught me that." One clodhoppered foot thudded down onto the next tread. "In fact—" then another "—sometimes, you can hear far more when you ignore the words and pay more attention to other things." And... another. "Words can be controlled, see. Feelings can't. Not completely." He turned away, took another step, then pivoted back. "I would never hurt you, Galen. Not intentionally. Which means I won't let something get started that I know you really don't want."

Oh. He was being a good guy, right? Making a sacrifice. Or maybe not, considering she had no idea if she was really any good in bed. But in any case, he was being very noble, wasn't he? A regular hero, in fact.

Then how come she felt like slugging him?

Her arms crossed, she ventured a foot or two away from her door, calling down the stairs, "What about the floor?"

He looked up, puzzled.

"The tiles?" she reminded him. "You said I could start hacking away at them today."

"Oh. Right." He shifted his gaze elsewhere. "Mike'll show you what to do." Then he clunked the rest of the way down in that graceful, awkward way of his.

He was long gone by the time she got back downstairs herself. Mike showed her the ropes; fifteen minutes later, she'd taken up exactly one square foot of tile, was sweating like a thoroughbred after the Derby, and had figured out exactly what was bugging her about Del's "noble" gesture: He was making the decision *for* her.

He was telling her that good girls, nice girls, old-fashioned girls didn't go around lusting after their contractors.

Let alone consider seducing them.

That he was right was totally beside the point.

She wants me to make love to her.

Del swung the truck into the Bustamentes' driveway, but he didn't get out right away. Instead, he sat there, holding on to his head, listening to Bruce Springsteen on the truck's radio, willing his libido to cool off and back off and generally forget about it.

She might not know that's what she wanted—he had the feeling her body was a couple steps ahead of her brain in that department—but it hadn't been *that* long that he couldn't read the signals. He'd felt that tremble, boy, and it had taken powers he didn't know he had to keep from planting a good one on her.

And if he had, he'd've been no better than the bastard—or bastards—who'd messed with her head so badly to begin with. He *wouldn't* hurt her. And the easiest way to hurt her would be to get in the way of whatever it was she had to do.

Now he knew why he'd resisted touching her for so long.

Besides, although he admired her—yes, he did, despite his teasings—and ached for her, he wasn't in love with her. He'd been in love, and what he felt for Galen felt nothing like that. With Cyndi, it really had been rockets and flares and blaring trumpets, of feeling so damned lucky, every time he looked at her and realized she was his *wife,* he couldn't quite believe it. When he looked at Galen...well, it was just different, was all. Hell, he wasn't any good at putting these things into words. He just knew it wasn't love, what he felt for her.

Couldn't be.

Just as he figured, that part of the emotional factory had been shut down for good. And Galen needed a man who'd love her. She didn't know that, yet—and would undoubtedly throw something at him for even suggesting it—but she did. The right way, this time, though. Someone good and kind and strong, someone brave enough to let her have her head, even if she shot herself in the foot in the process.

He sure didn't have the guts to deal with her on a full-time basis, that was for damn sure. Ah, jeez...it was already killing him to watch some of the stunts she pulled, and they weren't even involved. He'd be one step away from suicidal if there were more going on between them. So...no, uh-uh. Not in this lifetime.

Besides, letting things get out of hand would be tantamount to betraying a trust she probably didn't know she'd even put in him. But she had. Or rather, he'd assumed it. She'd been betrayed once. No way was he setting himself up to be the next on that infamous list.

He knew she wanted him to make love to her. Even if *she* didn't. But what she really didn't know was that she really *didn't* want him to make love to her.

She just thought she did.

"Oh, Galen, Galen, Galen," he let out on a long, frustrated sigh. He'd do anything for her, but not that. No way was he getting that close to the edge.

That close to something never meant to be his.

Chapter 11

Wendy insisted on delivering the invitation to her birthday party herself.

Figures, the first day in months he didn't *have* to see Galen, and here Wendy was dragging him over there anyway.

"What if the mailman loses it?" she'd signed. "Or you do?"

So much for unfailing trust in dear old Dad.

He parked the truck around the corner, in the shade, the May afternoon sun already hot enough to turn steering wheels into torture instruments. Wendy spotted Galen before he did, bending over one of the large cement urns in front of the restaurant, planting flowers. Long, pale legs stretched to the sidewalk from baggy shorts, while a two-sizes-too-large scrub top billowed around her torso. Wendy broke away from his clasp, making a beeline for her new best friend.

Galen glanced up at Wendy's enthusiastic approach, her face breaking into an enormous smile. Woman and child hugged each other fiercely for a long moment, then Wendy pulled back far enough to hand Galen the invitation.

When she noticed Del, though, the smile faded around the

edges. Just like it always did. She rubbed a gardening-gloved hand on her shorts, then swiped at a strand of hair, smearing dirt from cheek to chin. She hesitantly signed "I'd love to come" to Wendy—since Wendy regularly strong-armed Del into bringing her over to play with the two kitties who were still left, Galen had begun to learn sign in self-defense— which, natch, earned her a huge smile.

It didn't seem to matter that they couldn't speak the same language.

It didn't seem to matter that Del and Galen couldn't figure out what, exactly, they were to each other. Although it did. More and more each day.

Nothing had changed, nothing was any more defined, than it had been weeks ago, when he'd nearly kissed her. She still kept sending out those damned mixed signals—desire and fear and caution, all mushed together the way Wendy liked to smash up her ice cream before eating it. They couldn't be friends, they couldn't be lovers…they couldn't be in the same room for more than five seconds without the air going all crackly around them.

He'd meant what he'd said, about being able to deal with a woman on a non-sexual basis. Theoretically, he was doing just fine on that score.

His body, however, regularly and repeatedly had some real choice words to say about the situation. Oh, yeah, it was spring all right, and the sap was running to beat the band. In fact, his was damn well about to overflow its banks. Especially when Galen looked at him the way she was looking at him right now.

"Can I go play with the kitties?" Wendy signed.

"For a minute," Del signed back. "I have to get back to work."

She scampered inside, leaving them alone. With no buffer of any kind to dull the sexual vibrations whining like pesky children between them.

"It's hard to believe she's nearly five," Galen said after two more beats than necessary.

"*You* find it hard to believe?" Del smiled; Galen cleared her throat, looked away.

"What I find hard to believe," she said, swiping pointlessly at her hair, "is that this—" she nodded behind her, indicating the restaurant "—is almost done." The grin was cocky, still, but a little dull. "*Ahead* of schedule, too."

He grinned back, even though his heart wasn't really in it. "Do I detect a hint of smugness in that comment?"

"Maybe," she said with a slight nod.

"Nothing doing today?"

She shook her head. "Upholsterer's coming next week. And the carpet. And Belinda, who's doing the mural, has classes all day today." He watched something flicker over her features, before she suddenly dodged his gaze, turning back to her flowers.

"Those look very nice. Great color. Red."

"Thanks."

It was then he noticed her movements had gone all jerky, the way she was very deliberately avoiding looking at him.

"Galen," he said softly. "What is it?"

"Nothing," she said, jabbing the trowel into the soil deep enough to bury nuclear waste. She looked around, almost frantically, like she'd lost something. On a hunch, he picked up a small potted flower of some kind—a geranium, maybe?—and held it out.

"Looking for this?"

Her eyes darted to his, then to the flower. With a sharp nod, she took it from him, tapping it out of the pot and sinking it into the hole she'd just dug.

"Ah. You're scared to death, aren't you? About the restaurant?"

He saw the halt in her movements, her shoulders stiffen. "Nothing I can't handle," she muttered, then continued to till her soil.

Oh, brother. "I'm sure," Del said, his arms crossed. Looking elsewhere so he wouldn't see the surreptitious swipe at her check. "But you know, before I hung out my shingle? God—I don't think I slept for two weeks before. Or after."

He looked at her, aching for what he knew she was going through. "It's okay to be scared, honey. And to admit it. That's what friends are for, y'know. To buck you up when you need it."

Even in profile, he saw her chin tremble with the effort not to cry in front of him. "I'm fine," she insisted, stuffing the last plant into the soil. And irritation flared inside him, that she couldn't even let herself cry in front of him anymore. That this new *control,* or whatever she thought it was, was preferable to honesty.

That she'd be willing to trust him with her body, but not with her feelings.

"For God's sake, Galen," he bit out, "it's not a sign of weakness to be scared, y'know? Or to let somebody just bloody care about you!"

Her eyes shot to his, wide with terror.

Something snapped, way down deep. He stormed inside to collect his daughter, who didn't understand at all why they had to leave in such a hurry.

Tears burning Galen's eyes, she hugged Wendy goodbye, then watched Del practically yank the poor little thing around the corner.

Oh, Lord. This was one of those moments when being a grown-up wasn't at all fun. This new persona of hers, she decided, didn't like things all nebulous and unsettled like this. She didn't like making other people nervous or uncomfortable, and she clearly made Del both.

As did he, her.

She couldn't wait for this project to be finished. Six weeks—longer even—they'd both ignored the goofy hum that buzzed between them whenever they came within fifty feet of each other, their conversations stilted, unnatural. And things were ten times worse whenever they got closer.

But she wanted to be closer, didn't she?

Oh, for crying out loud—would you cut it out with the euphemisms already?

You wanna have sex with the guy so badly your teeth ache!

Her cheeks flared redder than the geraniums.

Yes! she mentally answered the stupid little voice. *Okay! You happy now?* But, well, wouldn't it be nice to see what it was like with someone who really cared? About *her?* Not someone who saw her as a means to an end.

And she should have her head examined for lugging around this preposterous fantasy like a white patent purse in December. Even if he was amenable and she was that foolhardy, jumping into bed—or anywhere else, she thought as her cheeks flamed anew—with the guy was hardly going to clarify the relationship, was it? If anything, things would be even murkier than before.

Which would be pretty darn murky.

Galen gathered her trowel and the empty plastic containers, dragged herself back inside, and finally let the tears come.

He was right about her being scared. More than right. Dead on. She was absolutely petrified, now that they were so close to opening. What if nobody came after opening night? What if she had *too* much business? What if some reviewer ripped the place to shreds?

Sniffling, she planted her fanny on a dropcloth and stared up at the fresco through a scrim of tears, willing her heart to slide back down where it belonged. Galen was thrilled with what Belinda was doing: a vista of the Mediterranean, so patrons would feel like they were dining *al fresco* at some charming place in Sorrento, instead of in Spruce Lake.

Hmmm... *Al Fresco?* Grinding her palm against her soggy cheek, Galen made a mental note to add it to the list of possible names. The staff was hired, the menus planned; Rod had donated his marketing expertise, and come up with some really wonderful—and cheap—ways to promote the new place. Nameless though it might still be.

Then Rod hit on his most brilliant idea yet: deliberately *not* name the restaurant at first, letting customers drop ideas into a fishbowl by the front door on their way out, or something. Until then, it could be known as the No-Name Cafe. Or something. Winning name earns a free dinner for two. Or something.

Which pretty much described her relationship with Del, didn't it?

She let out a trembly sigh, then opened Wendy's invitation, printed in Del's oversize block writing. For Wendy's sake, she wanted to go more than anything. For her sake, she'd just as soon have her leg hairs pulled out, one by one. It was stupid, she knew, but she lifted the envelope to her nose to see if it smelled like Del. She convinced herself it did.

Which in turn convinced her she was losing it.

She remembered the way his knuckle had felt against her cheek the way a fourteen-year-old girl remembers her first kiss. Except she'd been nearly seventeen when she'd had her first kiss, and she couldn't remember it at all. Oh, she remembered it happening—in the linen closet at Granata's, while the staff was all on break before the evening rush—but she couldn't remember how it felt.

Her first kiss from the man who eventually became her husband, and she had no earthly recollection of it.

Confused. That's what she was. In so many ways, so full, so happy, so…complete, as far as *this*—her gaze swept the restaurant—went. And yet, not. Not so full, or happy, or complete as she figured she'd be at this point.

Oh, Lord. It would be so easy to lean on Del. Let him be strong for her. But she couldn't. Didn't dare. Because she knew, still—if not even more intensely than before—that her hold on her self-confidence was still very new and shaky and tenuous. The second she let go, it would be all over. Instead of struggling through on her own, making her own decisions, she'd go to him. Ask for his advice. Men liked that sort of thing, didn't they? Fed their macho egos or something. And she saw how Del lit up whenever one of his guys would come to him about something, ask what he thought.

Del was definitely one of those men who liked to be in charge.

And Galen was definitely one of those women who didn't dare let a man be in charge of her, ever again. Even if it was Del.

Especially if it was Del.

And just think what would happen if they slept together—

Rapping on the glass door jerked her to attention. Shaking herself out of her mental ramblings, Galen pulled herself up and walked to the door, her feet like lead.

There stood Snow White and Rose Red, aka Elizabeth and Nancy, grinning like a pair of just-fed cats and obviously up to no good. Except their grins vanished when they got a load of Galen's face.

"You've been crying!" "What's wrong?" they said simultaneously.

"Nerves," Galen lied. "About—" she shrugged "—stuff."

"That settles it, then," Nancy said after the briefest pause, then pushed her way inside. "We're kidnapping you. It's a glorious Friday afternoon. The mall beckons, the plastic glistens, the kids are all properly dispersed and all's right with the world."

Stunned and flattered and very, very tempted—she didn't dare tell them she'd never just, you know, gone shopping with gal pals before—Galen looked from one to the other. And sighed. "I'm hardly dressed for the occasion."

Elizabeth scanned Galen's scrub top and shorts, shrugged. "You look as good as anybody else out there." Galen took in Elizabeth's pink silk shell, her white linen shorts, the Italian sandals, and thought, "Uh-huh."

"Better," Nancy added, sweeping her heavy hair out of her face. Now, Nancy *was* wearing jeans, but hers were tiny, fashionably baggy and topped by the cutest little cropped cotton sweater with little roses embroidered along the neckline.

These two didn't exactly look like they were on the dole. Whereas Galen looked, understandably enough, like she'd been making mudpies for the better part of the morning. Not to mention she felt like she'd been eating them.

And it was high time she got out of *that* funk, she decided.

"Give me five minutes," she said, then dashed upstairs, sending cats and dog into a tizzy as she madly scrubbed and combed and yanked and tossed and groaned—a lot—until she could feel reasonably sure people wouldn't look at the three of them and wonder when Galen was due back at the home.

She even rummaged through three drawers until she found that lipstick she'd bought on impulse in 1993. Or thereabouts.

Then, actually feeling a little better, she grabbed her purse and went back downstairs. The other two simply stared at her.

"Ohmigod," Nancy finally said, "where the *hell* have you been hiding those breasts all these months?"

Galen looked down. Oh, my. Had she really bought this T-shirt that size? She fought the urge to hug her purse to her chest.

"Don't you dare," Elizabeth put in, snatching at her hand. "And that skirt—"

"That skirt is to die for," Nancy agreed.

Galen looked down, again, this time at the flowing, triple-tiered white cotton she'd picked up for cheap somewhere but had never worn because it came down nearly to her ankles and had always seemed too free-spirited or New Age or something. Before today, anyway.

Then she gasped. "Good grief! Is it my imagination, or can you see clear through to Lansing?" She spun around to go back upstairs. "I've got to get a slip—"

But Nancy hooked her arm through Galen's and tugged her toward the door. "Don't be ridiculous. With those legs, who cares?"

Galen put up one hand as she shuffled along behind. "Me?"

Nancy and Elizabeth looked at each other, then burst out laughing.

"You, honey, have some serious loosening up to do," Elizabeth said, settling her sunglasses on her cute little nose as soon as they got out onto the street.

"And we're just the ones to help you do it," Nancy added, opening the passenger side door to Elizabeth's Lexus.

Galen looked from one to the other. Munchkins with a mission. Great.

"I have no say in this, do I?"

"None," they both said at once, then pushed her into the car.

"Hey, boss—someone to see you!"

Del turned from watching the foundation being poured for

the Metzgers' new family room, squinting at the gray-suited man walking toward him.

"Del Farentino?" the man yelled over the sound of the grinding cement mixer.

"Yeah?"

"Todd Sullivan," the middle-aged man said, extending a hand. "I called you earlier?"

"Oh, right—of course." Del took the proffered hand, which gave his one firm shake. He'd gotten the call maybe an hour before. Something about bidding on a large project, the man had said, which had certainly piqued Del's curiosity. But what with checking on the four projects he already had going, he'd completely forgotten about the call.

Until now.

Sullivan glanced at the belching mixer, then at Del. "Someplace we can talk?" he shouted.

Nodding, Del led him around through mounds of dirt and gravel to his truck, parked on the other side of the property where the noise level was more tolerable. "We could have met in my office," he began, but the older man shook his head.

"No, I'm headed back to Cinci this afternoon. Figured I'd just catch you wherever I could. I got your name from Sidney and Louise Golden," he said.

It took a second before Del remembered the Goldens had chosen someone else to remodel their house. "I don't understand. I've never done any work for them. I bid on their project, but I didn't get it."

"Which, from what I gather, Sid and Lou regret to this day," Sullivan said with a grin. "Especially when they saw the work you did for the Martins, their neighbors. And, since Sid sits on Spruce Lake's Chamber of Commerce, he's also gotten an earful about the wonderful job you're doing renovating some old diner in town. And the Bustamentes' old place out on the highway. And the new gym for the elementary school."

Del crossed his arms, a smile tugging at his lips. "Nice to

hear I'm making a good impression.''

"Mmm. In any case, I hear renovations and remodels are your specialty?"

"I've done a lot of them, yes."

"No complaints on the work?"

"I try not to give guarantees that are going to come back to haunt me."

"So I hear. So the question is, you ever take out-of-town projects?"

He couldn't have told anyone why those words made his gut clench. Or why Galen's face popped into his brain. Of course, Galen's face had a bad habit of popping into his brain on an irritatingly regular basis.

Not to mention her smile, her laugh, her scent...

Don't go there.

Del lifted his chin, like a dog catching a scent. "In Cincinnati?" Sullivan nodded. "So how come you're not using someone local?"

"Oh, I'm asking a couple outfits to bid. But I'm more interested in reputation and quality. Not convenience."

The sun beat down on his hard hat, seared his back. "Big project, you said?"

Sullivan glanced toward the house. "A helluva lot bigger than this."

"How long you expect it to take?"

Underneath an expensive suit, a pair of broad shoulders lifted. "A year? Maybe longer. Maybe more work down the road, too, if this goes well."

Del rubbed his hand across his jaw. Relocate? Uproot Wendy from her family, her schooling? Then he thought of the terror in Galen's eyes earlier. Their mutual inability, after all this time, to come to terms with whatever the hell *was* going on between them. And how, every day, every time Wendy saw Galen, the bonds between *them* grew tighter.

Was this the answer?

Del turned back to face Sullivan, nodded. "I'm listening," he said, leaning against the truck.

* * *

Within ten minutes of hitting the mall, Galen had decided her companions regarded shopping as a religious experience.

And that she was well on her way to being converted.

The first half hour was spent shopping for birthday presents for Wendy—Nancy decided that Del was giving Wendy the half-grown kitten, even if Del didn't know it yet—but once that little chore was dispatched, things got really serious.

"The first rule," Nancy declared when they hit Lord & Taylor, "is that you may not buy anything that looks like my mother would wear it."

"Or mine," Elizabeth added.

"What's wrong with the way your mother dresses?" Galen asked Elizabeth, since she couldn't remember anything strange about Maureen's attire the couple times she'd met her.

"Nothing. If you're a middle-age Realtor."

"But don't you two wear the same sort of—"

"Oh, look! Lingerie!" Nancy said, dragging Galen into the intimate apparel department, where she said in a hushed voice, sweeping her hair out of her face, "*You* know they dress exactly the same, and *I* know they dress exactly the same, but Elizabeth is clueless. So we who love her simply don't bring it up anymore. Okay," she said, changing subjects with an ease Galen had come to dread, "you need some new underwear."

"No, I don't. I just bought some, a few months ago."

"Ah. You forget. I work with Cora."

Took a moment. Then she gasped. "She told you about my *underwear?*"

"What can I tell you? She thought it was a crime against nature. Just couldn't keep it bottled up inside her, you know?" By this time, Elizabeth had wandered in, shopping bags banging against her bare legs, and was beginning to drool over some very pretty nightgowns hanging on a rack. "Oh, good. You're here," Nancy shouted across the department. "Help me find some new underwear for Galen." She turned, stared at Galen's chest. "Let me guess—38C?"

Galen wondered if she could will herself invisible. "You know, I really don't need—"

"Something a lot more feminine than what she's wearing now," Nancy blithely continued, snatching a leopard-print push-up bra off a rack. She held it up to her own chest. Which was not, by any stretch of the imagination, a 38 anything. "Whaddya think?"

"Fine," Elizabeth said, having drifted in their direction, "if you're going for the Lion King look. Which I somehow doubt Galen is."

"You don't think she'd look fabu in leopard print?"

Galen opened her mouth to protest again, but there was little point. Nobody'd hear her anyway.

"I don't think jungle beast is exactly what she had in mind, Nance."

Nancy looked genuinely perplexed. "What's wrong with that?"

With a loud sigh, Elizabeth steered Galen over to a rack of bras and panties ranging from white to cream—pretty, delicate little confections frosted with lace. "Feminine," she said pointedly, tracing one pale pink fingernail over a satin cup, "is not the same as wanton."

"I heard that!"

Galen fingered a pair of panties she couldn't believe was supposed to be her size, two scraps of satin held together by two scraps of lace. But still white.

Aha. So we're getting into this, are we?

She frowned. "I don't know. This isn't it, somehow."

Which was the first indication she'd had that there was an "it" to begin with. That, for all her protests, maybe the world wouldn't shift on its axis if Galen Granata ditched her white cotton underwear.

Then again, maybe it would.

That, um, maybe, well…if something really bizarre happened and she did somehow, maybe, end up in an intimate situation with…a man…

Oh, brother.

…that maybe *she* might feel prettier? sexier? in something besides white cotton.

"Hey!"

They both turned to see Nancy waving something tiny, bright red and sequined. "How 'bout this?"

Even Galen had to laugh. "Uh, no. I don't think so."

"Fourth of July's coming up, you know…"

But a display several feet away *had* caught Galen's attention. Even as she floated to it, her heart pounding, she couldn't quite believe she was doing this. Contemplating buying something like that. But it was perfect. She could picture it against her fair skin, knew this, of all things, would make her feel…like a woman. Like a grown-up. Not like a child with breasts.

Or a *de facto* nun.

She flipped through until she found her size—which Nancy had guessed more closely than Galen wanted to admit— yanked it off the rack, then turned to face the two ladies.

"How about this?" she said, which elicited a dual, "Ooooh, yeah…"

Galen caught her breath, then quickly carted the items to the checkout before she could chicken out. This was for her, she told herself, just like Cora had said. And this time, nobody was going to tell her to take them back.

Or that good girls didn't wear things like that.

Because, as of right this moment, *this* good girl wore whatever the heck she wanted. In fact, after this? She might even lop off her hair.

You go, girl.

Hugh leaned against the porch railing on Guy and Elizabeth's side porch, his arms crossed as he apparently watched Wendy scampering around the sun-dappled yard with the Sanford kids, occasionally stopping to scoop her new kitty away from Einstein, who kept bowling the little thing over and giving her very messy doggy kisses. Del couldn't tell from his father's expression what he was thinking, but he could probably guess.

"Have you told Wendy yet?"

"There's nothing to tell yet, Dad. I don't have the job."

Hugh turned, his dark eyes boring into Del's. "Good as."

Del let out a huge sigh, crammed his hands in the pockets of his khakis. "It's the opportunity I was waiting for—"

"An opportunity I could have given you, ten times over, for God's sake! And it wouldn't have meant leaving Spruce Lake, ripping Wendy out of school, away from her family—"

"It's just in Cincinnati, Dad. Not cross country. We'll be back every weekend—"

"Oh, don't be so naive, Del. It never happens that way."

Del said nothing, his stomach churning, hardly prepared for his father's next words.

"Why are you really taking this job?"

Stunned, Del blinked at his father. "I already told you—"

"You told me bunk, is what you told me. Even without my help, you were really beginning to get things off the ground here. You think I don't keep track? So why're you leaving, Del? What're you running away from?"

Something cold ran up Del's spine, despite the warmth of the day. He heard the "this time" at the end of his father's sentence, did everything he could to push it away. "I have no idea what you're talking about—"

"Got anything to do with the pretty redhead over there handing out pieces of cake to the kids?"

He didn't want to look. Didn't need to, since Galen's image was now permanently etched in his brain. First off, she'd cut her hair. Not drastically or anything, just feathered it around her face, framing her huge eyes, that angular jaw. No more barrettes or clips or headbands.

Then, too, she was wearing a sleeveless dress, nearly the same color as her eyes, in some soft, weightless fabric that molded to her figure every time she moved or the breeze shifted. Damn thing floated around and teased her long legs, flirted with her ankles, showed off her breasts. His eyes drifted back up to her hair, floating and flirting, too, with her neck, her cheekbones. His libido.

No more Ms. Convent, that was for damn sure.

But Galen Granata was not why he was going to take this job. If he got it. He wanted this job because it meant more money, more challenge, more opportunity. And less interference. He loved his family, his friends, dearly. But man-oh-man, could they get on a guy's case or what?

A little freedom…yeah. It would be nice, wouldn't it?

And if moving away meant breaking this pointless whatever-it-wasn't between him and Galen, shutting up various and sundry relatives praying that something might blossom between them—and yes, nipping Wendy's hopes in the bud, but before disappointment led to heartbreak—well, he'd be the first to admit that maybe that wouldn't be such a bad thing.

But that wasn't the *reason* he was leaving. Just a fringe benefit.

Then Galen looked up and caught him watching her—which he hadn't realized he was doing—and everything he'd just told himself suddenly made no sense whatsoever.

"She's nothing like your mother, you know," his father said, startling him.

"What?"

"Or Cyndi, either. If that what's keeping you from going after her?"

Del's voice simply vanished for several seconds. "I'm not 'going after her,' as you put it, for several reasons," he finally managed. "The main one of which—not that it's any of your business—is that we simply wouldn't…work. Together."

"So. You've thought about it?"

Oh, hell. Del looked away, knowing no matter what he said, he was going to get in trouble.

Speaking of trouble…Wendy ran up to the table, signing something to Galen. Galen apparently asked Ashli to translate, after which Galen's entire face lit up in an enormous smile as she knelt on the grass, the dress billowing out around her, to give his little girl a hug.

Which was enthusiastically returned.

"She adores Wendy," Hugh said softly.

But not him. Not enough to trust him.

The thought caught him up short, his heart twisting so painfully inside his chest, he could barely breathe.

"It wouldn't work, Dad," Del replied, banging his hand against the railing, twice, before walking back into the house.

Something was going on. She could tell.

Frowning, Galen watched Del leave the porch, caught his father giving her a shrug. Now, what on earth d'you suppose that meant?

Cora tromped over, helped herself to a piece of cake, blatantly watching Galen watch the space where Del had been.

"You're some kind of fool, girl, you know that?"

Galen whipped her head around so fast her neck cracked. "Excuse me?"

Cora shoveled in a forkful of cake, stopped to wipe a splotch of whipped cream icing from the corner of her mouth. "You got the hots for the man. You're single. He's single. Ain't nuthin' stopping you but...well, actually, I have no idea what's stopping you. Except maybe that damn pride of yours."

With narrowed eyes, Galen threatened Cora with the mucked up cake knife. "You know, if I didn't love you so much, I'd smack you."

"Huh," Cora said on a chuckle, dropping into a nearby lawn chair. "Sounds to me like somebody got her spunk back."

"Which is *all* I want back. I'm not in the market for a relationship, Cora. You know that. I don't want a man—"

"To get on your case, to interfere, to tell you what to do. Yeah, yeah, I got all that, weeks ago. So who's talking about something permanent? What's the harm in just having a little fun, for heaven's sake?"

Galen looked away, shaking her head. "I can't believe I'm hearing this."

"Well, believe it child, because I'm not going to say it twice. You've spent your entire life doing for others, listening to others, not ever doing anything for you. Least, that's what you told me. Now I see you looking at the man like you want to eat him alive. And, honey, in case you missed it, he looks at you the same way. So what the *hell* are you waiting for? A voice booming down from the clouds?''

"Are you saying I should just…?"

"Jump the man's bones, baby. Yes, I am. Do you both a world of good and maybe erase some of those tension lines I see growing deeper by the day between your pretty little eyebrows.'' She shoveled in the last bite of cake. "Besides, if he takes that job in Cincinnati—''

Galen did the whiplash number again. "What job in Cincinnati?''

"He didn't tell you? That some developer down there has offered him big bucks to go supervise the restoration of an entire block of old houses downtown?''

Galen could barely hear her answer over the ringing in her ears. "No. He didn't.''

"Well, I suppose maybe he figured on waiting until the deal was signed and all that. I only know because I heard Maureen talking about it to Hugh, on the phone.''

In a daze, Galen looked back at the house, only of course Hugh was no longer there. Had that been the cause of the altercation between father and son a few minutes ago? If it was, clearly Hugh was none too happy about it.

Funny thing. Neither was Galen.

Now, this made no sense. On the surface, what could be a more perfect solution? I mean, if the man left town, there'd be no more running into him, no more smelling him. Or hearing him tease her. Or praise her.

Would he even be here for the opening?

And why hadn't he told her? He was her contractor, for heaven's sake. Didn't he owe her that much?

"Excuse me,'' she said, plunking the cake knife among the squished blobs of cake on the cardboard tray, "I need to, um, use the ladies' room.''

From their vantage point over by the swing set, where they were helping their toddlers play, Elizabeth and Nancy watched Galen head toward the house.

"You think?" Nancy asked, peering over her sunglasses at the retreating redhead.

"Only one way to find out," Elizabeth replied. "Watch Chloe, okay?"

Ignoring Chloe's screeches for a kiss, Elizabeth hot-footed it over to Cora, who was sitting with a supremely smug look on her face.

"Did it work?" Elizabeth asked.

"Like a charm, baby." Cora chuckled, smoothing her skirt over her broad thighs. "Like a charm."

With a big grin, Elizabeth turned back to Nancy, giving her a thumbs up.

You could hear her *"Yes!"* clear to Battle Creek.

Chapter 12

By the time she got into the house, Galen had no idea what it was she thought she was going to say to Del. After all, how was it her business what he did, where he went? She was his customer. Period. Okay, maybe a smidge more than that, but it was a tiny smidge.

So why did hearing about his potential move hurt so much?

A dozen breezes, balmy and rose-scented and at cross-purposes to each other, swirled through the high-ceilinged house. Voices drifted to her on one of them, coming, she thought, from the powder room tucked underneath the stairwell.

Del's and Wendy's. Laughter and giggles, respectively, over the sound of running water.

She took several baby steps closer, drawn by that laughter. By sounds she only vaguely remembered from her own childhood. Her father hadn't been around all that much, but she did remember, when he was, the way he and her mother kidded and laughed and teased.

Her mother was a strong woman, she thought suddenly. Maybe she missed Galen's father when he was gone, but Galen was suddenly bombarded by memory fragments—of her mother, on the phone, firmly insisting a bill was wrong; of her mother fixing a flat tire herself, more than once; of her mother going to bat for Galen in the first grade when Tommy Zwiekowitz kept badgering her on the playground.

Self-determining. Self-sufficient. Self-confident.

And, Galen realized, thoroughly, completely, unselfishly in love with Galen's father.

Del's voice cut through her thoughts.

"Stay *still,* goose," he said, laughing. "You've got more cake on you than in you. Hey! What'd you do that for?"

More giggles. Flat, nasal, but definitely delighted. Galen crossed her arms over the ache, even as she smiled at the exchange. Her eyes burned with tears for what she'd lost. For what she'd never have.

It was best, that Del was leaving. Before she loved Wendy too much.

Before—

"Hey! Get back here, you little monkey!"

Galen ducked into the living room just in time to see Wendy tear down the hall in front of her, back out the front door, a very wet Del in hot pursuit, towel in hand. At the door, however, he stopped, then shook his head, chuckling. Wiping his face with the towel, he turned, spotted Galen.

Nearly six months, they'd known each other. Worked alongside each other. Yet, here they stood, in Elizabeth's entryway, as awkward and unsure of things as they'd been on Thanksgiving.

Something like guilt flashed across Del's face.

"Galen! You startled me!" He finished toweling off his face, then pointed to his wet shirt. "Word of advice. Don't let a four—nope, sorry…*five*-year-old anywhere near water unless you tie her hands first." The towel clutched in his hands, he nodded toward her. "I like it. What you did with your hair."

Her hand lifted, sifting through the feathery bangs. "Really?"

"Yeah."

She tried a smile, but felt like crying instead. "I'm still not quite used to it."

"You do it yourself?"

"Oh, no…does it look—?"

He laughed softly. "It looks great, honey. Listen, there's something—"

They were interrupted by a thundering herd, better known as Guy's kids, storming through the side door, a grinning—and drier—Wendy in their midst.

"Uncle Del?" asked Ashli, shoving her dark blond hair behind her ear. "C'n Wendy spend the night with us? Mama says it's okay if it's okay with you."

Galen saw the hesitation, the apprehension, that momentarily froze Del's features, even as the kids all chorused "Please? Please? Please?" and jumped up and down in front of him.

"Kids! For heaven's sake!" Elizabeth wended her way through the crowd, Chloe ensconced on her hip, glanced briefly from Galen to Del, her face expressionless. On that count, at least. "We'd love to have her stay. She said she's never been on an overnight before."

As he always did, Del signed as he spoke, keeping Wendy part of the conversation. "She's been too young before, for one thing," he said. "And it's…" He hesitated. "Not like I can just leave her anywhere."

Elizabeth laid a hand on his arm. "Time to start hacking away at the cord, sweetie," she said gently.

So much family. So much love. Yes, even as the two boys started bickering in the background. Something Galen had never had, not like this.

Something she'd never *have*. Not like this.

Before anyone could see the tears, she quickly left the room.

The herd swarmed out again, including Elizabeth, who'd taken an in-the-midst-of-potty-training Chloe to the bathroom. Del looked for Galen, couldn't find her anywhere. He did, however, find Cora. Or she, him. He wasn't sure which.

"She left," she said from about ten feet to his left as he stood on the porch, scanning the yard. He turned, startled.

"Who?"

Cora heaved herself up onto the steps. "Honey, you are too damn old—not to mention big—to play coy." He expected whatever came out of her mouth next to have something to do with the aforesaid missing person. "Heard the baby's gonna spend the night here."

Fooled him.

"Yeah. I was outvoted. It'll be her first night away."

Cora chuckled. "And you feel like someone's just cut off your arm, right?"

A half smile twitched across his lips. "That pretty much sums it up."

Several seconds passed.

"So. You're a free man tonight."

He refused to answer. Not that Cora needed verbal encouragement. The mere fact of their sharing an air pocket on the same planet was the only opening she needed. "Seems to me, this might be a good opportunity."

He knew better. He really did. But he said it anyway. "For?"

"Well, now, baby—if I have to tell you, seems to me you're in far worse shape than I thought."

And with that, she went on into the house, just like that's what she'd been planning all along.

It wasn't fair, the way her heart bounded into her throat when she saw, all the way from the end of main street, Del's truck parked outside the restaurant that evening.

Nor was it fair the way her legs picked up the pace, of their own accord, completely ignoring her brain's protests to slow down.

But what was especially unfair was the way she went all gooey inside when he noticed her approach and turned, the breeze teasing his hair across his forehead. No, no—it wasn't his hair that made her go all gooey, though it might well have, on another day, under other circumstances. It was the look on his face.

He'd come to tell her he was leaving, hadn't he? He'd been about to, back at the party, but he never got the chance.

So he'd come to tell her in person. Alone.

And that's what made her go all gooey inside.

"I was just about to leave you a note," he said when she got within earshot.

"Oh?" She was close enough to smell him, now. Touch him, if she'd been of a mind. Instead, she crossed her arms. She hadn't changed since the party, and the temperature was dropping, now that the sun was going down, raising a flock of goosebumps on her arms. Or was that a gaggle?

"I don't know why I assumed you'd be here," he said.

She pushed her hair out of her face. Smiled a little. "Maybe because I usually am?" They both laughed, the laughter sputtering out when she realized their gazes were hooked together like a pair of kissing teenagers' braces.

Jeez-o-man. If the sexual tension was any heavier, they'd choke on it.

Just a professional relationship, her fanny.

Deep breath. "It was such a nice evening, I decided to take a walk in the park." She nodded back toward the end of the street.

"Ah." Del jingled his keys in his pocket. He hadn't changed either, still in his khakis and the navy polo shirt he'd been wearing earlier. She saw a muscle ticking in his jaw. Wanted to touch it. Knew she was being foolish for even thinking that. Knew, in what had to be one of the world's brighter epiphanous flashes, exactly what she was going to do if the opportunity presented itself.

Maybe.

"Wendy all settled in?" she asked.

"What? Oh. Yeah." He grinned. "In hog heaven."

"She needs that. To get out, to be on her own, a little."

Brown eyes met hers. "With that crowd? She's hardly on her own."

Galen smiled. "She doesn't know that, though."

Giles and Roberta from the bakery passed, nodded greetings.

"Look, would you like to come inside—?"

"Do you think I could come inside—?"

Another bout of nervous laughter preceded Galen's murmured, "Sure," as she dug the keys out of her pocket, unlocked the door.

Silence enveloped them, as deep and warm as the humid air in the closed up building. In the confined space, she was even more profoundly aware of Del, of his clean, comforting scent, his size, his masculinity, and felt dwarfed by it.

No. Not dwarfed. Not diminished at all. Empowered.

Feminine.

Her heartbeat thrummed in her throat, her pulse echoing the chant—sweet, achy, determined—low in her belly.

"Would you like a beer?" she asked, casually heading for the back. Not even looking over her shoulder. As if inviting men up to her apartment was something perfectly natural, perfectly normal.

He'd followed her as far as the kitchen, hesitated when he realized where she was leading him. As if he knew she'd never had a man alone in her house before. Not one she wasn't married to, at least.

"Galen."

She turned, one hand on the banister.

"I've been offered a job in Cincinnati."

She waited a moment until the jab of realization—that it was true—dulled. "A good one?" she asked quietly.

"Very."

Then what's with the anguish in your eyes, Del Farentino?

"Is that what you came to tell me?"

"Yes."

She smiled. It was the least she could do. And she held out her hand. "Then I'm sorry I don't have anything fancier than beer to celebrate with."

He stared at her hand for a long moment, then rammed his own through his hair. "Galen...honey..."

She lowered her hand. Inside her stomach, flocks of razor-winged butterflies took flight. "Don't you *want* to go to bed with me, Del?"

His gaze shot to hers, his expression flummoxed. She might have laughed, if she could have gotten the sound out past those boogying butterflies.

"I mean, if you don't, just say so—"

His eyes darkened. "Yes."

Something like triumph flared through her. And heart-stopping fear.

Not because he would take her to bed, but because, if the set to his mouth was any indication, he wouldn't.

Unless she changed his mind.

She left the stairs, started back toward him, not sure how her knees were carrying her. It occurred to her they'd never even kissed. Or dated. And here she was, determined to get this guy naked and inside her within the next...well, she didn't have that part figured out. But soon.

Very soon.

Less than a foot separated them. Del hesitated, then lifted his hand, cupped her jaw, his work-rough thumb gently tracing her cheekbone. With a soft sigh, she leaned into his calloused palm, her heart now beating so fast, so hard, she could hear it.

She knew what he was thinking.

"You don't have to be my protector, Del," she said softly, rubbing her cheek against his palm. "I know what I'm doing."

With a soft sigh, he drew her into his arms, his hand warm, strong on the back of her head, his heartbeat strong, sure, underneath her ear.

"I'm not going to be around."

For a moment, she shut her eyes against the stab of pain, then lifted her eyes to his. "My life. My body." She swallowed. "My decision what to do with both of them."

"Galen...you're not the type—"

"For what, Del? To have a fling?"

He touched her cheek. Smiled sadly. "No."

"Because I'm a good girl?"

Now his caress extended to her hair, brushing it off her forehead, followed by his lips. Gentle. Circumspect. "Yes," he whispered against her temple.

"And good girls can't want sex, is that it?"

His eyes met hers, his brows tightly drawn. "That's not what I meant."

"Then what did you mean?"

"That women like you...deserve more than a toss in the hay."

"But I don't *want* more than that, you idiot!" she practically shrieked, pulling away from him. Away from his determination to protect her from herself, from her own needs and desires. "I don't want permanent! Or haven't you heard a word I've been saying these past months? I'm not looking for happily ever after! I just want...now."

His eyes clouded. Darkened. "As in, you just want sex. For tonight."

She nodded, afraid to speak.

His expression told her he didn't believe her for a minute.

That, she could ignore. What was harder to ignore was her heart's concurrence with that expression.

For several seconds, he just stood there, his hands in his pockets, his gaze locked with hers. He was frowning slightly, as if considering whether or not to bolt.

She felt her pulse jump at the base of her throat.

"There's been no one since Cyndi," he said quietly. Then, on a sigh, he added, "And there weren't a helluva lot before her, either. If you're expecting ..."

She shook her head. "No expectations."

He closed the space between them, slipped his hand underneath her hair. His lips barely brushed hers, like a breath, his tongue flicking out to tap her bottom lip, then her top. Every nerve cell in her body screamed. She thought she might have moaned.

Again, he barely joined their mouths, sliding his lips across hers, gently tugging at her bottom lip with his teeth. Teasing. Tormenting.

This time, she definitely moaned.

Then he *really* kissed her.

She was already damp for him. And he hadn't even touched her yet. Not really.

Not physically.

He was going to be a careful lover, she realized.

And thorough.

Have fun, honey.

For the rest of his life, he'd wonder about this night. Which he would regret more—what he was about to do, or not doing it?

The walk upstairs had interrupted things just enough to give him—both of them—a little breathing space. A chance to gather their wits. A chance for one or both of them to turn to the other and say, "You know, now that I think about it…maybe this isn't such a hot idea."

But neither of them did.

Galen kicked off her sandals onto a small, heavily patterned rug by the front door, then padded across the nearly bare living room floor to open the windows, turn on a couple of lamps to chase away the dusk. He hadn't seen the apartment since she'd moved in, he realized. Somehow, he'd expected frills and gee-gaws, dried flowers and lace. Although, he didn't really know why he'd expected that. Galen wasn't frills and lace; why should her apartment be?

Early garage sale, he thought with a half chuckle. As half of the restaurant would be. Once she'd conquered Marv, she was hooked. If there was a bargain to be had, she got it.

Baby trotted over, then promptly flopped on her back to get her tummy rubbed. Del did better than that. He picked her up, scratched her underneath her hairy little chin. He thought the dog was going to swoon. The cat, however, simply sat in the kitchen doorway, looking vaguely annoyed.

Del glanced around, nodding. "Nice."

Galen stood by one of the windows, her arms crossed. An almost weightless breeze, slightly floral-scented, messed with her hair. "I figure, the less I have, the less I have to clean."

"Good philosophy."

A smile flickered across her mouth.

And her hand lifted to her throat.

Oh, man. Were there ever two more clueless people? They'd

come up here to have sex. They'd already done the should-we, shouldn't-we dance downstairs. Yet here they stood, like a couple of twelve-year-olds at their first mixed dance.

No. Like a pair of thirty-somethings who hadn't slept with anyone else since their spouses died.

"I'll get the beer, then," Galen said, her dress floating around her legs as she walked to the kitchen.

"I don't need it."

"Fine," she called from the kitchen. "More for me."

Seconds later, she returned, a cold bottle in each hand. It was that "Lite" stuff, but oh, well. He hesitated, then dropped the dog—gently—and took the beer, smiling when she tilted the bottle to her lips.

"This part of the new, liberated Galen Granata?"

She actually laughed, her skirt whooshing around her as she slid down the wall, landing in a heap of long limbs and yards of fabric—knees up, legs spread, the full skirt chastely covering everything. He found the position extremely erotic, as only something that innocent can be.

The thought of undressing her made him very, very hard.

Took a second before he realized the laughter had fizzled out, replaced by a serious sort of calm that put him on guard. She'd speared her hand through her hair, her elbow resting on her knee, regarding him thoughtfully.

"Your wife," she said quietly. "How did she die?"

He nearly dropped the bottle. "Why on earth do you want to know that? And why *now,* for God's sake?"

One shoulder hitched, that sad gesture of the little girl who still lurked inside that very grown-up body. And head. "I know this may sound strange…but…" She looked down, toying with the hem of her skirt where it brushed one instep. Then she lifted her eyes, peering out at him from underneath those long auburn lashes. "Because I figure that's the most intimate thing you could share with me. Because, somehow, I'd feel more comfortable…later…if I knew…"

Her hand lifted to her cheek, gone red, as usual.

Del crossed to her, joining her on the floor, his back, like hers, braced against the wall. He tipped back the bottle, downing half of it at once, then stared at it for a long moment.

She was right. Talking to her about Cyndi was far more intimate than sex.

Definitely more intimate than he'd planned on being tonight.

Heaving a great sigh, he reached over, took Galen's hand in his, then kissed it, a thin smile stretching across his lips when she leaned her head on his shoulder.

"Cyndi had a hidden heart problem." He hesitated, waiting for the pain, anticipating it welling up inside him like some living thing. "Something that didn't show up until she went in for her first prenatal appointment. We'd...been trying for five years to have a baby, see, so she really, really wanted this kid. I did, too, of course—I remember I walked around in a daze for at least two days after she took the pregnancy test, and for the first time, it was positive. But not..."

He dragged a palm over his face, regained control.

"She didn't tell me. About the heart condition. She didn't tell me the doctor advised her to abort, fearing if the pregnancy didn't severely tax her already weakened heart, labor might. She couldn't take any medication, see, because of the baby..."

Five years, and it still ripped him apart. That she'd taken that risk.

That she hadn't told him.

Trusted him.

"Would she have lived," Galen asked softly, "if she hadn't had the baby?"

Del sucked in a breath, shook his head. "Nobody knows for sure. Maybe. They tell me she might have lived in any case, if they'd gotten the baby out before she went into labor, perhaps. I didn't even know what was going on until then. I was busy, during the pregnancy, working for a huge contractor in Chicago, and she insisted I didn't need to go with her to her doctor's appointments. She was real tired the whole time, but I thought that was normal. I had no idea..."

He hesitated, gathering his thoughts.

"I got home that night, three weeks before her due date,

found her having hard contractions. By the time I got her to the hospital—remember, at that point, I still had no idea anything was seriously wrong—she could barely breathe.''

Like a booted foot, the memories rammed into him, again and again. ''Cyndi went into cardiac arrest before they got her prepped for the C-section, which apparently cut off Wendy's oxygen supply, which they tell me caused her deafness. They told me they tried to revive Cyndi, but...''

He clamped his jaws together to keep control, then heard a faint rustling at his side as Galen shifted, rubbed her cheek against his shoulder. ''She wanted that baby enough to risk everything for it, didn't she?''

''You know what she told the doctor?'' he said, the words ripping from his throat. ''She told him how much *I* wanted the baby. That it would have killed *me* if she had to abort the child! That since there was a chance, if she took very good care of herself, that everything would work out, the risk was worth it.''

After several seconds, Galen asked, ''Would you have insisted she terminate if you'd known?''

He nearly crushed her hand as emotions and doubts roared through him, screaming like banshees. ''You have any idea how many times I've asked myself that? I don't know, Galen. I honestly don't know. But if she'd told me, if we'd decided to see the pregnancy through together, then maybe I could've taken better care of her than she clearly did of herself. I can't say whether she would have lived or not, but if I'd known, if I'd been allowed to be part of the decision, I wouldn't have felt so...damn...*helpless!*'' With each word, ground out through a clenched jaw, he banged the now-empty bottle against his knee.

Galen slipped her hand out of his, but only so she could wrap her arms around his waist, snuggle against his chest. ''Oh, Del,'' she breathed, ''you can't take care of everyone, all the time. You weren't responsible for what happened. You weren't.''

There would be no point in arguing with her.

But, through the resurrected agony of remembering that

night five years ago—oh, God! Five years ago tonight!—when he became both a father and a widower, filtered an odd sort of peace.

An acceptance, maybe.

For several minutes, he simply held Galen close, drinking in her softness, her fragrance, her unselfishness.

The least he could do was to return the favor.

If it killed him, he would take his time with her. Figure out what she most needed, then do his best to oblige. From now on, tonight was for her.

As long as he kept that in mind, he just might come out of this alive.

He kissed her hair, gently rubbing her shoulder. How long had it been since he'd wanted something so badly, something he knew he shouldn't even be thinking about? She leaned back to look up at him; he could see her heartbeat hopping at the base of her throat. His knuckle traced her jaw, then swept down, toying with the scoop neckline of her dress. She sucked in a quick breath; he watched her pupils dilate, her lips part.

His own need, so long ignored, slammed into him, jacking up his own heart rate to the danger point. He pulled her onto his lap, deliberately tormenting himself. On a sigh, he kissed her, deeply, letting his hand sweep up a thigh as slick and smooth as marble, but a helluva lot warmer. Softer.

She shifted. Inviting.

Trusting.

Heart stuttering, he touched his forehead to hers, stroking her jaw. "Tell me what you want."

Her breathing quickened, her breasts rising, falling, beneath the brilliantly hued fabric of her dress. "As in?"

"As in…" Carefully, lightly, he swept one finger alongside her breast, then up over the peak, feeling the nipple bud, just that fast.

"You mean that?" she asked, like a child not believing it was really Christmas eve. Some odd, out-of-place emotion—anger, maybe?—raced through him. Not at her—no, never at her—but at whoever had put such insecurity behind those words.

He smiled. "As long as it doesn't involve chains and whips. Sure."

There went the blush. And for a moment, a pair of lowered eyes. When she raised them again, however, he saw traces of devilment. And anticipation.

"First, I want you to undress me." The words trembled.

"I can handle that. And?"

Eyes averted again, she tucked one corner of her lower lip between her teeth, even as she traced his collar with one fingertip. "Then I want to undress *you*," she said, so softly he could barely hear her. She lifted her face, embarrassment and need for acceptance fighting it out in her eyes. "I want to…touch you. I mean, if you don't mind—"

Again, she looked away. Again, anger zipped through him. He snagged her chin, held her until their gazes were locked. "Good girls do touch, honey," he whispered. "Kinda takes the fun out of it otherwise."

That got a smile. And a nod. And a very deep breath.

"One more thing?"

He laughed. He couldn't help it. "What?"

"When we…I mean, when it gets to that point…could I be on top?"

Oh, Lord, it was everything he could do not to crack up completely, but her earnestness, her obvious fear that he'd—somehow—find her request unseemly or something squelched any desire to laugh. But honestly—what kind of sex life had this poor woman had?

He didn't want to know.

What he wanted was to kiss her. Slowly. Thoroughly. He tilted her backwards, onto the rug, and did just that. She made little murmuring noises, deep in her throat, as her hands threaded through his hair. Holding him, encouraging him. Finally, he lifted his mouth from hers long enough to say, "I'm sure we can manage that. At least, for one of the times."

He'd never seen anyone's eyes go that wide. "*One* of the times?" she squeaked. In fact, she was so startled, she hadn't even noticed he was unbuttoning her dress.

Del chuckled. Behind her ear. She shivered; he could see,

even through two layers of fabric, her nipples harden. This was not going to be easy, going slow. But boy, was it going to be fun—

Something poked the back of his head. "What the...?" He lurched up onto his elbow to find Baby standing six inches away, little more than a wagging blur. When Del tried to shoo her away, she charged him, yapping and snapping.

Galen laughed, low in her throat. "Either she's trying to protect me, or she thinks we want to play with her."

Del glowered at the dustbunny with teeth. "What? You've never seen two people make out before?"

Baby yapped and scampered away, only to scamper back ten seconds later and *ptooey* a rubber ball in Del's face.

Galen lost it.

"So much for romantic," Del grumbled. He got to his feet, scooped up dog and ball, depositing both in the extra bedroom, then returned to where Galen was waiting for him, sitting up, her arms linked around her folded knees.

Del stood over her, hands on hips. "Now. Where were we?"

Still flushed with laughter, she looked down at her chest. "Mm...the third button?" Then she looked up, grinning. "I saved the rest for you."

He lifted her to her feet, brushing his lips over her soft, shiny hair as his hands clumsily negotiated a seemingly endless row of buttons. The room pulsed with her intoxicating woman/child scent, sex and innocence all tangled up, drugging him. Healing something in him he hadn't realized needed healing.

Pushing him frighteningly close to thinking this was real.

"I'm going to go slowly," he said.

She tensed, slightly, making him smile. "Whatever," she finally murmured, as he peeled back the dress, from her shoulders, her arms, letting it float to the floor.

His eyes shot to hers, a grin breaking out at her blush.

He wasn't sure how the fragile-looking, lacy bra was holding everything in, let alone up, but he didn't really care, to be honest. His interest in architectural engineering only went so far. But the effect was so...so...

Well. Let's just say that he almost didn't want to remove it quite yet.

Almost.

"Your underwear matches your eyes?" he said, reaching for her hand.

She touched one bra strap, worry brimming in her eyes. "Do you like it?"

On a sigh, he tugged her to him, fingering the delicate satin straps, even as he was suddenly and extraordinarily aware that a beautiful, willing woman wearing nothing more than a film of lace was pressed tightly against his erection. "You look luscious," he whispered against her neck, and she giggled. Relieved, he thought. His lips found hers again, melting into a dizzying, endless series of kisses. "And all this time, I had you pegged as a white cotton type of gal."

"Mmm," she murmured into his mouth. "You should see my top drawer."

With a quiet laugh, he touched her hair. "Your turn," he whispered.

He wasn't sure whether to grin or groan at the sudden set to her mouth, like this was something else she had to get through before she could claim her prize. But his chest constricted at how much her hands trembled as she tried to undo the single button a few inches below his neck. He thought of a thousand things to say, decided against all of them. After all, this was her idea. So he simply combed his fingers through her hair, then placed a gentle kiss her on the temple.

She burst into tears.

He should have known.

"Okay, that's it." He stepped around her, gathering her dress up off the floor. "Arms up, honey," he commanded, slipping the dress over her head, yanking the front closed, though not buttoning it.

The hurt and confusion in her eyes nearly sliced him in two.

"No, I'm not rejecting you," he quickly reassured her, guiding her to the single armchair. He dropped into it, pulling her onto his lap. "But, in case you missed it, you're not as ready for this as you think you are, sweetie pie."

Which just made her cry harder.

He just held her, let her sob. When he figured she might be able to hear him, he said, "Why are you trying so hard?"

Sniffling, she lifted her head. He reached over and handed her a tissue from the box on top of a pile of magazines beside the chair. She wiped, then said, "Trying so hard?"

"Yeah. To be this *femme fatale* or whatever it is you think you have to be. I mean, you want to undress me, you want to be on top, you want to handcuff me to the damn bed, it's all fine with me. Long as that's what you really want." He fingered a tear from her cheek. "Not because you feel you're trying to prove something, okay?"

She scrambled off his lap, then stood awkwardly in the middle of the room, as if she realized she had nowhere else to go.

"Vinnie..." she started, then sucked in a breath, started over. Her face was splotched, her arms tucked tightly against her ribs. "Vinnie had very...definite ideas about a woman's role in the bedroom. About this woman's role in the bedroom, in any case. Anything even remotely aggressive was a big no-no. I always felt...like there was something wrong with me. Like I was perverted or something. That I had all these feelings inside me, things I wanted to try or do, but they weren't 'right' somehow."

Neither spoke for several seconds. Del, for one, didn't dare. Then he stood, wrapped one arm around her waist, and led her back to the bedroom. "Tell you what," he said softly when they got there. He turned on the bedside lamp, turned down the bedclothes. Then he began undressing himself. Not too fast, not too slow, watching her watching him, her arms strangling her waist. Peeking out between the edges of the unbuttoned dress, her magnificent cleavage seemed to wink at him. "Why don't we start out slowly and work our way up to adventurous, okay?"

He flung his shirt onto the chair by the bed, toed off his shoes, removed his socks. Unbuckled his belt, smiling at her gaze, riveted to his crotch. The cat jumped up on the bed; he unceremoniously shoved her back down, ignoring her indignant *mrrrowp* in reply. "Let's just play this whole thing by ear. You want to touch—" he unzipped his pants, pushed them down "—you go right ahead and touch. There are no 'rules' in *this* bedroom—" he kicked the pants aside, now standing in nothing but his underwear "—got that?"

Galen lifted red-rimmed eyes to his. Then pointed, laughing. "You said black!" she shrieked. "They're *white!*" she said. "White *boxers!*"

"And now—" Del hooked his thumbs into the waistband, slipped them down, tossing them handily off to the right. "Tada! They're *gone*—!"

A muffled thumping caught their attention. Startled, they looked around to see the cat spinning around backwards, trying to fight her way out of his drawers.

Del took advantage of Galen's collapse into laughter to pull her down onto the bed.

He wasn't kidding about slow.

Not that she was complaining. Not after—

Hey! How many people are in this bed, huh?

She drew in a deep breath, smiling as Del traced kiss after kiss over her belly. Her hips. Skirting, flirting with a hundred areas of her body that were whistling and stomping and yelling, "Hey! Over *here!*" And in the process, courting a hundred other areas she'd never known could be so grateful for a man's touch.

She could get very used to this.

Uh, no. She couldn't.

He's taking very good care of you, isn't he?

She stiffened, forced herself to relax when his mouth returned to hers, his kisses soft as rainwater. And as nourishing. By now—well, actually, for some time already—she'd been quivering with need, making all these little whimpering noises which seemed to please Del quite a bit. Don't ask how she knew that. She just did. Her nipples strained, aching for his hands, his mouth, *anything.* But what did he do? Stroked her arms instead. *Her arms!* Deliciously, she had to admit, but maddeningly, occasionally grazing a nipple with the underside of his wrist. She wriggled. Whimpered a little more. Hinting. Hoping.

Doing this silent little *pleasepleasepleaseplease* mantra inside her head.

Except the creep caught on. Chuckling, he deliberately moved his hand a half inch east.

She smacked him. Hard.

"Would you *please* get on with it!" she hissed, only to nearly choke when he obeyed, rolling one nipple between his fingertips. Sensation shot to her belly, lower, spreading and warming and setting things on fire, and all she could manage after that was a little string of shaky "ohs". Jiminy Christmas—her *toenails* were throbbing!

"Oh, you mean like this?" he whispered. Or at least, that's what she thought he said. Between the roaring in her ears and the fact that he was speaking with his mouth full of her other breast, she couldn't be quite sure.

Praise all the saints, how could anyone think of this as anything but bleedin' miraculous? She arched and cried out and did all those things she'd always wanted to do but never could, thoroughly enjoying herself for *the first time in her life*. She didn't feel afraid or vulnerable or awkward with this man: she felt completely and forever free. If nothing else, he would leave her with this.

Even as he would leave her.

She pushed out the thought, letting herself drown in a red haze of pure, sweet sexual pleasure—the kind of pleasure that only comes, she realized, when sex becomes the means of expression, not the goal. And yet, as she clutched blindly at sheets and pillows and her lover's shoulders before she flew off the bed, another emotion also broke its bounds, roaring through her, fueling her climb to what she knew, without a doubt, was about to be the most incredible climax any woman had ever had, anywhere, in the history of sex:

Anger. At being cheated out of her due. At having to wait so long.

At being made to believe this could somehow be wrong.

Del caught it. Somehow. Here they were, both breathing so hard she momentarily worried about hyperventilating, and he reached up, winnowed his fingers through her hair. Through the haze, she caught the edge of his frown. "He wouldn't let you—?"

"No," she bit out. "Never."

Del's own eyes darkened as he shifted them so she was on top. "Allow me."

And with one sharp thrust, they were joined.

Yes!

It should have hurt, after all this time without. It didn't. It should have bothered her, on some level, the way Del had just taken control, guiding her onto him, setting the rhythm. Possessing her.

It didn't.

She sucked in a breath, her teeth between her lips, then sighed with soul-deep contentment as wonder eclipsed reason. Del cradled her breasts in gentle hands, playing her, loving her, murmuring words she more felt than heard as he drove higher than she ever thought possible. At her core, every muscle tensed, prepared for liftoff, and she smiled, welcoming it. Del pulled himself up to take a nipple in his mouth; a shudder of anticipation streaked along her nerve-endings—

This one's for me, Vinnie! ME! she thought on a scream as that oh-so-long-awaited climax—fierce, vicious, and absolutely glorious—blasted through her, leaving her feeling, at last, like a real, live, normally functioning woman.

And, oddly enough, not the least bit *bad*.

Well, he had the answer to his question. The one about what he'd regret more? Yeah. This had to win, hands down. No way could he possibly have felt worse, if he'd walked away, than he knew he was going to feel that he hadn't.

She murmured drowsily in his arms as he held her more tightly, not wanting to let her go. Wishing…wishing…

Wishing life would just play fair, for once.

Three times, they'd made love. She'd been on top. And underneath.

And once…well, he wasn't sure who was where, exactly, but it worked.

Spectacularly.

But now it was well after midnight and they were both starving. So he suggested maybe they should eat something so they wouldn't be found dead in the morning. And somehow, he managed to let go of that fragrant, soft, cuddly body long enough for her to throw on some silky robe or something and make her way to the kitchen.

She wasn't walking any too fast. "You sore?" he called out.

Her laughter filtered back through the darkness. "Oh, that's romantic."

But he caught the edge in her voice.

Del hauled himself out of bed, pulled on his pants. He found her staring into the refrigerator, clearly regretting what they'd just done. He slipped his arms around her waist from behind, pressing a kiss to the back of her neck. He wanted her again. Well, soon, anyway.

He wanted her forever.

Oh, *hell.*

He felt her swallow, hard. "Omelettes?" she said thinly, and Del twisted her around, shutting the refrigerator door. A street lamp cast streaks of anemic light through the slats of her miniblind, not enough to see by, really, if you were looking for something, but more than enough to see her ravaged expression.

"I take it this isn't because you're sore."

A single tear, silver in the dim light, raced down her cheek. "No."

"You know," he said softly, "if I hadn't just had such a good time in there, I might be tempted to be real ticked off with you." He backed her against the counter, bracketing her with his arms, one on the counter edge, the other gripping the refrigerator door. "What's wrong *now?*"

Her laugh was a weak, pathetic little thing, and Del's heart twisted in his chest. "I'm screwed up?"

"Nope. Can't use that as an excuse," he said, touching her hair. Feeling strangely like…

He loved her.

Nope, uh-uh. Not an option.

"We're *all* screwed up, babe," he said, tamping down the emotions surging to and fro in his chest. "Even Elizabeth, although she'd be the last to admit it."

Galen tried to laugh again, but this time she couldn't even manage pathetic. "You make me feel so safe," she whispered.

Del went very still, then brushed his lips over her hair. Understanding. But not. "Let me guess. That's the problem."

She sighed, kissing the hollow of his throat. "That's the problem."

"Okay. I know I'm going to regret this, but…because…?"

"Because when I feel safe, I let down my defenses. I become the weak little girl who ran from her problems, who let the big, brave man take care of her, who believed in someone other than herself."

He simply took her in his arms, fighting back the urge to rail at her for her idiocy. Knowing it would do no earthly good. "You're not that same person anymore, honey."

She rubbed her cheek against his bare chest, then turned back to the refrigerator. "I'm not so sure. All I know is, I'm never in more danger than when I feel safe."

Del pulled away, opening the refrigerator himself, pulling out this and that for these omelettes which he could have felt less like eating. "Then it's a good thing this is just a fling, isn't it?" Oh, man—was that bitterness in his voice? "That I'm leaving anyway. I mean—" he slammed shut the refrigerator door, turned back to her "—God forbid a man should care about you, right? I mean, really, truly care. Not because you serve *his* purpose, because he gets his kicks from manipulating someone he supposedly *loves,* but because he just *likes* you. *Respects* you. Thinks maybe you're a nice, funny, sexy, pretty lady. How is that a threat to you, Galen? How? Yes, you're *safe* with me. I would never, ever stand in the way of what you wanted to do. And I should think you'd've figured that out by now, for God's sake! Why can't you *trust* me?"

He took her shell-shocked expression in for several seconds, then realized what he'd said. Or good as.

And how he'd just shot himself in the foot, bigtime.

He didn't want to be mad at her. It wasn't her fault she was gun-shy. It wasn't her fault he'd—

He'd fallen in love with her.

None of this was anyone's fault.

He reached up, smoothed her hair back from her face. "You're one helluva woman, Galen Granata," he said softly. "And I'm gonna miss you like nobody's business."

Then, before either of them could say something stupid, he strode back to the bedroom, yanking on the rest of his clothes, his heart racing in his chest. When he turned to leave, Galen was standing in her doorway, her hands rammed into the robe's pockets. The lonely, sad little girl who didn't know how to make things right. Tears tracked down her cheeks.

"Please understand, Del—it's not you I don't trust," she said, her voice quavering. "It's *me*."

She smelled like flowers, and lovemaking, when he brushed past her on the way out.

"I still can't believe you're doing this."

Del glanced at his stepsister, leaning in his bedroom doorway, her car keys dangling from her hand. Until he found someplace to live in Cincinnati, Wendy was going to stay with Elizabeth and Guy. He'd come back in a week to finish off the move, collect his daughter.

Ten days had passed since he'd seen Galen. Slept with her.

Fallen in love with her.

Ten days in which every thought about work or Wendy or packing or this new job had to fight its way into his brain, shoving aside thoughts of Galen.

And you know what was the kicker? He couldn't believe he was doing this, either. But what was the alternative?

He stuffed another pair of jeans into his duffel bag. Packing was not his strong suit. "Did I tell you about St. Rita's?"

"Several times. And I'm sure it's a great school and Wendy

will just love it. But it's *there*, Del. Not here. Besides, what's wrong with Crawford's?''

''Nothing,'' he said, looking around for his toiletries kit. Ah—the bureau. He stepped around the bed to get it, tossed it into the bag as well. ''But it's here. Not there.''

''Which is neither here nor there,'' Elizabeth said, and Del groaned. ''Sorry. Couldn't resist.'' Then she came on into the room, only mildly wincing at the disaster-area decor, and dropped onto the edge of his bed. In her glasses—which she donned on the odd occasion when she couldn't wear her contacts—a pair of shorts and T-shirt, her long blond hair pulled back into a ponytail, she looked about fourteen. She did not, however, sound fourteen. ''You're going to miss Galen's opening, leaving now.''

Ignoring the crushing sensation inside his chest, he reached around her for his extra pair of shoes, shrouded in a plastic freezer bag. ''Can't be helped. Sullivan wants to start in two weeks. I've got to start preliminary work now.''

''You could come back—''

''Liz!'' He glared at her. ''Back *off!*''

She smiled.

Oh, *hell.* He yanked the zipper closed on the bag, the harsh sound grating on his nerves.

''You got it bad, doncha?'' she said.

Del stood silently contemplating both the window and how long a sentence he might get for strangling his stepsister, then slapped the top of the overstuffed bag. He counted to ten, then looked over at her. Unfazed, she pushed her glasses back up onto her nose, her arms neatly crossed over her ribs. ''Well?'' she said.

''I don't want—''

''Uh-uh-uh…''

''I don't need—''

''Nope.'' She reached over, grabbed his wrist. ''Repeat after me. I. Love. Galen. Granata.''

''Really? Does Guy know?''

She huffed a little sigh, recrossed her arms. ''Honest to Pete, Del—''

"Sorry. Couldn't resist."

Elizabeth pulled a face, and he imagined, just for a moment, what it would have been like if their parents had somehow managed to find each other twenty years ago, to have been around her growing up.

"So do you? Love her?"

Then again, one of them would probably be dead by now.

"Since the lady said she's not interested, it doesn't much matter what I think, now does it?"

That got narrowed eyes. Oh, Lord.

"And you believed her?"

Del just stared at her. "Well, yeah, since that's what she said and I didn't peg Galen as being much of a game player—"

Elizabeth let out a single, high note of utter disbelief. "Men are so damn clueless," she muttered, more or less to herself, then to him, "I can guarantee you she's interested, Del. She's just scared, is all."

Del lugged his bag off the bed and headed toward the living room, leaving his stepsister to hop up from the bed and trot along behind. "Well, guess what, Dr. Brothers?" He dumped the bag on the floor by the front door. "That ain't exactly a news flash. I know she's scared. That's why she's not interested, y'know? And I'm not nearly as clueless as you might believe, either." He peered over to the end of the room where Wendy was watching TV and playing with Snickers, the kitten. "She's got identity issues, see, because of the way her husband treated her." He grinned at Elizabeth's lifted eyebrows. "Surprised you, huh? That I know the lingo?"

The brows fell. "No. Surprised you're buying into that crap."

"Aw, Liz—"

"Oh, don't 'Aw, Liz' me. You've giving up without a fight, is what you're doing. If you leave, how she's supposed to know she can function while you're still on the same planet with her, huh? I mean, what the—" she glanced over at Wendy "—dickens does it prove if you go away?"

Del started toward his daughter, touching her head to get

her attention. "It proves, dear sister, that I've got enough re-spect for the woman to stay out of her way. Let her work out whatever it is she has to get through on her own."

"Conveniently sidestepping any possible risk to your own person in the process."

Keeping his expression neutral, he signed to Wendy to go get her things, which he'd packed before. She glowered at him before stomping off to her room; he snatched the half-grown kitten off the sofa back and stuffed her into a cat carrier, which he handed to Elizabeth, taking advantage of the distraction to cool down. Wendy returned, not looking at him. She was only five—how could she understand that this was best, in the long run?

"Think what you like," he said wearily to Elizabeth as Wendy slowly made her way to other side of the room to get Snickers's catnip mouse. "I'm taking this job for me. And for Wendy—"

"Oh, right," Elizabeth said, arms crossed. "For Wendy. Just look at the joy and excitement rolling off the child."

Del rammed a hand through his hair. "Okay, so maybe we have some things to work out on that score. But I'm also taking it for Galen, in a way. So we don't have to keep running into each other at family gatherings or on the street or in the supermarket. So I don't have to see the fear in her eyes, ev-erytime she looks at me and sees…"

He held up one hand, forestalling the inevitable, "What?" from Elizabeth. "She doesn't need me in her life, Liz. So I'm conveniently removing myself from it. And if you say another word, so help me God, I'll deck you where you stand."

After a second, Elizabeth smiled, then lifted her hand to pat him on the cheek. "Awww…it's just like having a real brother and everything. And to think I managed for thirty-one years without having someone threaten me with grievous bodily harm."

"Did it work?"

She shrugged. "Maybe. Maybe not." Then she bent over to Wendy, signing, "Ready?"

The little girl nodded, the corners of her mouth turned

down. Elizabeth herded her outside, then turned back, briskly rubbing Del's arm while Snickers had a panic attack in her suspended cage. "Call us when you get in, 'kay?"

"Yeah. Sure." He gave his sister a hug, then crouched down in front of Wendy. "I'll be back in seven days," he said and signed. "You be good for Elizabeth?"

He cringed at the tears cresting in her big brown eyes. "Why do you have to go?" she signed. "Why do we? I don't want to leave." She circled her heart. "Please, Daddy. I don't want to leave everybody."

He grabbed her tiny hands, kissing them before pressing them against his chest, choking back his own tears. But he had to let go to sign, "I know, baby. But sometimes we have to do things we don't want to do."

Tears streaming, chin wobbling, she signed, "When I'm a grown-up, I'm *never* going to make anyone do something they don't want to do!"

On a groan, he drew his daughter into a fierce hug, hoping she'd understand, if nothing else, how much he loved her, even if he was a royal doodyhead. Ever since he'd brought her home as a tiny but spunky newborn, they'd never been apart for more than a few hours, except for the night of her birthday, ten days before. She'd kept him going, during those horrendous first weeks after Cyndi's death, when grief and rage threatened to pull him under. In many ways, this little girl had saved his life, even as she'd unwittingly taken her mother's.

But she hadn't, he quickly amended, burying his face in her sweet-smelling hair. Even at the beginning, when he roared at the doctors, the hospital, the heavens, so desperate for someone to blame for ripping his life apart, he'd never once blamed Wendy for her mother's death. And as one of the doctors had pointed out to the rampaging new father in his office, there was no way of knowing how long Cyndi might have lived, even if she hadn't become pregnant.

Life offered choices, but no guarantees.

Finally, nothing resolved, he let Wendy go, watching as she climbed into Elizabeth's car, as they drove off, until they were out of sight. Still, he stood for another full minute, staring into the space where they'd been, before loading his gear into the back of his truck. He slammed the tailgate shut, then slammed his hand against it for good measure.

He could have stayed. Could have probably continued the affair with Galen. Could have done all sorts of things that might have made him feel better than he felt right now—which was pretty crappy—but he didn't. He'd chosen to take this job. He'd chosen to leave.

He'd chosen to give up.

For her, he told himself sharply. *I'm doing this for her.*

He got into the truck, gave the key a vicious twist, cursing when the truck roared to life.

Like hell, he thought, tires squealing as he gunned the truck out of the parking space.

Chapter 13

Six hours to go.

Out front, a bevy of well-meaning women were scurrying about like the critters in Disney's Cinderella, setting tables and arranging flowers and arguing about God knows what, while Galen quietly went mad in the kitchen.

A state with which she'd been flirting ever since Del—looking like a kid who'd just been handed an F on a test he'd studied for for three days—walked out of her apartment two weeks before.

Why had she thought if he left, if she no longer saw him every day, things would be easier? Instead, she saw or heard or felt or smelled him *everywhere*. Her bed linens. The beer bottle he'd drained and left on her living room floor. The bill he'd had his bookkeeper send for the balance due on the project, signed personally with a big "Thanks" at the bottom.

Every detail they'd argued about in the restaurant.

Her sleeveless cotton blouse stuck to her back, Galen zipped from spot to spot, tasting sauces, checking supplies, answering the phone, smiling and nodding and trying to fend off the bad, bad feeling that she'd just made a horrible mistake.

Oh, Wendy. She'd had dinner at Elizabeth and Guy's a couple nights ago. Her heart nearly broke at how unhappy the child was, knowing she was going to be moving away in a few days.

"But I wouldn't feel so bad if you could come with us."

Galen had lost her breath when Elizabeth translated Wendy's signing. Helpless, she'd looked to Del's stepsister for a clue, but only got a shrug in reply. Until later, after Wendy and the other kids were asleep, and Elizabeth had said, simply and directly, "Just remember it's not only the two of you battling this out."

It was true. When Galen pushed Del away, she'd also pushed away his daughter. Who might have become her daughter as well, if things had been different.

If she'd been different.

Too late now, in any case. They were leaving, and she had to stay. Del would probably find someone else, someone who'd be a better example for Wendy than Galen was, someone strong and confident, like Elizabeth and Maureen and Nancy were. He'd get over her, would eventually understand she'd done the right thing. For both of them. She had.

Hadn't she?

"Galen?"

Startled, she looked up to see Nancy's frothy-haired head poked through the kitchen door.

"Don't ask me why, but the ladies' room john just backed up. You want me to call a plumber?"

Galen dragged sweaty palms across her capri pants, nodding weakly, just as the butcher's rep, Andy, rang the back buzzer. Her stomach heaved, but she couldn't throw up. There was no time, for one thing. She couldn't understand how, considering how carefully she'd planned to make sure there were no last-minute glitches, how many of the suckers still managed to pop out of the woodwork, like roaches from the baseboards of a slum apartment.

Her brain on serious overload, she watched blankly as Andy unloaded the cooler which contained three-quarters of tonight's main courses.

The toilet was just the most recent thing to happen. One of the bakery ovens had gone on the fritz, so she was only going to have half as much bread as she'd planned; there wasn't, for God knows what reason, a single decent tomato to be had within a hundred-mile radius; her still-under-warranty car had broken down on her way back from the greengrocer's, so she was running two hours behind; one of the waitstaff had called in sick; and now, she realized as she came to enough to actually look at what was on the table, Andy was trying to pawn off old chicken on her.

She prayed to God this *wasn't* a sign.

She sniffed at a package of chicken breasts, then shook her head. "Sorry, but these aren't fresh," she said in a reasonable voice, jumping when Brad, her second-in-command, clanged his spoon on the side of the marinara sauce pot. By this point, her stomach was churning so much, she'd barf butter.

Andy, a heavy-lidded little man with an overabundance of hair, belly, and cockiness, looked at her like she'd lost her mind. "Whaddya talkin' about? I swear to you, yesterday, these chickens were struttin' around the yard, completely oblivious to their imminent fate."

Good girls don't lose their tempers.

Right.

She picked up the tray of fillets, shoving them underneath the rep's nose. "Would you pay $18.95 for a dish that started out smelling like this?"

He backed up, but still had the audacity to say, "Eh, that's just because they were wrapped in plastic. Let 'em air a couple minutes, they'll be fine."

Six months ago, she would have probably backed down, avoided the confrontation, just gone and gotten fresh ones somewhere and swallowed, as it were, the loss. Six months ago, she wouldn't have heard Del Farentino's voice saying, "Are you crazy? You gonna let this creep get away with this?"

Criminy. He was even in her *head.*

"They're not fine, and I'm not paying for something I can't use." Her cheeks blazed, but there wasn't a whole lot she could do about that. "So I suggest you get me something I *can* use. Please."

"Lady, there's not a damn thing wrong with this chicken. You just got an oversensitive nose or somethin'."

It got so quiet, you could hear the sauces bubbling. Galen took a single steadying breath, then crossed her arms. "If you think I'm either paying for or serving anyone chicken that smells like this, you're outta your mind. Take it back," she said softly, "and bring me something else."

The little guy narrowed his eyes at her, then snatched the chicken from the table. "We was doing you a favor, you know. Agreein' to supply a small potatoes operation like this. Fancy place like this, in a small town? Pffh…" He shrugged. "You'll be lucky to last three months, you know that? No skin off my nose, honey, believe me. You wanna find someone else who'll supply an operation this small, you go right ahead."

He turned, heading toward the door, but she sidestepped in front of him, her arms crossed to cover up her shakes.

"Excuse me. Nobody forced your company into agreeing to be our supplier. But you did, and we have a contract. For *fresh* meat, delivered daily, as per my specifications the day before, *subject to my approval.*" Del had suggested she put that bit in the contract; she'd reneged at first, rebelling against his telling her what to do, until she finally realized the man was right. As, she'd come to discover, he usually was about most things. "Well, guess what? I *don't* approve. But that doesn't alleviate your obligation to fulfill your part of the bargain. *Within the hour.* Now, unless your boss wants his butt dragged into small claims court for breach of contract, I suggest you honor every damn clause in it."

His face, she was sure, at least a notch or two redder than hers, the little man pushed past her, smelly chicken and all, mumbling something about "damn women's lib" and "not what they meant by belonging in the kitchen" and "should be home having babies, not giving men ulcers".

He just managed to get the door closed before the ladle she

hurled at him crashed against the screen, splattering marinara sauce all over creation.

All three of her kitchen staff immediately went very, very still.

She didn't have time for a breakdown. But as it seemed she was about to have one, whether she wanted it or not, she decided it would be better to fall apart in the privacy of her apartment, with only the cat and dog as witnesses.

"Be back in a minute," she said. Then fled.

And when she got to her apartment, her haven, the one place where no one could stick their nose in her business, she threw herself across her bed—the bed she'd always think smelled like Del—and sobbed her heart out, only barely aware that both pets had curled up beside her to offer solace.

Her gold leather sandals flashing against the pebbly carpet, Nancy skittered back to the booth where the entire female complement of Millennium Realty sat, turning linen napkins into little bishop's hats. They all knew their help was completely superfluous. But nothing on earth would have kept them away.

Elizabeth looked up, brows lifted. Judging from Nancy's expression, her friend was every bit as good at spying as she was at nagging. "Well?"

"I didn't catch all of it. Move over," she commanded Cora with a little flap of her hand before wiggling her spandexed fanny back into the booth, "but she threw the butcher person or whoever he was out on his keister." She shoved her wild hair behind one ear, leaned over. "And she *swore*."

The other three "ooohed" appropriately.

"Then she took off upstairs."

"Crying?" Maureen asked, her delicate blonde brows crumpled.

"About to, maybe. I didn't have a clear view."

All four sat in silence for several seconds.

"Well," Maureen said, tugging at the back of her linen skirt as she pushed herself out of the booth, "I think Cora should go talk to her." Elizabeth's mother grabbed her share of hatted napkins and headed for the far corner of the restaurant.

Cora peered over her reading glasses at Maureen's retreating form. "Why me?"

"Because the rest of us have husbands who would mourn our passing," Nancy said.

"I'll get you for that, little girl—"

"But the main thing is," Elizabeth said, halting the potential bloodshed, "how do we get my sorry-assed stepbrother here by tonight? I mean, we all agree that's why Galen's such a mess, right? Because Del left?"

Murmured assent all around. But before anyone could throw out a suggestion, Elizabeth snapped her fingers. "I could call him, tell him something's wrong with Wendy! That'd get him up here!"

"If he didn't have a coronary first," Nancy put in. Elizabeth noticed that Nancy, who was definitely no threat to Martha Stewart, was still torturing the same napkin she'd started on twenty minutes ago. "Barring that, once he found out you'd *lied,* you'd have to go into hiding for like twenty years or something."

"True." With a huff, Elizabeth finished folding her last napkin, then got up as well to place them at the linen-covered tables in the middle of the restaurant, each one flanked with deliberately mismatched chairs, set with its own china and crystal patterns, lovely odds and ends that Galen had found on her yard sale forays. Textured, parchment-colored walls, arched windows, and the stone fountain nestled in an oasis of live plants made the restaurant warm and homey and inviting. Even if it was still nameless. "But we have to figure out some way to get him back here, right?"

"Elizabeth."

Oh, Lord. She knew that tone of voice. Brows raised, she twisted to face her mother, calmly setting little hats. "Has it occurred to any of you that maybe, if everyone backed off, Del and Galen might work things out on their own?"

Nancy let loose with a sharp "Hah!", which pretty much summed it up.

"And isn't that going to be a little tricky," Elizabeth said, "what with them being in two different cities and all?"

Maureen waved away her daughter's objection. "If it's right—"

"Oh, for heaven's sake, Mother. I've never seen two people more bullheaded about admitting what everybody else has known for months already."

That got a "You're one to talk, Missy," look. Which was well-deserved, since she'd kinda dragged her heels about Guy there, a few years back.

"All the more reason to stay out of their way," her mother then said. "Hugh tells me Del's always been like this, having to come round to things in his own time."

"And I can vouch for Galen being the same way, honey," Cora put in. "Even when she was little. Nobody could tell that child *anything*."

Nancy finally tossed down her still-flat napkin in disgust, then looked over at Cora, chin in hand. "Not even you?"

"Did I say that?" Cora said, sliding out of the booth, tugging her boldly patterned polyester tunic down over her hips. "Just because she's stubborn doesn't mean she can't use a good talking-to."

And that went for Mr. Del, too, Elizabeth thought. The instant Cora disappeared, Elizabeth walked back to the booth, grabbed her handbag with her cell phone inside, then headed to the ladies' room before her mother could ask her just what she thought she was doing.

As the agent droned on about amenities, Del snuck a peek at his watch. Five and a half hours until Galen opened her doors to the public.

He felt like he was about to miss the birth of his child. Or something. Well, Galen's child, anyway.

"...the carpeting and drapes were updated just last year..."

This was not working. Hell, the longer he was away, the more he ached for her. All he wanted to do was support her.

Not suffocate her.

Listen. Not dictate.

To be whatever she needed him to be.

If she needed him at all.

Ah.

Oh, this opportunity was nothing if not convenient, wasn't it? Hadn't it been easier to walk away, to avoid facing his feelings, to avoid facing the definite possibility that, no matter what he said or did, he'd never be able to convince Galen she was wrong? That he wasn't Vinnie, or her grandfather, or whoever the hell else had tried to quash her independence over the years?

"...and from this unit, the gym and pool are just a couple hundred feet away..."

What a crock, believing he'd left because of some altruistic motive that he was doing *her* a favor, that getting out of her hair would be best for *her,* when the simple fact was she'd gotten close enough to break his heart.

Only twice before had another human being ignited feelings this rich and intense and overwhelming inside him. Losing Cyndi had nearly killed him; that, along with the inexorably entwined joy and fear that Wendy brought to his life, had made him leery of taking risks, he realized. Not in his career, maybe. But emotionally? Brother.

Sure, he could physically remove himself from Galen's presence, but how the hell was he supposed to get her out of her his heart? Leaving might have been the easiest thing. The most logical, on some level. But had it been the best thing? For *anybody?*

"Mr. Farentino?"

Del looked over at the agent, dazed.

"Do you have any questions?"

Yeah. Yeah, he had a lot of questions. But none this guy could answer.

He shook his head, clapped the man on the arm. "I'll...let you know, okay?" He walked out of the empty apartment, jingling his car keys in his hand.

"I wouldn't take too long to decide, if I were you," the agent called after him. "These units are going like hotcakes. If you don't act fast, you'll regret it!"

Good point.

* * *

The knock on her door sounded like it was coming from about three blocks away. Galen glanced at the clock by her bed—she'd only been up here ten minutes. *Oh, God, please— not another crisis.*

Feeling half-drunk—or what she imagined it would feel like to be half-drunk—she clumsily dragged herself off the bed, wiping at her face with the back of her hand as she weaved to the door. "I'm coming, for Pete's sake," she said in response to another round of knocks. "Keep your blinkin' shirt on."

Still sniffling, she opened the door, not even caring who it might be.

"Okay, baby, you wanna tell me what's goin' on, or do I have to drag it out of you?"

Then again, maybe she did.

Galen leaned against her door frame, suddenly too weary to stand on her own steam. "You lose the coin toss?"

Cora frowned. "Huh?"

"Never mind," Galen said, backing up before the woman trampled her on her way in. "But nothing's going on, Cora. Except your normal, everyday, I'm-about-to-open-a-restaurant-and-everything's-going-wrong stress."

"Uh-huh," Cora said, just waltzing on into the living room, her steps heavy on the uncarpeted floor. "So why don't you get yourself on in here and take five minutes to tell me all about whatever this is that's not going on."

Still leaning against the doorjamb, Galen eyed her uninvited guest. "Anybody ever tell you you're the nosiest woman on God's earth?"

"It's my life's calling, baby. Especially when that look you've been lugging around on your face all week's enough to make me want to smack you upside the head." One dark, imperious hand jabbed at the floor by her feet. "Git, little girl."

Galen stood her ground. Trembling, but she stood. "I'm not your 'little girl'. Or anybody else's."

"Then stop acting like one."

They glowered at each other for several seconds. Then, with a heavy sigh, Galen kicked the door shut with her foot and slouched inside, feeling, if not like a *little* girl, an awful lot like the petulant teenager she never got to be.

Nothing like being a late bloomer.

"Okay," Cora said. "Now, before we even get into this, let me tell you right now, I've seen that look before, on my daughters' faces more times than you wanna know, on Elizabeth's face, on Nancy's. I do not know what it is about women that they think they can be in love and nobody's gonna know it—"

"I'm not—"

"And you can stop right now and save yourself a trip to the confessional for lying."

Her mouth clamped shut.

"That's better. So. Now that we got that cleared up—"

Galen glared at her.

"—you can tell me just why you're fighting this so all-fired much."

It was like having someone poke at a festering sore. Galen uncrossed her arms, but only so she could stab one hand through her hair. Baby whined at her feet, more of a noodge than Cora. Galen ignored her.

Would that she could have ignored Cora.

"*Are* you in love with the man?"

After a long moment spent studying the wood pattern in the floorboard underneath her right foot, she finally nodded.

"Well, hallelujah."

"Oh, right, let's sound the trumpets." Galen finally looked up at her old friend, bitterness and confusion lodged unpleasantly in her throat. "The only other time I felt like this about someone," she said, each word scraping her heart like a rusty knife, "I ended up losing myself. It was just easier to let Vinnie do everything, be everything... Instead of learning to rely on myself, I just...disintegrated. And because of it, I was an emotional and social cripple when he died."

"Uh-huh. And then you took care of your grandmother for three years, which didn't help things any."

Galen sighed, then walked over to her window. In a few hours, there'd be cars in the parking lot. Or at least, she hoped there'd be. This was no time for a personal crisis. Let alone an interrogation by the Emotional Awareness Committee. "No," she admitted. "It didn't."

"So answer me one thing. Is this woman standing in front of me, this woman who's about to open her own business, who negotiated nearly every single detail of the whole shebang on her own, the same sheltered young woman who ran away with the first man to pay some attention to her, seventeen years ago?"

She turned to Cora, tears streaking down her cheeks. "You don't think I've asked myself that a million times, tried to convince myself I'd changed? Well, guess what? I look at Del, and I crumble inside. He gives me those looks he does—not the ones where he looks at me like I've gone off the deep end, the other ones, like he could eat me up—and I feel just like that naive eighteen-year-old all over again. I look at everything I've done, what I'm about to do, and instead of feeling proud that I did it on my own, instead of feeling strong and independent, you know what's going through my head? How much I miss Del, how much I want to share this with him! A thousand times this week, whenever a question would come up, I'd find myself wishing I had him around to give me grief, to tell me what to do. Whether I listened or not, without even wanting to, I became dependent on him. Oh, Cora," she sobbed, "I miss him so much, I feel like my insides are going to explode. How can that be a good thing?"

Cora stayed still for a long moment, her arms folded across that prodigious bosom of hers, then shook her head. "Child, you are one messed up female, you know that?"

On a brittle laugh, Galen swiped at her nose. "So tell me something I don't know."

Cora let out a long sigh. "You miss the man because you love him, you fool. And you love him because, unless I'm

way off, he's the first man to treat you *right*. Not because
you're dependent on him.''

Galen jabbed her hands out to her sides. ''But how do I
know that? In here—'' she pointed to her head ''—it's all
mixed up, see. I just don't know...'' Exhausted, she sank into
the armchair, her head clutched in her palms. ''Besides,'' she
said to the floor, ''he's gone. I drove him away.''

''You really think you did that?'' she heard. Gaze still
pinned to floor, Galen nodded.

''Then you're more full of yourself than I thought.''

By the time Galen lifted her head to ask Cora what on earth
she was talking about, she heard her front door slam.

''Excuse me...''

The man's hand tenderly supporting his pregnant wife's
back, the youngish well-dressed couple paused, probably wondering who the idiot was standing by the restaurant's front
door waiting to accost them. Del took a chance they'd be
willing to take part in a romantic subterfuge.

''There's a very pretty blonde in there somewhere, her hair
probably up in a French twist, sitting with a guy wearing an
earring and, in all likelihood, a very odd tie.'' He tried to hand
the husband a note. ''She's my sister. Could you get this to
her?''

The man stared at the folded up piece of paper for a second,
then asked, reasonably enough, ''Why can't you just go on in
and see her?''

Del shook his head. ''It's a long story, and I'm sure your
wife wants to sit down as soon as possible. Let's just say...it's
a matter of the heart.''

The guy's face relaxed into a grin. ''Ah. Somebody else is
in there you don't want to see?''

''Not just yet.''

''Gotcha.'' Then, with a little salute, he guided his wife
inside.

Thirty seconds later, Elizabeth came roaring out.

''What is this, a James Bond flick? I tried to call you, but
your phone was dead. Why didn't you get here sooner—?''

"I left in plenty of time, but there was some accident involving a truck full of pigs or chickens or something—" At her raised eyebrows, he hurriedly added, "No one was hurt, I gathered, but the interstate was closed for two hours while they rounded up livestock. But never mind all that. How's it going?"

Elizabeth relaxed, a little, smoothing non-existent wrinkles from her the front of her pink—he thought, in the dim light—dress. "It's going great. Up until a little bit ago, people were waiting as much as an hour to be seated. Or making reservations to come back another night. Rod's advertising campaign worked like a charm, apparently. You heard about the Name the Restaurant contest?"

He shook his head.

"There's a fishbowl by the front door. Everyone's being asked to suggest a name for the place. Winner gets a free dinner for two." She grinned. "No purchase necessary, but one whiff, and who's not going to eat?"

He walked up to one of the windows, keeping far enough back so he couldn't be seen. And he saw her, laughing with some customers, her feathered hair brilliant in the glow of the soft overhead lighting. A simple, sleeveless black dress hugged her figure, ending just about her knees; when she turned, he could see it dip to below her shoulderblades. Confidence radiated from her, from her smile, from the way she held herself. A few months ago, he knew, she'd never worn a dress that revealing.

His chest tightened with pride. And longing. And the fear of knowing the risk he was about to take.

"She's absolutely in heaven, isn't she?" he whispered.

He sensed, more than saw, Elizabeth come up beside him. "Not quite," she said softly. "But she will be. Soon."

"She needed tonight, Liz. To shine on her own. If I'd been here..."

"I know, I know. But you're here now, aren't you?"

After a moment, he nodded. "But don't tell her, yet. Where's Wendy? At your place?"

The blonde nodded. "We figured we'd bring the kids next week sometime—"

"Good." He glanced back at the window. "I'll come back later, then."

"But—"

He turned and met the confusion in Elizabeth's eyes. "Trust me." Returning his gaze to the window, he smiled, even over his cramped heart. "Trust me," he repeated, but more to the graceful woman serving the pregnant couple, now seated at a tiny, glittering table near the fountain, than to his stepsister. Slowly, he withdrew his little pad and pen from his pants pocket, scribbled something down on a sheet, ripped it out, folding it into quarters. "Here," he said, handing it to Elizabeth.

"What's this?"

"A suggestion. To put in the fishbowl."

She took the paper, tucking it against her ribs as she hugged herself. "She loves you, Del. She does. Even if she doesn't know it yet."

There was little point in answering her. Instead, he briefly squeezed his sister's shoulder, then sent her back inside.

"What was that all about?" Nancy asked.

"Del's here," Elizabeth whispered, repositioning her napkin on her lap.

"What?" Nancy cried, but Elizabeth snagged her wrist to shut her up. Then glanced from one husband to the other, her mouth set. "He says not to tell Galen, that he's handling this his own way. Whatever that means."

Guy nodded toward her hand. "What's that?"

Elizabeth looked at the folded up piece of paper clutched in her fingers. "Oh, shoot. I forgot to stick this in the fishbowl. It's Del's suggestion for what to name the restaurant." Since the paper wasn't sealed or anything, she flipped it open, then burst out laughing, holding it out for the others to see.

Guy chuckled. "I think we now know how he's 'handling' it."

"And it might just work," Rod added.

Nancy smacked him in the arm. "To get her attention, maybe. You'd really think she'd *use* it?"

They all looked at each other, then laughed all over again.

"She asleep?" Del asked Hannah before he was even fully inside Elizabeth's house.

"Yeah," Rod's daughter said, leading him down the hall, fluffing a hand through her short hair. "She conked out in front of the TV about eight." They went into the jumbled family room to find Wendy snoring on the popcorn-littered floor, snuggled against Einstein, the kitten snuggled against her, the other kids blithely watching some video or other around her. Einstein rolled his eyes in Del's direction and thumped his tail as Del gently lifted Wendy off the floor and carried her to the living room.

She awoke groggily, as usual, frowning when she realized whose lap she was in. "Why are you here?" she signed on a yawn.

It wasn't an easy sign to do with his arms full of sleepy child, but he managed to brush his knuckles against each other, twice. "To fix things," he said.

After a drowsy moment or two, Wendy smiled, then threw her arms around his neck.

Well. She'd done it.

The kitchen was clean, linens gathered, chairs upended on tables, and she was alone, at last. A mixture of garlic and oregano and about a hundred different perfumes hovered in the humid air, suspended like dust in the silence. She'd shut down the air conditioner about a half-hour ago, and the thick June night had seeped in, plastering against her like a long-haired cat.

Balancing a glass of wine in her hand, Galen slipped off her pumps, then slid bonelessly into one of the booths, weary and amazed and *this* close to tears.

One trickled down her cheek, in fact, spawned of a soul-deep ambivalence she just couldn't shake. She had every right to be very, very proud of herself. And she was. Sure, it was

a little early to use the term "rousing success", but judging
from the contented groans of customers leaving, a notebook
well sprinkled with future reservations, she was definitely on
her way.

She lifted the glass in an imaginary toast. "Thanks, Gran,"
she whispered.

And if it weren't for this little niggling, nagging business
about Del Farentino, she'd be happy enough to burst. But there
it was, niggling and nagging.

Another tear followed the first. She swiped at them, then
lay her over-burdened head down on her folded arms.

Yes, she missed him. Yes, she loved him. No, she didn't
feel any differently than she ever had, about not wanting another man in her life.

Except she felt very differently, for all that.

But in any case, he was gone. So why couldn't she just
forget the guy, already?

She closed her eyes—briefly, or she'd fall asleep where she
sat—and thought about this for a second. Decided she'd ask
for one more favor...

"Oh, God, please? Give me a clue what I should do about
this balled up feeling inside me."

She waited, swaying slightly with exhaustion.

Psst—the fishbowl?

"Huh?" she said aloud, lifting her head, her eyes drifting
to the Name the Restaurant suggestion bowl filled with some
little forms Nancy had made up, over by the front door. Oh,
right. Elizabeth had bugged her about being sure to look
through them before she went upstairs.

So, with a sigh, Galen crawled out of the booth, hobbled
barefoot across the room, then hauled the bowl back to the
booth and dumped it out. There were maybe a couple dozen
or so. She laughed out loud at some of the suggestions,
moaned at others, then came to a rigidly creased piece of lined
paper. She slowly unfolded it, her heart jumping to life as she
read the single, block lettered name:

"Farentino's."

Her hand flew to her throat, not so much because of the

implication of the word itself, but because the only way it could have gotten into the bowl was if—

"Hey, lady," came through the glass door, accompanied by three sharp raps. "Got any leftovers?"

With a soft cry, she got up, made her way slowly to the door. She mouthed his name, her shaking hands hardly able to unlock the bolts.

Then she didn't know what to do. Or say.

She swallowed, trying unsuccessfully to blink back the tears. All those balled up feelings rushed through her, gathering momentum with every second longer he stood there, giving her that seesaw smile. "Well, um, there's some chicken parmigiana, I think. And cheese tortellini with pesto sauce …"

"Later," Del growled, reaching for her.

Every nerve ending roared to life the instant his hands touched her bare arms. "Later?" she managed a split second before his mouth covered hers.

Oh, my. Suddenly, she wasn't the least bit tired.

She lay, naked and sated, her lover molded to her back, his breath warm and lovely against her neck. One arm draped over her shoulder to claim her hand, their fingers now as entwined as their limbs had been, minutes before. Baby had slunk off to her bed in the corner of the bedroom a half hour ago, but the cat, figuring the thrashing was over for the moment, had hopped up onto the bed to curl by Galen's stomach, her placid purr weaving in and out of their breathing, their heartbeats, the soft whirr of the ceiling fan overhead.

"You came," she said softly.

Del chuckled. She swatted his arm. "Not what I meant."

He pressed his lips between her shoulder blades, sending little tendrils of renewed desire slithering from here to there and everywhere.

Funny, the way sex solved nothing.

"You're too quiet," Del murmured into her hair. "Thinking?"

"Mmm," she said, kissing his hand.

"You want me to cut to the chase?"

She smiled, remembering. "I thought you already had."

He disengaged their hands to skim her bare hip with his palm. "That was unexpected," he said, grazing his lips over her shoulder. "I'd planned on talking. No, really," he said when she chuckled, "I swear."

She swiveled around, met his gaze, dark and...what? Worried, maybe. Hopeful? Yeah, definitely hopeful.

Shoot.

She remembered the piece of paper in the goldfish bowl. What he'd written on it. She frowned, but more out of curiosity than pique.

"So tell me something," she said. "Why would I name *my* restaurant 'Farentino's'?"

He grinned, his teeth flashing white in the moonlight. His hair, as usual, was a mess. Of course, this time she had something to do with that. I mean, when a man's doing...well, what Del had been doing...where else is a gal supposed to put her hands, huh?

"Got your attention, didn't it?"

Her eyes widened until she realized *he* was talking about the piece of paper. "Not as well as the kiss, but, yeah. It got my attention."

"Well, think about it."

She didn't have to. She knew what it meant. She also knew...

Nothing. Not a single blessed thing. Except, she loved this man with her whole heart.

Which was the problem.

He combed his fingers through her hair, his gaze roaming her face, then lower, his hand following suit. A knuckle grazed the top of one breast, avoiding the nipple. Barely. "These are truly a miracle of nature, you know that?" he said, and she laughed through the tightness constricting her heart.

"I've never known anyone who could combine lust and reverence in the same sentence before."

He just grinned, then propped his head in his hand, skimming his other hand up and down her arm. Tender. Caring.

He *was* the first man to ever treat her right.

"Well?"

She drew in a breath, snuggled closer, tucking her head underneath his chin. Far more dangerous than sex, this. Far more intimate. But for just this moment, she needed to feel safe. "You're asking me to marry you."

"Ten points to the redhead with the beautiful—"

She jerked up her head, the corners of her mouth turned down.

"—eyes," he said, grinning. Then he sobered. "I turned down the job in Cincinnati. Took some fast talking, but Sullivan said he understood. So I—we're—not moving."

Took a good five seconds for that one to sink in. "You *what?* Why—?"

"Because you just opened a new restaurant here."

Her breath lodged somewhere between her throat and her chest. His not being here full-time was supposed to be her safety net, the only way she'd ever be able to sort out all these confused feelings in her head. Her heart.

"Oh, God. Oh, Del...no..."

Somehow, she sat up, then got up, grabbing the first thing she could find to put on, which happened to be Del's T-shirt. A shirt which she had nearly ripped off of him not all that long ago. She shrugged into it, only to immediately sink onto the foot of the bed, her arms wrapped around her middle.

"I can't...I'm not ready..."

"I know that, baby."

Confused, she twisted back around. Del was sitting up, the sheet discreetly draped over his lap. "But if you knew I'd say no..." She shook her head, wishing she could shake something loose inside it. "Why on earth did you—?"

He was close enough to stroke her cheek. "*Are* you saying no? Or are you saying, *not now?*"

She drew her knees to her chest, trying to squeeze out the panic. "It frightens me, how much I love you," she whispered, shutting her eyes when she felt his strong arms close around her, draw her once again to his chest. "How easy it would be for me to slip back into old habits. To lean on you—"

"I won't let you do that. Ever. Hell—you even *try* to lean on me, I'll set you straight so fast it'll make your head spin."

She stilled.

"No comment?"

His chest hair tickled her ear as she shook her head.

"Good. So just sit here and listen." His chest rose and fell as he sucked in a breath. "It was funny, you know? I had it all figured out, that after what I'd gone through with Cyndi, the way she'd go off half-cocked all the time, that if there ever *was* another woman in my life, I'd want someone I could predict. Someone who'd actually listen to me from time to time. Take my advice. Someone I could count on to not scare the bejesus out of me every five minutes."

His hand, so large and rough and gentle, stroked her shoulder as he talked. Galen let her eyes drift shut, hoping. Praying.

"And then there was my mother," he said quietly. "She died when I was a kid, did you know?" She shook her head. "Yeah. Got mugged coming home from volunteering at a homeless shelter in a rough Chicago neighborhood. Nobody could talk her out of going down there—she said she had so much, those people had so little. We all thought she was reckless, when what she was, was courageous. Unselfish. Just like Cyndi was, in her own way. Then I met you, and I thought, aha! Here's this lovely, sweet woman who's not going to do anything stupid, who's not going to give me *agita*—"

Galen smiled, kissed his chest. "And then I go and blow a quarter of a million bucks to open a restaurant."

"Exactly. But you know what? Somewhere along the way, as I watched you blossom into this incredibly efficient, competent woman these past few months, I realized, hell—I'd die of boredom with a woman like what I thought I wanted. My mother wasn't to blame for her death. And neither was Cyndi. Not really. It was just like the doctors said. There weren't any guarantees, either way. So what I'm trying to tell you is, I love you too much to let you revert to that scared-of-her-shadow creature you were when we first met. I don't want that woman. I want this one."

She knuckled away a tear, realizing she was frowning so hard she was making her head hurt. "You think I'm strong?"

He tightened his hold. "Think, hell. I *know* it."

"How can you be so convinced of something I'm not?"

She felt him shrug. "Can't answer that one, babe." Then he said, "I actually got here a couple hours ago, did you know that?" Eyes burning, she shook her head. "Yeah, I did. But you know what? There was no way I was barging in on your show, distracting you. This was your night. Your triumph. You didn't need me...no—let me finish. There's a difference between needing someone because you feel incomplete, and needing someone because you want to share your life with that person." He chuckled. "Okay, I came up with this analogy, but don't laugh, okay? Say you have this pair of beautiful candlesticks, right? My mother had a pair, silver, really fancy. Sometimes, she put each one in a different room, as part of some decoration or other. Sometimes, she put them together, like on the dinner table. Each one was perfectly fine by itself, but together, they gave off more light. When she separated them, it wasn't like they were incomplete or anything, or they couldn't function. Together, they worked with each other, yeah, but they didn't have to borrow each other's light or anything...oh, hell. Sounds stupid, doesn't it?"

"No, Del," Galen whispered, knocked for a loop by his eloquence. "It doesn't sound stupid at all." Then she said, "But it's about this protecting business—"

He chuckled in her hair. "Nancy swears I was a Jewish mother in a previous life." She laughed, too, snuggling closer. "It's only natural to want to protect the people we love, honey. To look out for them. I can't change who I am, Galen. That part, you'd have to deal with."

They sat in silence for several seconds, Del caressing her hair, before he said, "I'll do anything for you, honey. Anything but leave you. Because, see, the way I figure it, the only way you're ever gonna see that I'm no threat to your independence is if we're together. Being apart proves nothing."

Well. What could she say to that?

* * *

Del held his breath, even as he held her in his arms. Protectively, yes. He'd always protect her, whether she liked it or not. But not possessively.

Baby jumped up on the bed, flopping down beside her. Galen reached out, slowly, to scratch the dog behind her ears. "I don't know how long this will take," she whispered.

Hope flared in Del's chest, sweet and warm. "S'okay, babe. I'm not going anywhere."

She reached up, twining her arms around his neck. "Thank you," she murmured, then aggressively pressed her mouth to his.

Epilogue

Del had insisted on a formal wedding—white gown, altar boys, bridesmaids, the whole nine yards—since she hadn't gotten one her first time around. That was about the only thing they hadn't argued about in the past seven months, two weeks and three days, but only because she'd had the idea first. And because the restaurant had done well enough for her to pay for the whole shebang herself.

That, they'd argued about. Sort of. Until she pointed out that he'd paid for the lot for the house he was going to build for them, so this was only fair.

With a grin, he'd backed down, hands up.

Of course, seven months, two weeks and three days planted their wedding smack in the middle of winter, but it would have taken far more than ten-degree-below temperatures to keep folks from attending *this* wedding.

Wendy was out of her mind with happiness, Galen thought with a smile, watching her new daughter chase after her step-cousins in the crowded restaurant. Galen knew how she felt. Del's hand entwined with hers as they sat at the head table, she hoped the photographer was taking lots of pictures, because the day was just whizzing past. Of course, they had the reception here, at the restaurant. And of course Del had given her grief because she'd insisted on doing most of the cooking herself, yesterday and this morning, rushing into her gown at the last minute and barely making it to the church on time. But after all, it was her restaurant. That's what it said, on the two huge neon signs on either side:

"Galen's".

She'd just gone ahead and given free dinners to everyone who'd made a suggestion. Seemed only fair. She also supposed it was ironic that her husband had still ended up naming the thing, but she decided she could live with it.

Her husband. A year ago, a husband was the last thing she thought she needed. And now...

Well.

The husband in question leaned over, nuzzling her cheek. She giggled. And blushed. "You look absolutely extraordinary in that dress," he said softly, fingering a fold of crisp, creamy silk taffeta, the gown a creation of a relatively new bridal designer out of Atlanta. It seemed very fitting, both literally and figuratively, that she should pick a Fairchild gown to be married in.

She'd read Brianna Fairchild Lockhart's profile in a recent *Entrepreneur* magazine, how the former bridal consultant had built her manufacturing business from the ground up, all on her own, without so much as a penny from her wealthy business tycoon husband—a man to whom, Galen could easily read between the lines, the smiling blonde in the photograph was completely devoted.

Two days after reading that article, Galen told Del she was ready to do this for real. And forever.

Now she smiled up at the man who she knew would always support her efforts to be the best she could be, eyeing a lock of dark hair that was still too long. "You clean up pretty good yourself," she said, flicking a speck of lint off his tuxedoed shoulder.

"Okay, you two," the photographer prompted, "let's get a

photo of the bride feeding the groom the wedding...pie?'' The man turned. "That's it? No cake?''

"That's it," Galen said with a grin.

Poor Cora. The woman had nearly lost it when she walked into the restaurant and saw twenty chocolate cream pies instead of a traditional wedding cake, lined up on a long, lace-draped table. Galen would explain it to Del later. Maybe. Sometimes, a girl just likes to have secrets, you know?

She caught another glance of Wendy as they moved toward the table, fought back the concern that still needled at her, now and then, about whether or not she'd be around enough for her, with the restaurant 'n' that. Except Wendy had pointed out that having a mother around some of the time was still better than not having one around at all. Especially if the mother was Galen.

Galen had bawled for a half hour after that one.

But there was more. The instant they told Wendy they were getting married, she put in her order for a baby brother or sister. When Galen gently explained she couldn't have children, Wendy had simply shrugged.

"My best friend Ling Mei is adopted," she'd signed. "So why can't we adopt a baby?''

And Del had said, "Why stop with just one?''

Oy, as Nancy would say.

"Okay, Galen," the photographer directed. "Do your worst!''

Grinning, she shoveled a huge bite of pie into her new husband's mouth, deliberately smearing half of it all over his face, thinking how even he had finally realized he could carry stubbornness too far. And pride. The last time Hugh offered him a job, Del had graciously shut up and accepted it.

All those signs she'd asked for—and gotten? They'd all led to this moment, she realized. This outcome. She was meant to be here, to be with Del and Wendy. She admitted to herself some time ago that she'd probably fallen in love with Del right around the time he herded her into the ladies' room at the airport so she could upchuck. It just took awhile for her head to come to terms with that fact. She wasn't quite sure when she'd stopped being afraid. When she realized loving Del was no threat to her self-ness. That he never had been.

And he'd helped her to understand, as well, how strong she'd been all along. How often she'd made conscious decisions about what path to take—to run off with Vinnie and away from her dictatorial grandfather; to stay with him through his illness; to move back in with her grandmother.

To spend her entire inheritance on opening a restaurant in a strange town.

These were not the actions of a weak woman, he pointed out. A crazy one, yes, he'd added with a devilish smile, but not a weak one.

"Hey, you," he growled through his laughter, his touch searing the small of her back as he pulled her close. He pointed to his face, pure wickedness dancing in the depths of his dark eyes. "Now you have to lick it off!"

Galen laughed back, grabbing a napkin to undo the damage. "Good girls don't lick whipped cream off their husbands in public," she whispered.

"And in private?"

She pretended to consider. "Throw in some chocolate sauce, and we'll talk."

Applause resounded through the tiny restaurant as Del planted a good one on her, sharing the whipped cream.

* * * * *

Don't miss this great offer to save on *New York Times* bestselling author Linda Howard's touching love story

SARAH'S CHILD, a must have for any romance reader.

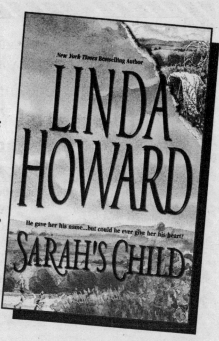

New York Times Bestselling Author

LINDA HOWARD

He gave her his name...but could he ever give her his heart?

SARAH'S CHILD

Available December 2000 wherever hardcovers are sold.

Don't miss this great offer to save on *New York Times* bestselling author Linda Howard's touching love story

SARAH'S CHILD, a must have for any romance reader.

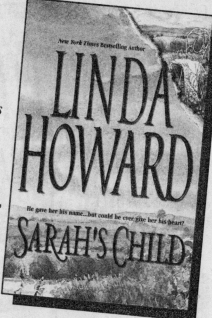

Available December 2000 wherever hardcovers are sold.

SAVE $2.00

off the purchase price of SARAH'S CHILD
by Linda Howard. Available wherever hardcovers are sold.

MIRA

5 77506 00082 2   (8100) 2 00177

MLH620US

Coming in January 2001 from Silhouette Books...

ChildFinders, Inc.:
AN UNCOMMON HERO

by

MARIE FERRARELLA

**the latest installment of
this bestselling author's popular miniseries.**

The assignment seemed straightforward: track down the woman who
had stolen a boy and return him to his father. But ChildFinders, Inc.
had been duped, and Ben Underwood soon discovered that nothing
about the case was as it seemed. Gina Wassel, the supposed kidnapper,
was everything Ben had dreamed of in a woman, and suddenly he had
to untangle the truth from the lies—before it was too late.

Available at your favorite retail outlet.

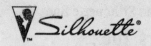

COMING NEXT MONTH